CRUISING IN YOUR
EIGHTIES IS MURDER

CRUISING IN YOUR EIGHTIES IS MURDER

MIKE BEFELER

FIVE STAR

A part of Gale, Cengage Learning

Detroit • New York • San Francisco • New Haven, Conn • Waterville, Maine • London

GALE
CENGAGE Learning·

LIBRARY OF CONGRESS CATALOGING-IN-PUBLICATION DATA

Befeler, Mike.
    Cruising in your eighties is murder : a Paul Jacobson geezer-lit mystery / Mike Befeler. — 1st ed.
    p. cm.
    ISBN 978-1-4328-2581-2 (hardcover) — ISBN 1-4328-2581-X (hardcover)
    1. Retirees—Fiction. 2. Murder—Investigation—Fiction. 3. Memory disorders in old age—Fiction. I. Title.
PS3602.E37C78 2012
813'.6—dc23   2012028698

First Edition. First Printing: December 2012.
Published in conjunction with Tekno Books and Ed Gorman.
Find us on Facebook– https://www.facebook.com/FiveStarCengage
Visit our website– http://www.gale.cengage.com/fivestar/
Contact Five Star™ Publishing at FiveStar@cengage.com

Printed in Mexico
1 2 3 4 5 6 7 16 15 14 13 12

For Wendy, Roger, Dennis, Laura,
Paige, Asher, Kaden, and Adam

ACKNOWLEDGMENTS

Many thanks for the assistance from Wendy Befeler and Laura Befeler and my online critique groups and the editorial support from Deb Brod and Tracey Matthews.

CHAPTER 1

As I awoke, I stretched my arms and my right hand brushed against a woman lying next to me in bed. I eyed my companion, admiring her silver hair cascading over the pillow. My ticker started thumping lickety-split. What was an attractive old broad doing in bed with a geezer like me?

I tried to recollect what had transpired the night before. A big void. In fact I couldn't remember anything from the day before. Think, you old poop, I told myself. I could only dredge up that I was Paul Jacobson and had been kicking around the planet for eight decades or so.

I looked around the room. It seemed to be a spacious place with plush blue carpeting, a desk and several chairs. Nothing familiar here at all. I looked in the corner and spotted two matching suitcases on stands. Must be a hotel. Did I run off somewhere with the woman next to me?

I regarded this young lady who I estimated to be in her seventies. Who the hell was she? My wife Rhonda had passed away, so this wasn't her. I realized I could remember the distant past perfectly. But what had transpired recently had disappeared into my cobwebs.

She let out a contented sigh, and her left hand rose to her face above the covers. She had on a wedding ring. Damn. I was sleeping with a married woman. Then I happened to look at my left hand. I had a wedding ring as well. I turned my ring with the thumb and index finger of my right hand. It was gold with three small imbedded diamonds. When Rhonda and I tied the knot, she gave me a simple gold band. How strange that I could remember that but not how I ended up in this room. So I appeared to be a secondhand married man. By the process of elimination, I deduced that I must be married to my snoozing companion. I considered waking her, but she was sleeping so peacefully I didn't have the heart to interfere.

I lifted my aged body off the mattress and ambled into the bathroom to take care of peeing and then splashed some water on my puss. Next, I ran water in the sink and raised the stopper in preparation for scraping off my overnight whiskers. When I turned the spigot off, the bowl quickly emptied out. I jiggled the stopper. No luck. One thing hadn't changed even if I couldn't remember yesterday: hotel sinks still didn't hold water.

When I dried my face on a towel, I spied an insignia that read *Lincoln Hotel.* Now I was making progress even though I didn't know where the Lincoln Hotel was or why I was there.

I peeked out the curtains and saw other buildings. I'd ended up in some downtown of a major city. After throwing on some clothes and a light jacket I found in the closet, I had one other idea. I checked out the desk and found a brochure welcoming me to the Lincoln Hotel in Seattle. How'd I end up in Seattle? The last I remembered I lived in Hawaii and before that raised my son in Long Beach after growing up in San Mateo. I could recall all that ancient stuff fine. But yesterday—poof. Then a note on the nightstand caught my attention. It stated: "Read this you old fart. You'll wake up not knowing which end is up. You remember fine during the day, but overnight your memory goes zotto from the day before. You're in Seattle with your new wife Marion and going on an Alaskan honeymoon cruise."

What a shocker. I should have read this evidence sooner as it would have eliminated some of my confusion. I replaced the note and regarded Marion. My heart started thumping again as

I admired her. I was half-tempted to return to bed and do a little reconnoitering under the sheets, but it wasn't fair to interrupt her peaceful slumber.

Instead I decided to take my daily constitutional and explore some of the byways of Seattle. I hadn't been here since the eighties when Rhonda and I took two weeks to drive up the West Coast and back. I remembered eating some good seafood and visiting the Space Needle.

I found a room key card on the desk and dropped it into my pocket. Then I hung a "Do Not Disturb" sign on the outside handle and checked the number by the door, noting I was on the seventh floor, so I'd know where to return. Then I moseyed down the hallway to find an elevator. The ride down to the lobby was uneventful, without even being subjected to elevator music. I emerged into a pleasant room containing a fireplace surrounded by bookshelves, flower-patterned couches, a glistening black baby grand piano and a potted palm tree. Even a slightly worn gray carpet made it look homey. I nodded to the desk clerk and headed toward the door. At that moment a man juggling a large metal box with a TV-like screen on top shot out of a side room.

"Here. Let me hold the door for you," I said as he charged out toward the sidewalk. I followed him out, but by that time he'd disappeared around the corner.

Young people. Always in so much of a hurry. When they reached my heights in geezerland, they'd slow down.

I crossed the street and turned back to lock in the image of the Lincoln Hotel: a green awning over the lobby, green canopies over second floor windows and the red brick structure reaching up twenty stories or so.

I accosted a man in an overcoat and asked, "Which way to the bay?"

He pointed down the street and I followed his directions.

11

After half a dozen blocks I spied a sign that said "Pikes Street Fish Market." The street was bustling with people carrying baskets and bins and setting up food at long counters inside an open-air market building.

Crates clattered, laughter echoed and the aroma of bacon wafted by. Damn. I was hungry, but I'd wait until I returned to the hotel to eat anything, and then Marion and I could have breakfast together while we renewed our acquaintance.

I turned at the crunching sound of crushed ice being poured into one of the stands. I watched as seafood was placed on the counters—crab, fish, clams.

I passed a large metallic pig that looked like a piggy bank on serious steroids. I patted its cold surface. There was actually a slot to put coins in, but I didn't have any change with me.

As I strolled along the street watching the early-morning collection of vendors and tourists, a man emerged from a doorway. He wore a tattered brown flight jacket and had a red bandanna wrapped around his head. He stopped in front of me, and I noticed a large mole on his left cheek.

"Can you spare some money for a disabled vet?"

Before I could answer, a man in an apron and holding a broom emerged from a shop. "Move along, Lumpy. I've told you not to bother people in front of my store."

Lumpy muttered something I didn't hear and then turned to stumble down the street, mumbling as he went.

I continued along the street and came to a park that overlooked the harbor. A sign indicated this was Victor Steinbrueck Park. I wondered who the heck he was.

People sat on benches, and I ambled over to a railing to look over a lower level of roofs toward a cruise ship moored alongside a pier. I suspected that might be the one waiting for me. It rested there three times the length of a football field, shiny white with a dark blue smokestack and white radar gear poking out on top. It looked large enough to stay afloat and keep my feet dry. I liked the idea of a cruise except for the fact that I hated the ocean. Oh well. I'd be fifty feet above the water unless they stuck us with one of those lower level porthole rooms.

I looked up at a totem pole, where two pigeons rested on a wing-like protrusion. On the sidewalk below them accumulated some of their little gifts. A sign informed me not to feed the pigeons, but right next to it sat a plate full of crusts of bread. A seagull held a piece of bread in its beak. I guessed it was okay by Seattle standards to feed the seagulls.

I felt a thumping on my shoulder and turned to see another vagrant with a scraggly beard standing inches from me.

I flinched.

His rheumy eyes seemed to be searching for something to focus on, and he made a smacking noise with his lips. Then he cleared his throat and in a raspy voice said, "Hey, Mac. You got some change for a cup of coffee?"

I patted my pockets. "Sorry. I don't have any money with me."

His expression changed from benign to a snarl. "I'm always hearing that. I know you have money."

"Sure, but not with me."

"I need money."

"Cool it. I told you. I don't have any money with me."

As if planning to grab my collar, he moved his hands, but I slapped them away.

"Asshole tourist!" he shouted.

Now he had me heated. "What the hell's your problem?"

The guy acted like he was going to reach for me again, but another man stepped between us and said, "Easy, you two. We don't need any fighting here."

My assailant backed off, turned and shuffled away. He

13

stopped once, looked over his shoulder and again shouted, "Asshole!"

I turned toward the man who had broken up the confrontation. "Your street people always this aggressive?"

He shrugged. "Some get a little carried away."

"So who's this Victor Steinbrueck?"

The man smiled. "He was an architect who talked the city into keeping the Pikes Street Market. In the nineteen-sixties, a group wanted to 'improve' the waterfront by tearing it down."

"Good decision to follow Mr. Steinbrueck's advice. What's that peninsula jutting out in the water?"

"Across Elliott Bay is Duwamish Head. Behind that you can see the Olympic Mountains."

"Thanks for the geography lesson."

I decided I'd continue my morning stroll to cool down from my encounter with the aggressive homeless man. I shook my head and let out a sigh. That but for the grace of God could have been me. With my faulty memory and my quick temper I could have ended up as a street person. I took a deep breath. He'd really ticked me off, and I needed to regain my composure.

I found another overlook and viewed the cruise ship once more. I checked my watch and figured it was time to head back to the hotel to eat some vittles with my new wife. Hiking up a hill, I spotted a block covered with vegetation. A sign indicated it was a public garden maintained by people in the neighborhood.

I entered and ambled through a section with flowers. No one else was around, so I sniffed the lilacs and admired the petunias. Then toward the other end of the garden, I spied something that looked like a shoe sticking up. Being a nosy coot, I headed over to investigate. I parted a bush. A face attached to a bloody body stared vacantly up at me.

CHAPTER 2

I stumbled backward, stepping smack in the middle of a flower patch. Extracting my foot from the crushed daisies, I looked wildly about, trying to find someone to help me. My heart thumped double time, and I felt drops of perspiration forming on my forehead.

At that moment a man appeared carrying a hoe and shovel.

"Where can I find a phone to call nine-one-one? There's been an accident. A man is dead."

The man dropped his implements. "Where?"

I pointed to the body on the ground. "There."

He approached and gasped, then reached inside a jacket pocket, extracted a little electronic thingy and punched his finger into it three times. Then he began yammering. While he talked, I regarded the body. Scraggly beard, ragged clothes . . . crap. It was the street guy who had accosted me in the park earlier. I looked closely. Blood covered his chest and had formed a pool in the dirt. His shirt was torn. He had obviously not died from a heart attack or stroke. Now my stomach tightened.

Within minutes I heard a siren. A white van pulled to the curb, and two EMTs hopped out. I waved to them and they raced over to where we stood. They began ministering to the fallen man, but I could tell it was too late. The gardener and I stood in silence watching the proceedings.

The siren had attracted attention, and a crowd began to gather.

15

Then a man in a suit and overcoat strode toward us. He spoke in a firm commanding voice. "We received an emergency call from a Mr. Jason Buchanan. Is he here?"

The gardener put his hand up, and the guy in the overcoat went over and spoke to him in hushed tones. After a moment the gardener pointed to me.

Next thing I knew the overdressed guy was standing inches from my face. He said, "I'm Detective Bearhurst. I understand you found the body."

"Yes, sir."

His dark penetrating eyes bore in on me. "Please show me some identification."

I patted my hip pocket. "Sorry, Detective. I didn't bring my wallet with me on my morning stroll."

He stared at me. "And you are?"

"I'm very surprised to be in this situation."

He almost smiled. "I want to know your name."

I gave him my most genuine smile. "Well, why didn't you ask? I'm Paul Jacobson."

A pregnant pause ensued.

"And your current address?"

"I'm not quite sure. I have a short-term memory problem."

He jotted something on a notepad.

Just then a woman stepped out of the crowd and motioned toward the body. "It's Curly who panhandles over at Victor Steinbrueck Park. I saw him there earlier this morning." Then she pointed at me. "And that old man was fighting with him."

"Wait a minute," I said. "We weren't fighting. He accosted me and started shouting at me."

Detective Bearhurst eyed me intently. "Very interesting. You and the victim had an altercation and then you report finding him dead."

"Hey. I just came across the body. Nothing more."

"Where are you staying, Mr. Jacobson?"

"At the Lincoln Hotel."

He regarded me again. "I thought you said you had a short-term memory problem."

I sighed. "Detective, I can remember everything that's happened this morning clearly, but last night has disappeared into the mist."

He shook his head like he was the one with a memory screw loose. "How about if I give you a ride to the hotel so I can check on a few things with you there?"

"I'd appreciate the lift. I think I've had enough excitement exploring Seattle."

I followed him to his Crowne Victoria parked half a block away, glad to be no longer tripping through the tulips.

"You going to lock me in the back seat?" I asked.

"That won't be necessary. You can sit up front with me." He chuckled. "Just don't make any sudden moves."

"I'm too old for sudden moves."

"You're also too old to be a criminal."

"Exactly. And you're too young to be a detective."

"Touché."

"Could you turn on the siren?" I asked.

He gave me a look that convinced me to shut up.

Detective Bearhurst drove in silence, so after I had given him a few minutes to forget about locking me in jail rather than going to the hotel, I opened my yap. "Do you have a lot of homeless people in your fair city?"

"Yeah. Probably not like San Francisco or Los Angeles, but we attract our share of people who live on the streets."

"This guy Curly seemed awfully aggressive when he accosted me earlier. Is that common?"

"No. Most of the homeless stick to themselves, panhandle a little and don't cause trouble."

"Are many assaulted?"

"We periodically have attacks that result in injury or death. Why all the interest, Mr. Jacobson?"

"Just trying to figure out why someone would have attacked Curly."

When we arrived at the red brick building, Detective Bearhurst accompanied me to the front desk. The clerk I had seen earlier stood behind the counter.

"I need to verify that this man, Paul Jacobson, is staying here." Bearhurst held out his identification.

The clerk squinted at the ID and then looked up. "I saw him leaving this morning, and he is a registered guest."

"You feel better now, Detective?" I said.

He only stared at me.

The clerk cleared his throat. "There is one thing though. We had a theft this morning. A man stole one of our computers. Mr. Jacobson may have inadvertently assisted his escape."

"What?" I shouted.

The clerk held up his hands as if to calm me. "Someone entered our administrative office, disconnected a computer and headed toward the door. Mr. Jacobson held the door open for the thief. An officer was here half an hour ago to take my report on this incident."

"Very interesting," Detective Bearhurst said, eyeing me again. "What do you have to say for yourself, Mr. Jacobson?"

"I was only trying to be polite. I didn't know he was a thief."

"I think we better check out your room, Mr. Jacobson."

"Fine with me. I have nothing to hide."

We took the elevator to the seventh floor, and I led him to the room I had left earlier.

"Let me look inside first to make sure my wife is up."

I entered and saw the lights were on.

"Marion, we have a visitor. Are you presentable?"

"I'm dressed and will be out of the bathroom momentarily."

I ushered the detective into the room, and the attractive old broad who had been in bed with me earlier emerged from the bathroom.

"Damn, you look good," I said. Then I pointed. "Detective Bearhurst is here because I found a dead body in a garden this morning."

Marion gasped. "You aren't getting involved in a murder investigation again, are you?"

"Again?" Detective Bearhurst and I said simultaneously.

"What are you talking about?" I added, with my heart rate approaching the zone where bad things could happen to geezers like me.

"Calm yourself, Paul. Let me explain for you and the detective."

I took several deep breaths.

Detective Bearhurst raised an eyebrow. "Yes, please enlighten us, Mrs. Jacobson."

"My husband has in the past been accused of crimes when in fact he was an innocent bystander."

"I've heard that before," Bearhurst said, crossing his arms.

"But in Paul's case it's true. In fact, in each case he was instrumental in helping the police finally solve the crimes involved."

Bearhurst's eyes rolled upward. "Great. I don't know what's worse, an old criminal or an old busybody interfering in police work."

"Watch who you call old," I added helpfully.

Bearhurst wrinkled his nose and Marion continued. "Paul has happened upon crime scenes before. First in Hawaii, then in Colorado and recently in Southern California." She wagged her finger at Bearhurst. "I'd suggest you listen to what he has to say, as he's been one hundred percent accurate in all three jurisdictions."

Now Bearhurst let out a deep sigh. "Give me a break, lady. Your husband reports a dead body when he is seen publicly arguing with the victim thirty minutes earlier."

Marion held her ground. "Paul has a bit of an anger problem and does engage in debates with people, but he's not violent."

"What's that bruise on your arm, Mrs. Jacobson?"

Marion flinched. "A bag fell out of the overhead compartment on our flight yesterday and struck me."

"You sure it wasn't caused by your husband?"

"Just one minute, Detective. I may not remember yesterday from chicken fricassee, but I don't attack women."

"How about homeless people?"

"I admit I got a little heated today when Curly confronted me, but no, words are as far as I go."

Bearhurst locked in on my eyes, and I stared back at him without flinching.

"Now Mr. Jacobson, I'd like to see the identification that you neglected to take with you this morning."

"It should be around here somewhere."

"Paul, look in the drawer of the nightstand on the right side of the bed."

"There you go, Detective. My bride is on top of these things." I scurried over and opened the drawer to find a worn brown billfold. Inside rested an identification card with a picture of a dazed me. I whipped it out and handed it to Detective Bearhurst

His forehead wrinkled. "This has an address in Hawaii."

I shrugged. "I used to live there."

"Paul, I forgot to remind you to change your address," Marion said.

"Now don't you start forgetting things," I replied.

Marion reached for her purse. "Detective, you can copy our

address from my identification."

Bearhurst jotted down what he needed and turned back to me.

"We'll speak again, Mr. Jacobson. Now I'm going to have to ask you not to leave the city for the next two days."

"But that's not possible," Marion said. "We have a honeymoon cruise beginning this afternoon."

"Honeymoon?"

"Yes. Paul and I were married two weeks ago." Marion held out her left hand.

Detective Bearhurst shook his head like he was trying to clear away annoying flies. "May I see your tickets?"

Marion retrieved a packet from her purse. "Here are our two tickets on Scandinavian Sea Lines and our passports."

He scanned the documents, wrote a note on his pad, then looked up at me. "I'll know where to find you, Mr. Jacobson. And when you return to Seattle next Sunday, I want you to call me." He handed me a card.

"You could always come down to the dock to greet us," I said.

He smiled. "I just might do that, Mr. Jacobson."

"You can even bring me a present, as long as it's not handcuffs."

"We could always add a little extra tour on the end of your cruise—King County Jail." He nodded toward Marion. "Mrs. Jacobson, nice meeting you." With that he turned and exited the room.

I stared at the closing door.

"That's a heck of a way to get ready for a cruise," I said.

Marion hugged my arm. "There's nothing we can do now."

"What an intense fellow that Detective Bearhurst is. You'd think he was trying to track down a terrorist."

Marion pursed her lips. "This isn't a laughing matter."

"I'll say. He seemed on the verge of locking me up."

"I'm just glad he didn't try to prevent you from going on the cruise ship."

"That would have been a problem. Now, my stomach is growling. Are you ready for some feasting?"

"First, you have one thing to take care of. It's time for your pills."

"Pills?"

She retrieved a rack of containers from the dresser, opened one labeled "Sunday Morning" and handed me three horse pills.

"Are we going to play marbles?" I asked.

"No. You're going to be good and swallow these."

I eyed the three rocks in my hand. "You've got to be kidding."

"Now don't be such a sissy. Take your medicine."

"How do I know you're not trying to poison me and run off with all my life savings?"

Marion exhaled an exasperated sigh. "Just swallow them or I might consider some form of bodily harm."

"Since you put it that way, yes, ma'am." I filled a glass with water and managed to down the pills somehow.

"I have to go through that every day?" I asked.

"Twice a day. Once in the morning and once around dinner time."

"Are these supposed to help my memory?"

"The doctor says they prevent your memory from getting worse."

"How can it get worse if I can't remember yesterday?"

"You still recall things fine during the day."

"I guess you're right."

"Now I have another thing to help your memory."

"A new set of brain cells?"

"No. A journal." She pulled a notebook out of her suitcase and handed it to me. "Every day during our cruise you can write down what happens. Then you can leave a note on top of this diary to remind yourself to read it the next morning to review what happened the day before."

I shook my head to try to see if I could loosen up my tangle of uncooperative brain cells. Made as much sense as anything else that had transpired so far today.

Marion laughed. "Why don't you watch TV while I finish getting ready? Then we can go down to breakfast."

"I'm sure set for some culinary delights after my hike this morning."

I turned on the tube and clicked through several channels before stopping on one with a dog show. Not having anything better to do, I watched a line of trainers and beasts including an Australian shepherd, boxer, Dalmatian, Shih Tzu, Welsh Corgi and golden retriever prance by to try to win Best in Show.

When Marion stepped out of the bathroom part way through her beautifying, I said to her, "I don't get this dog show program. They're trying to choose between such different types of animals. It's like trying to select the best fruit between an apple, orange and banana."

"I guess it's not any different than picking the best husband." She patted my arm.

"Or picking your nose."

Marion swatted me.

"Careful. I don't want to become an abused husband."

"Then don't tell dumb jokes."

"Yes, ma'am."

While Marion continued her powder and putty application process, I opened the curtains and sat down in a chair to admire the view of downtown Seattle. I should have been relaxed watching the traffic below and seeing the Space Needle poking out in

23

the distance, but my insides were still churning. Here I'd tried to take a calm early-morning promenade and look what happened. Images of a dungeon in some institutional building out there in the jungles of Seattle danced in my head. I had to get a grip. I knew I was innocent no matter how Detective Bearhurst acted. I took a deep breath. Think. Was there anything I'd missed that would demonstrate my innocence? I'd have to noodle on it today. From what I'd learned, by tomorrow all of today's activities would disappear from my befuddled brain. I definitely would have to write in the journal Marion had given me. I'd need any recollection I could muster to stay ahead of a determined detective. In the meantime, I'd prepare for the cruise. At least I hadn't been detained.

Marion emerged from the bathroom.

"Damn, I'm a lucky man to be married to you."

She smiled. "I consider myself lucky as well."

CHAPTER 3

After a trip down to the restaurant for a large cheese and mushroom omelet, we returned to the room to finish re-packing.

We lazed around until eleven o'clock when Marion said, "Oh, I just remembered something we need to do."

"Go get on the ship?"

"No, besides that. I'm supposed to remind you to call your family to let them know we arrived safely in Seattle."

"I don't know how safe our arrival is, given the events of this morning."

"Just phone them."

"Okay." I reached for the room phone and then realized I didn't know my son Denny's phone number.

"Don't use that telephone." Marion reached in her purse and handed me a tiny object the size of two matchboxes. "Here."

"What the heck is this?"

"Your granddaughter Jennifer gave this to you as a present on the condition that you use it to call her while we're on the cruise. She wants a full report of all our activities."

"All?" I arched my eyebrows.

Marion crossed her arms. "In particular, the ones where you get in trouble with the police."

"Oh. How old is my granddaughter, anyway? I last remember a little girl of six or so."

Marion tsked. "She's now twelve, Paul."

I shook my head. "How time flies when you're having fun." I

eyed the electronic gadget in my hand. It had numbers; I understood that part. Then I saw a red button, a green button, some arrows and a window that displayed the time.

"Okay, so this is like a clock. How am I supposed to make a phone call?"

"My grandson Austin programmed all the relevant phone numbers in it for us. He also showed me how to find them. I'll fetch the number for your family and show you what to do."

She grabbed it back, punched some keys and returned it to me.

"Now all you have to do is hit the green button and it will dial your family's number in Boulder."

"Then I have to yap into it like all those people I saw today wandering around with their hand to their ear like they were talking to themselves?"

"That's it."

"And it's magically going to send my voice through the air?"

"Yes."

I sighed. "Next you'll try to convince me to use one of those computer things."

"Both Austin and Jennifer have been trying to talk you into that, but you're too stubborn."

"Darn right. A geezer like me has to retain some of his old-fashioned reluctance."

I pushed the green button and thrust the hunk of plastic and metal to my ear. I heard ringing and then I recognized the sound of Denny's voice.

"Hello to you too. This is your father, safe and sound."

"Dad, I'm glad you called. You sound so far away."

"That's because I'm in Seattle."

"No. I mean you're not speaking directly into the phone."

I adjusted the dad-blamed gadget. "Is this better?"

"Now I can hear you clearly."

"I'm calling to tell you Marion and I are about to head off on our honeymoon cruise, and I wanted to see if that grand-daughter of mine was around."

"She's here. Hold on."

I heard some background noise, then, "Grandpa!"

"You got me there. I'm up in the Northwest ready to see some whales."

"There are supposed to be whales everywhere up there, Grandpa. Be sure to take pictures."

"Well, I haven't seen any yet because we're not on the ship."

"Have you found any dead bodies yet?"

I almost dropped the phone. "What's that supposed to mean?"

"Grandpa, you have this way of bumping into crimes. I've helped you solve them in the past."

"As a matter of fact, I did find a dead street person."

"Cool."

"No it wasn't. The detective thinks I had something to do with it."

"You'll solve it, Grandpa. You're good at figuring out these things."

"Well, I have no clue this time, not that I can remember any previous bodies with my soggy memory."

"That's why you need to keep your journal, Grandpa."

"Marion gave me a diary. You think it's a good idea to write in it?"

"Absolutely. That way you know what's happening to you. Add to it every day. Then you can read it every morning to refresh your memory. For you it's like having a battery in a cell phone."

I pulled the thing away from my ear and looked at it, then thrust it back against my ear. "Speaking of which, why do they make these damn phones so small?"

27

Jennifer sighed. "Grandpa, I don't know what I'm going to do with you. Cell phones are small so you can easily carry them with you. Now, don't change the subject. Tell me all about finding the dead body."

I recounted the morning's activities.

"And because you argued with the victim, the detective thinks you might have killed him."

"That's right. Circumstantial evidence, but the best he has so far."

"Maybe someone had a grudge against the street person."

"That makes more sense than an old fart like me doing it."

"I know you had nothing to do with the murder, Grandpa."

"I appreciate the vote of confidence. Will you be a character witness at my trial?"

"It won't go that far." There was a pause on the line. "Grandpa, did you look carefully at the dead body?"

"I saw a shoe and then the rest of the appendages attached to it."

"Think back. There must be a clue in something you saw at the crime scene."

My daytime photographic memory clicked in, and I recreated the image of the man sprawled in the posies. "Yeah, I can visualize him lying there."

"Anything unusual?"

"Yeah. He was dead."

Jennifer clicked her tongue. "I know that. What else?"

"He was dressed like a bum."

"There might still be a clue there somewhere. Keep thinking it over."

"I better do it today. From what I've learned, my memory is great at what transpired today, but overnight it goes in the crapper."

"Grandpa, what a way to talk." Then she giggled. "You're so

old-fashioned. The kids I hear swear don't use any of the funny words you do."

"Well, don't be like me. Speak nicely."

"Don't worry. I don't have to prove anything by swearing. I think it's gross."

"Good for you. Just as long as you don't think I'm gross."

"You're a denizen of a different era."

I almost swallowed the phone. "Where'd you learn a phrase like that?"

I could picture a shrug. "I've been doing a lot of reading this summer. It popped out from some book."

"I'll noodle over it. In the meantime if you have any other suggestions, let me know."

"I'll put my brain to work. You and I are a great investigative team, Grandpa. I'll see if I can come up with any new ideas. I'm going to be a private investigator when I grow up."

"I'm going to be a geezer when I grow up."

"You already are, Grandpa, and a darn good one. Now you be sure to call regularly during the cruise. Then we can discuss solving this crime."

"Yes, ma'am."

"And I'm glad you decided to use the cell phone."

"Fortunately, Marion knows how the crazy thing works."

"Just write a note in your journal to call me every several days."

"Will do. Tell me what you're doing this summer."

"Swim season is over, but I'm playing a lot of tennis right now. Whacking the ball pretty good."

"You keep at it. Tennis is a good sport for a lifetime."

"I've been improving. I've entered my first city tournament, which starts tomorrow. I'm playing singles and also entered doubles with my friend Patty."

"We'll have to talk during the week. I'll let you know how

Marion and I are enjoying the cruise, and you can keep me posted on your tennis results."

"Okay. And you watch for all those whales in Alaskan waters."

"I've heard a rumor they're waiting for me. I'll check them out from the comfort of a large ship. As long as I don't have to go near the water, I'll be fine."

"Oh, Grandpa. When are you going to learn to love the ocean?"

"Probably when I start loving lawyers and pills. You realize Marion stuffed three huge pills down my throat this morning?"

"You be brave and take your medicine. That's what my parents always tell me when I'm sick."

"But I'm perfectly healthy except for the fact I can't remember squat."

"That's why you need to take your pills. And another thing. Lawyers aren't so bad. You have a very good friend in Hawaii who was a judge and lawyer."

"I do?"

"Yes. When you lived in the retirement home. You and Meyer Ohana became good friends just like Patty and me. He's a retired lawyer."

"I'll be damned. Me, consorting with a lawyer?"

"Now that you have a cell phone, you should call him too. He'd like to hear about your cruise. He's living in a care home because he can't see very well anymore. He has macular degeneration."

"Kind of goes with my memory degeneration."

"Oh, Grandpa. You're still with it. You just need your journal and Marion to remind you of what's happened recently. Oh, I have to go. Patty and I have a practice match. We're playing two older girls to improve our game. Be sure to call me again."

"I'll remind Marion to remind me."

"Bye, Grandpa."

I handed the phone to Marion.

"You need to push the red button to end the call," she said.

"These new-fangled gadgets are too complicated for me."

"It's easy to use. Green on. Red off."

"Like my memory. Too bad my brain's set for red overnight. Say, Jennifer mentioned I have a friend in Hawaii named Meyer Ohana."

"That's right. I know him as well. You were buddies and he helped you catch a murderer." Her eyes lit up. "You should give him a call. He'll want to hear that you're once again being questioned by the police."

"Just as long as I don't have to ask him to represent me. Darn lawyers."

Marion pushed some buttons on the phone. "Here. Austin programmed in Meyer's phone number for you. You can call him." She handed the phone back to me.

"I know. Green." I pushed the blasted button.

A woman with a melodic voice answered. I assumed this wasn't Meyer, so I asked for him. She indicated he was at the breakfast table but would retrieve him.

I imagined a dog picking up a giant bone.

Finally, a male voice came on the line.

"This is Paul Jacobson of the fleeing memory. Am I speaking with Meyer Ohana?"

"Paul, it's great to hear your voice."

"I suppose it's good to hear yours except I don't recognize it from cream cheese. I understand we're friends from my Hawaii days."

He chuckled. "That's right. You sound like you're at the bottom of a well. Where are you calling from?"

I adjusted the useless container of electronic parts. "I'm in Seattle preparing to launch upon an Alaskan honeymoon cruise."

"You're quite the adventurer, Paul. Traveling all over, getting married, now preparing to brave the waters of Alaska."

"Brave is right. I'm the original landlubber."

"I remember that. But you've braved the ocean before."

"I don't recall anything other than sticking a toe in the surf."

"I'll recount the story for you sometime."

"Won't do any good. I'll just forget it again anyway."

"So have you found any dead bodies yet?"

I almost choked on my spittle. "I just spoke with Jennifer and she asked the same question. What's the deal with dead bodies?"

"Paul, some people have magnetic personalities, but in your case you attract other things."

"And here I thought I was just a harmless old geezer."

"Don't misinterpret what I'm saying. You don't do anything wrong, but you seem to have a knack for being the first on the scene when a murder has been committed."

"My kismet."

"Apparently so. Now are you going to tell me what happened or do I have to ask Marion to pick up the phone to explain?"

"There wasn't much to it." I proceeded to give him the gory details.

"And once again your temper put you in a bad spot because you were seen arguing with the victim shortly before his death."

"Yeah. That's the problem. For an old poop I shoot my mouth off at the wrong time. You'd think I'd know better by now."

"You'll never change, Paul. That's what I like about you."

"You, Marion and Jennifer seem to be my cheerleaders. If only Detective Bearhurst would pick up the pompoms."

"You have to provide the detective with some leads of other suspects to pursue."

"Since this all happened so quickly, I don't have any good ideas. Jennifer had me visualize the scene but nothing popped into my addled brain."

"Think of other connections, such as who might have been in the area around the murder."

"I'll keep working on it but so far no brainstorms, only brain farts."

"Keep at it and enjoy the whale watching."

I would have rubbed my hands together except I had to hold that stupid piece of junk next to my ear. "I'm looking forward to seeing pods and pods of whales."

"Paul, there's someone else here who will want to speak with you."

"A long-lost relative?"

"No. Henry Palmer. Henry used to sit with us at the dining room table in the Kina Nani retirement home. We were quite the threesome of eligible bachelors until Marion broke up the trio. You probably don't remember Henry though."

"Can't say as I do."

"Henry is short, squat and bald. He suffers from Asperger's syndrome, which leads him to be very focused on things he's interested in like his coin collection and baseball facts, but he lacks the social graces, so don't be surprised if he insults you."

"Great."

Meyer chuckled. "You two had quite the dialogue going at times, provoking each other."

"Since I mouth off too much, I can understand that."

"Henry had a heart attack followed by surgery and moved to the same care home I'm in for additional assistance. Let me bring him to the phone."

I heard the receiver clunk down and then waited. After some background mumbling a hoarse voice came on the line. "Hello, jerk."

"You sound like you have gravel in your mouth, Henry."

"My throat has never been the same after the doctor

crammed a tube down it during my open heart surgery."

"So you survived in spite of your acerbic personality?"

"Yeah, so I could continue to put up with morons like you."

This guy was starting to piss me off, but I kept my cool. "Well, I'm glad you pulled through even if it didn't improve your sweet disposition."

"Found any dead bodies lately?"

I felt like chewing up the cell phone and spitting out the pieces. "Don't start that up. Meyer can tell you what happened."

"Meyer's a useless old goat."

"He speaks kindly of you."

"You're all a bunch of retards."

"Don't take any wooden nickels in your coin collection and put Meyer back on the line."

There was a pause, and then in a quiet crunchy tone I heard, "I miss you." Then some shuffling noises and Meyer came back on the phone.

"Did I overhear Henry say he misses you, Paul?"

"Yeah. After insulting me up one side and down the other, he threw that in at the end."

"I've never heard him say something like that."

"Maybe he's trying to reform."

"Paul, you do have a positive impact on people. I miss you as well."

I sighed. "This memory loss is a pisser of a problem. I wish I could remember you. Thanks for the gracious words."

"Say hi to Marion for me and give a call again. It's always good to hear from you."

"Will do. And tell Henry what I related to you. He asked the same stupid question that everyone else has concerning me finding a dead body."

After we said our good-byes and I pushed the red button, Marion said, "I better call my daughter Andrea as well."

She used the cell phone and spoke for a few minutes. Then I heard her say, "Hi, Austin. Yes, we are." Marion alternately listened and talked for a few minutes then she handed the phone to me. "Here. My grandson Austin wants to speak to you."

I put the thing back to my ear. I might as well have glued it there.

"Hello, Austin. Your grandmother says you set up this tiny phone with telephone numbers of people we know."

"Yup. I figured you wouldn't use it otherwise."

"Well, thanks. This is the third call we've made this morning."

"Find any dead bodies yet?"

I almost threw the phone against the wall. "Why does everybody ask me that?"

"You have a reputation to uphold."

"To answer your impertinent question, I did find a dead man in a flower garden this morning."

"Cool."

"That was exactly Jennifer's reaction as well. Are you two in cahoots?"

There was a pause on the line. "We talk once in a while."

"Do I detect a budding friendship?"

"She's cool."

"I think so, too. Your grandmother and I will be boarding the ship soon to visit Alaska."

"There are supposed to be all kinds of whales up there."

"That's what I hear. I'm ready to spot them by the dozens."

"Now tell me more. You mentioned a body in a garden."

I sighed. "Everyone wants to hear the details. Okay. This is what happened." I went through the litany of events again. I was beginning to sound like a broken record.

"And the police detective suspects you because you were at the scene of the crime and had been seen with the victim earlier."

"Exactly."

"But you didn't do it, so some time between when you argued with the man and when you found his body someone else killed him."

"Precisely, Dr. Watson."

"Huh?"

"Just a saying."

"So who else could have been in the area?" Austin asked.

"I saw other people in the park earlier, fish and produce sellers, various homeless people and a few stray early-morning tourists like myself."

"Probably wasn't another tourist, not likely to be a regular park visitor or food seller. I'd vote for a homeless person."

"Jennifer's conclusion was someone with a grudge."

"There you go. Now all you have to do is make sure the detective checks out all the homeless people with grudges."

"Given the size of Seattle and the number of street people I saw this morning, that's no easy task."

"Still, it makes more sense than you doing it."

"My sentiments exactly. We'll see what the good detective comes up with by the time my ship comes in."

"Jennifer and I will talk it over and see if we can come up with any new ideas. She's planning to be a private investigator when she grows up."

"That's what she told me. How about you? What are your career plans?"

"I'm only in middle school, but I have some thoughts."

"Which are?"

"I think I'll become a lawyer."

"Useless attorneys."

"You're not a big fan of lawyers?"

"No. Why do you want to go to the Dark Side like that?"

"Lawyers have to be very logical, figure out a strategy and

convince people. Besides, I like to talk."

"I can tell. Do you want to speak with your grandmother again?"

"Sure."

I put Marion back on, and they yakked for another ten minutes. When Marion finally pushed the red button she said, "Austin has become quite a fan of yours."

"Sounds like a fan of Jennifer as well. Our grandkids make quite a pair."

"That's for sure. I think we'll be leaving the planet in good hands with those two."

With all of our phone correspondence caught up on, the next order of business was to check out of the hotel and catch a cab to the wharf.

We exited the taxi into a scene of mass chaos. We schlepped our bags to a line to check them in with hundreds of our closest new companions.

A boy of ten or so bumped into my leg.

"Be careful, Sandor. Don't run into the nice man."

"No problem," I said, patting the rascal on the head. "And thank you for calling me a nice man."

As we waited in line, I said to Marion, "Maybe I should enlist that boy's mother as a character witness if Detective Bearhurst keeps after me."

"I'll be a character witness as well," Marion said. "You are a certified character."

I raised an eyebrow. "I'll have to start swatting you for telling bad puns."

When we finally reached the front of the line and handed our luggage to a large gorilla in a uniform who tossed our bags on a conveyor belt, we were directed to go back outside and upstairs to wait in another line.

Following the lemmings, we mounted the stairs and re-acquainted ourselves with the mob of people. Shortly, a pleasant woman in a white uniform inspected our tickets. "These have the VIP seal," she said. "You can move to that station." She pointed toward a counter with no one else in line. All the other counters had fifty or so people waiting.

"Hey, this isn't so bad," I said as we once again handed over our tickets and passports. "I wonder how we rate such treatment?"

"You were given these tickets by a businessman you helped in Colorado, Paul. They certainly arranged the royal treatment."

"Nothing but the best for my bride."

After a moment of checking and stamping, a machine spat out two plastic credit cards.

"What are these?" I asked.

"You charge everything on the ship using these cards, and they are your identification when embarking or disembarking," the clerk informed me.

"So I better guard it with my life," I said.

She gave me a pearly white smile. "Not that extreme, but it's best not to lose it."

I inspected my card. It read Scandinavian *Sunshine,* the name of our home for the next week, had my name in crisp capital letters, the ship phone number in case I got lost and wanted to call the captain, and a muster station assignment.

"I haven't been assigned a muster station since I was in the Navy during World War II," I said to Marion. "I hope I pass muster again."

She swatted me.

The woman behind the counter who had watched our antics said, "Now please smile for the camera."

We each had our picture snapped.

Continuing to be nosy, I inquired about the photographs.

"It's part of our security system. When your card is scanned, your photograph is brought up on a monitor to validate the correct person is getting on or off the ship."

"Also to make sure I don't steal the captain's silverware."

She chuckled. "We do scan what you carry onto the ship, so be careful."

As we moseyed up a gangway, I finally had a view of a glistening white hull. Sure enough, it was the one I had spotted earlier in the morning.

I looked down as we passed over a small stretch of water separating the ship from the dock. I gulped. I wasn't afraid of heights, but the ocean always gave me a queasy feeling. And here I would be surrounded by water for a week. Anyway, this ship seemed large enough to stay afloat.

"So how do our suitcases get to the right room?" I asked Marion.

"Our cruise packet had luggage tags. I put them on and someone will deliver them to our place, Room 10610."

"I'm glad you're on top of all the details."

"My job is to make sure you arrive safely and stay out of trouble."

"Well, you haven't been doing your job very well. I've already stepped in the doo-doo in Seattle."

Marion squeezed my arm. "Now you're on the cruise so you'll avoid any more trying events."

"I sure hope you're right."

We worked our way along the deck and entered the body of the ship through large seaworthy doors to find a bank of elevators, one of which we took up to the tenth floor.

"We're in the high rent section," I said.

Once we deciphered the numbering scheme, we located our room mid-ship on the port side. I was starting to feel all nautical with visions of bows and sterns dancing in my head.

We tested both our key cards to our satisfaction and entered our room to find a cozy double bed, small sitting area and balcony. I stuck my head in the bathroom.

"Good thing we're both trim and fit." I patted my still-flat stomach. Next I slid open the patio door and discovered two chairs facing out across Elliott Bay. The sun reflected off the water, and I watched two small cabin cruisers motor past.

"Look, Paul, we have a newsletter with all the events for the day." Marion handed me a four-page missive that described a hypnotist show taking place at 7:30 and 9:30 that night, all the restaurants that would force food down our throats, a manda-tory lifeboat drill at 3:30 and numerous shops where I could invest my retirement savings.

"We're not going to be bored on this trip," I said.

"No, and I want to join the spa."

"Oh, pshaw," I replied.

Just then there was a knock on the door.

"Is the welcoming committee here already?" I asked.

I opened the door to discover a man approximately my height with flaming red hair. He wore a white suit with a Scandinavian Sea Lines insignia on the lapel.

"You here with our luggage?" I asked.

"No, Mr. Jacobson. I'm Norbert Grudion, head of security for the Scandinavian *Sunshine*."

CHAPTER 4

I wondered why the head of the ship's security would be making a call on little old me. I didn't know if I should join him in a Swedish polka or whip up some meatballs.

"Well, come on in and make me feel secure."

He raised an eyebrow but followed me into the cabin.

"Marion, we have a visitor."

Grudion introduced himself to my wife.

"What brings you to our part of the ship?" I asked.

He tapped his right index finger on the dark wood panel opposite the bed. "Yah, I wanted to meet you, Mr. Jacobson. I've received several conflicting reports about you."

"My reputation precedes me."

"So it seems. First, I was given a message that you were to be accommodated the full VIP treatment."

"My wife is interested in the spa. Is that like a spa treatment?"

He wrinkled his nose. "Yah, I was asked to make sure you received a special invitation to join the Captain's table tonight in the Discovery Room at seven P.M."

"I'm up for any new discoveries."

"Paul, that's wonderful," Marion piped in.

"Then my bride and I accept your kind invitation."

"But here's the incongruity." Grudion paused, pursing his lips. "I also received a report from the Seattle Police Department warning me that you were a person of interest in a homicide investigation."

I gulped. "Well, some people think I'm an interesting person. But regarding what happened earlier, it was just a minor misunderstanding. I happened upon a dead body in a garden this morning."

He tapped a finger on a notebook he held. "Yah, I also have a reference to a robbery at the Lincoln Hotel this morning, stating you were also at the scene of that crime."

"I was an innocent bystander."

He slowly nodded his head. "And completing a further background check on you, Mr. Jacobson, I found records indicating accusations in Hawaii, Colorado and Venice Beach, California."

Marion put her hands on her hips. "And if you check more thoroughly, you'll find that in all three locales Paul helped bring the true criminals to justice."

Grudion squinted at her. "Meaning what?"

"Paul was instrumental in uncovering evidence that led to the arrest of the real murderer in each case."

Grudion turned toward me. "Yah, why don't you recount the particulars of these incidents for me?"

"I'm afraid I can't, Mr. Grudion."

"And why is that?"

"I suffer from short-term memory loss. I remember all the details of what's happened today, but the last few years have gone 'poof.' "

"That's correct," Marion said. "Paul forgets overnight."

"Are you saying he won't remember this conversation if I question him tomorrow?"

"For most days, that's the case," Marion said.

I now regarded Marion. "For most days? You mean some days I might remember?"

"There is one particular circumstance when you retain your

memory." She gave me a Cheshire cat grin. "But back to your concerns, Mr. Grudion. I can assure you that Paul is no threat."

"We'll see. I'll check in with you again, Mr. Jacobson."

"First, the Captain's table and then all this special attention from you, Mr. Grudion. What's next?"

"I hope no trouble." He turned on his heels and left our honeymoon suite.

"Several things I don't understand," I said. "You, Grudion and my earlier phone conversations referred to crimes I had been involved with in other places."

"That's right, Paul. You were suspected of murder in each location but helped the police find the culprit."

"But I'm not trained in that sort of thing. All I ever did was push paper in the Navy and run an auto parts store."

"Well, in the last year you've also become an amateur sleuth."

I shook my head. "I don't remember one iota of that. And this oblique reference to most days that I can't remember what happened the day before. There's the implication that once in a while I do remember."

"There is one circumstance when you wake up recalling things from the day before." She waited a beat and then gave me a smile again.

"Don't keep me in suspense. What makes my faulty wiring work on some occasions?"

She leaned over and gave me a peck on the cheek. "It'll be a little surprise for you."

"I don't like surprises."

"I think you'll enjoy this one. Now let's go explore the ship."

"I'm for that."

"The first thing I want to do is find the spa," Marion said.

I picked up a map of the ship that had been left with the newsletter on our bed.

"All the way aft and up one deck, Admiral."

Marion giggled. "You sound so nautical."

"Just wait until this tub starts moving and I get my sea legs."

We sauntered toward the stern and took a flight of stairs up to find a marble-covered floor and an oak counter manned by two young ladies with gleaming black hair.

"We'd like to sign up for the spa," I told them.

"Names and cabin number?"

I gave them the particulars, and one of the girls thumbed through a list. Then she looked up at me with a broad grin. "My goodness. You two are already listed as receiving a complimentary spa registration plus a complete massage during the cruise, free."

"Paul, let's both have massages tomorrow, since it's a day at sea."

"Okay," I replied. "Sign us up."

"We have a regular massage or a hot stone massage. Which would you prefer?"

Marion smiled. "I've never had a hot stone massage."

"Whatever my bride wants. We'll go whole hog. Give us the full treatment."

"We can accommodate you at ten A.M. Would you like a tour of the spa facility today?"

"Lead on, but don't lead me astray," I said.

The taller and lankier of the two introduced herself as Georgette and guided us into a commons area with couches and then into a section with lounge chairs facing large windows looking out over the water. Soft music played, making me think of a nap.

"On each side is a room like this for relaxing," Georgette said. "This side is for the women."

We passed through a doorway into a spacious room with an indoor swimming pool, Jacuzzi and a hot bubbly pool. Again lounge chairs were lined up facing a set of huge plate glass windows on the stern and gigantic tropical plants growing out of urns. Here the soft music had been replaced by the sound of chirping birds.

Georgette pointed to doorways. "Locker rooms are off to the side. Just check in at the main desk, turn in your room card and you'll receive a locker key."

Then we entered a hallway with small rooms off to both sides. "These are the treatment rooms for facials, massage and acupuncture."

"I'll stick with being stuffed with hot rocks," I said. "I don't want anyone sticking funny little needles in me."

Georgette's eyes scrunched up and she laughed. "It's nothing like that. It's very relaxing."

After the grand tour, we walked up a staircase to find a fitness center. Twenty- and thirty-somethings were already pedaling, jogging and stomping.

We continued our exploration and entered a cafeteria. A woman in a dark skirt and blazer stopped us, pointed toward a blue globe and asked us to sanitize our hands. I thrust my hands downward to receive a globule, which I rubbed in. A sign explained that this was to prevent the spread of any infectious diseases during our cruise.

People were already stuffing their faces. I noticed that the people pigging out tended to be larger in girth than the ones pounding on machines in the fitness center. Oh well. This ship offered whatever entertainment you chose.

We each grabbed a banana and yogurt for a mid-day snack. Next we found the outdoor pools and hot tubs.

"We'll have our own private pool and hot tub in the spa," Marion said.

"Plus it will be warmer inside, so we won't have to freeze our tushes."

We climbed a set of stairs and found an area with lounge

chairs and a jogging and walking track that circled the ship.

"This will be perfect," I said. "I can stuff my face at meals and then take a stroll here to exercise."

"I may even join you, if it isn't too early in the morning."

"Really?"

Marion chuckled. "Probably not, since I like to sleep in. But you can do it on your own since you wake up earlier than I do."

Having toured part of our new home away from home, we returned to our cabin to unpack. Then a voice came over the intercom informing us that the lifeboat drill would begin in ten minutes. And at the sound of a horn we were to don our life jackets and dash to our muster station listed on our embarkation card. I located two orange life vests and dropped them on the bed.

As predicted, an irritatingly loud horn blasted, and Marion and I put on our life vests. We headed out into the hallway to join the throng moving toward the stairwell. We had to go down to deck seven and the staircase was jammed with orange-clad touristas.

Just as we approached our destination someone bumped into me, and I bashed into a woman in front of me, knocking her over. She tumbled down the remaining stairs and thudded to a stop.

She sat there dazed, a cane by her side. One of the crew members raced over, and he and I helped her to her feet.

"This man knocked me down the stairs," she told the young man in the crisp white uniform.

"I apologize," I said. "Someone pushed into me, and it caused a chain reaction."

"A likely story," she said, dusting herself off.

"May I see some identification, please?" the young man said to me.

I showed him my embarkation card and told him my name.

A man and woman in their thirties came rushing over, concern on their faces. The woman was attractive in an anemic sort of way, blond curls over a high forehead. The man was also skinny and had the serious expression of someone who didn't smile much. They fussed over the older woman who'd fallen, the man glaring at me as the young woman handed her the cane and helped her away. People continued to surge around us, so Marion and I got our butts in gear and proceeded to muster station Y3 Deck 7 Mid Port.

"That woman seemed awfully upset," Marion said.

"I can understand. I didn't like being bashed into either, and I'm sorry I knocked her down."

After the crew formed us in neat lines, a whistle blew and we returned to our cabin. Going up the stairs I stayed a ways behind anyone else and watched my back to make sure no one nudged me.

"That was a pretty fruitless exercise," I said as we approached our cabin.

Marion shrugged. "At least we know where our life vests are and where to go if there's an emergency."

"Not that I'd remember it anyway."

"But I know now, so I can lead us."

"We'll have to buy one of those kid leashes. You can tether me, and I can follow you."

"That won't be necessary. We can just hold hands."

"Like a pair of newlyweds."

"Exactly."

Back inside our home base I finished hanging up my clothes and stuffed my underwear and socks into a drawer. Then I slid our suitcases under the bed.

"Cozy but neat," Marion informed me as I passed muster for the second time that day.

"I hope we see some whales," I said. "That's something I've

never experienced."

There was a knock on the door, and I lumbered over to open it. Norbert Grudion stood there.

"Come on in," I said. "You here for a cabin inspection?"

"No, Mr. Jacobson. I just received a report that you pushed a passenger down the stairs during the lifeboat drill."

Marion came to my side. "I saw the whole incident. Someone bumped into Paul who stumbled forward, striking the woman who fell. It was just an accident. Too bad we didn't see who started it all."

Grudion stared at me intently. "Yah, you've only been on the ship three hours, and already you're involved in an incident. My concern is for the safety of all passengers." He wagged a finger at me. "I don't want to spend all of my time watching you, Mr. Jacobson, so please don't cause any more problems."

"I appreciate the special attention, but you probably have bigger fish to fry than little old me."

"Yah, I hope so."

After he left, I turned toward Marion. "I've found a way to alienate the local constabulary, and this guy Grudion will be breathing down my neck for the whole cruise."

Marion patted my arm. "Don't worry, Paul. I'm sure there won't be any more problems."

"Yeah, at least he didn't revoke our invitation to sit at the Captain's table tonight. Probably wanted me there so he can watch me."

The rest of the afternoon passed uneventfully; I didn't get in any more trouble. We watched from our balcony as we launched into Elliott Bay and headed north. I kept checking. No whales.

Marion went inside to use the little girls' room, and I continued to scan the seven seas. Too bad I hated the ocean. It was pretty from up here, but I had no desire to be in the water or close to it.

Then I began to ponder my fate. After the shock of this morning, I now had accidentally gained the attention of the intense ship security officer. A gust of air rippled past, and I shivered. An old coot like me should just be hunkering down in an easy chair without a care in the world, and here I was worried about a murder and a stairwell accident. I would have to keep my wits about me. With street people flopping over dead and ladies tumbling down stairs, I'd have to pay keen attention to what was going on around me.

When dinner time approached, I put on a tie and my dark blue suit, and Marion donned a flowered frock that showed off her attractive legs.

"Wow, you're a fine-looking old broad," I said.

"I guess I'll take that as a compliment."

"I'm a fortunate guy. I can't believe you decided to hitch up with an old fart like me and my soggy memory."

"It does make life interesting, Paul."

At dinner we sat at a table of eight with Captain Sanderson, a crusty seaman in his sixties with a neatly trimmed white beard and dancing blue eyes; an unattached woman, Mrs. Malloy, who yakked up a storm; a shipping executive named Samuels and his trophy wife; and another bigwig from some new-fangled technology company and his female companion.

I ordered one of those tall tropical drinks with pineapple and orange juice, coconut milk, and probably a little hot lava. I told the waitress to make it a virgin since I didn't want to kill any more brain cells. They were a scarce commodity.

Part way into the meal, Captain Sanderson nodded to Marion and me. "I received a special message from a friend of mine that the two of you were recently married."

"That's right," I said. "You're looking at a pair of newlyweds."

Everyone at the table raised glasses of champagne to toast us.

Samuels, who was sitting next to me, leaned over and whispered, "I'm into my third wife. Keep wearing them out so I thought I'd go with a younger model this time."

I whispered back, "I've only worn out one, and I go with the seasoned model."

Samuels straightened up and said in a voice that could be heard by others, "How'd you make your fortune, Mr. Jacobson?"

"I wouldn't call it a fortune, but the auto parts business."

"A supplier to the big three?"

"No. I ran an auto parts store in Los Angeles."

Samuels's eyebrows raised, and he turned to make a comment to his not-yet worn-out wife. I guessed he was trying to figure out why Marion and I were here with the upper crust.

After cleaning out a lobster shell and decimating some tiramisu, I asked Marion if she was up for an after-dinner stroll. We thanked the captain, excused ourselves and headed for the promenade deck to enjoy the outside air, which was still mild.

"What's our agenda for the rest of the evening?" I asked.

"I want to go to the hypnotist show."

"Fine by me. I've never put much stock in hypnotism, but I'm game to watch the show."

Half an hour later we entered a large theater and took seats toward the front center. When the program began, a glib young twerp, probably in his fifties, sauntered onstage.

He introduced himself and then said, "As I get older, I find I have more trouble with my sense of sight and hearing. Just yesterday I met a man who asked me if I had retired. I thought he asked me if I had expired."

Amid a round of chuckles, I elbowed Marion. "Hey, this guy tells dumb jokes just like I do."

"Ssh." She glared at me.

He told some other jokes and then explained about hypnotism. "Now, are there any newlyweds here tonight? Please raise your hands."

Marion grabbed my arm and lifted it along with hers.

The hypnotist spotted us and said, "Okay. I want all of you to come up on stage."

I looked at Marion. "Do you want to do this?"

"Sure. Be a good sport."

I shrugged. "Anything my bride wants."

We stood up, moseyed to the front and climbed the stairs to the stage along with half a dozen other couples, all in their twenties.

The hypnotist adjusted his tie and said to me, "Aren't you a little old to be a newlywed or are you the chaperone for these other couples?"

"I'm just getting started," I said. "And aren't you too young to be the entertainment?"

He smiled and launched into a preview of what he was going to do to us, stating that he could hypnotize people to help them remember things they had forgotten.

Marion raised her hand, and the hypnotist thrust the microphone toward her. "That wouldn't work with my husband. He suffers from short-term memory loss and doesn't remember things from the day before."

"Well, that's a challenge for me," he said. "I guess he'll have to be my first victim, I mean, volunteer."

He asked me my name and told me to take a seat in a chair facing a small screen. He snapped his fingers and a spot of light appeared on the screen.

I plopped down, my old ticker beating faster than a juiced-up bongo drum player. What was he going to do to me?

"Now I want you to relax. You will remember everything that transpires, so there's no reason to be tense."

"Easy for you to say."

He smiled. "That's better. Take a deep breath . . . and let it out. Good. Another deep breath . . . and let it out."

I felt like I was at the doctor's office having a physical.

"Now focus on the dot of light on the screen."

I looked toward the screen and my muscles relaxed.

"Just keep your eyes on the dot. You're getting sleepy and all your cares of the day are slipping away."

Like waking up not knowing where the hell I was, finding out I was married and then discovering a dead body. Right.

"Keep watching the dot as your arms and legs become heavy."

I suddenly felt very lethargic.

"Your head is heavy. Your neck is heavy. Your body is heavy. Your arms and legs are heavy."

He was right. I had the sensation that my whole body was lead.

"Keep watching the dot as you fall into a deep and relaxing sleep. You'll be aware of everything I say and will remember all of this after you wake up."

Now nothing bothered me.

"Now sense the weight flowing out of your body and you are as light as a feather."

It now seemed like I was floating around the room watching myself sitting there in the chair.

"Mr. Jacobson is fully hypnotized. He will respond to any request I make but won't do anything that is against his principles. Mr. Jacobson, your right arm has a helium balloon attached to it. It's going to rise straight up."

Sure enough, my arm acted as if it had a mind of its own and popped up like I was a school kid in class with the answer the teacher wanted.

"Now your raised hand will stick to the top of your head."

I found my hand searching for fleas in my wavy locks.

"Now I want you to pick your nose in front of this whole audience."

I heard laughter. No way I'd do that.

"As you see, Mr. Jacobson will not do something that he considers repugnant. Now if I had suggested he was in the privacy of his own home and his nose itched, he would have followed my command.

My hand shot to my face and scratched my sniffer.

Another titter of laughter.

"Now, Mr. Jacobson, please tell me what you did yesterday."

I felt my mouth pop open, but no words came out.

"Mr. Jacobson?"

"I don't know."

"Think hard. There must be something from yesterday."

"Nope. Nothing."

I heard Marion's voice. "I told you. He has short-term memory loss. You can ask him anything about today, but he doesn't recall things overnight."

The hypnotist cleared his throat. "Let's see if Mr. Jacobson can remember something unique that happened to him today. Mr. Jacobson, what was the strangest thing that you encountered this morning?"

"I found a dead body."

CHAPTER 5

A collective gasp rose from the audience at hearing that I had found a dead body that morning.

"Please recount what happened."

"I was wandering through a public garden in Seattle and spotted a shoe. When I went over to investigate, the shoe was on a foot of a man who had been murdered."

"Did you recognize him?"

"Yes. He was a street person named Curly who had accosted me earlier in the morning."

"Okay. I want you to describe him in detail."

"He wore brown trousers, black loafers, a red plaid shirt under a dirty blue windbreaker, had a gray scraggly beard and unkempt gray hair, liver spots on his left cheek and black nose hair sticking out."

A titter ran through the crowd.

"Now I want you to reexamine the man. There's something you didn't notice before that is important. You look carefully at him and you see the one thing that you didn't pay attention to before. What is it?"

I felt like I was back in the garden. My eyes focused on Curly's inert body. Then I noticed it. "There's a red bandanna poking out of his jacket pocket."

"And why is that important?"

My mind raced back to an earlier encounter that morning. "Because another homeless man who had also come up to me

54

earlier this morning wore a red bandanna."

The hypnotist turned to the audience. "You see, under hypnotism Mr. Jacobson is able to visualize more of what he saw in the past. He didn't realize he had seen the red bandanna before, but now he remembers exactly what he had seen."

He turned back to face me. "Mr. Jacobson, I want you to come out of your trance when I snap my fingers. You will remember everything that happened in minute detail." He snapped his fingers.

I immediately stood up and went over to Marion and whispered in her ear, "I need to call Detective Bearhurst in Seattle. That red bandanna may be the clue he isn't aware of. If that bandanna belonged to the other street person named Lumpy, he may be the murderer."

"What are you two conspiring over?" the hypnotist asked.

"Just newlywed talk," I said. "I want to thank you for refreshing my memory from this morning, but I need to take care of something important."

"Don't you want to see the rest of the show?"

"Another time."

Then I whispered in Marion's ear. "You stay, and I'll come back as soon as I get a message to Bearhurst. I have his card in the stateroom."

I left the stage and headed to the nearest exit sign to a round of applause.

When I reached our cabin, I located Detective Bearhurst's card and noticed a sticker by the stateroom phone indicating the astronomical price per minute to place phone calls to shore. Oh well, my life savings might be flying away, but I needed to do my civic duty.

I called, asked for the good detective and was told I would be transferred to his cell phone. I waited, tapping my fingers on the table and watching dollar signs flying past my face.

Finally, a crisp voice came on the line, "Detective Bearhurst here."

"Detective, this is Paul Jacobson."

"Mr. Jacobson. I thought you were on a cruise ship."

"I am. My bride and I are enjoying the wonders of the sea, but I have something important to pass on to you."

"A confession?"

"I confess that attitude is awfully negative, but no, I'm innocent as the pure driven snow. I'm calling because I remembered something that will be of use to you in your murder investigation."

There was a momentary pause. "You have memory problems but now recall something relevant?"

"Exactly. I had a little assistance from a hypnotist this evening."

"Is this turning into a crank call?"

"No way. I have something very specific. This morning in addition to being accosted by the victim and then finding his body, I was approached by another street person named Lumpy."

"Yes. Lumpy Holubar. He's one of the regulars who hang out by the Pikes Street Market."

"Didn't know his last name, but Lumpy was wearing a red bandanna when he unceremoniously buttonholed me. Later when I found Curly's body, I didn't make the connection, but under hypnosis I remembered that I had seen a red bandanna in Curly's pocket. It might not be anything, but on the other hand it might be a connection to Lumpy."

"That's it?"

"Check it out, Detective. You'll find the bandanna in Curly's jacket pocket, and it might prove that Lumpy was involved in Curly's untimely demise."

"Interesting."

"I think so. And there might be more of a motive with Lumpy than with little old me."

"I'll check it out."

"Good. I want you to catch the real murderer by the time I sail back into Seattle, so you won't have to waste your time suspecting an old fart like me."

"I'll see what I find. It's also interesting that I received a report late this afternoon that you were involved in an altercation on the ship. Seems a woman filed a complaint that you knocked her over."

I felt the heat rising in my neck. "That was an accident. Someone pushed me, and I bumped into the woman, who then fell down."

"People seem to have accidents when they're around you, Mr. Jacobson."

"I'm not planning on being around any more accidents for the rest of the cruise, Detective. I hope the information I've passed on to you helps."

After hanging up I sat there stewing. I'd only been trying to assist, and Detective Bearhurst made me feel like a Mafioso ready to drop someone tied to an anchor into the ocean. I took a deep breath. He was only doing his job, but it was disturbing that news of events on the ship had already reached him. This secret cabal of law enforcement should have better things to do than exchange stories of Paul Jacobson's adventures.

But my bride needed me by her side, so I returned to the hypnotist show. I found Marion back in her seat and plunked down next to her. On the stage four people were crawling around on their hands and knees, woofing like dogs.

"At least I didn't end up doing that," I said.

"You escaped lightly," Marion replied. "While you were gone, he tried to hypnotize me, but it didn't take. I was excused to return to my seat."

"And I thought I'd be the one who couldn't be hypnotized. You must have a stronger will than I have."

"I just need to be as conscious as possible so someone in the family can remember what's going on."

"And I gratefully accept the assistance."

After the show we strolled along the starboard side of deck seven and stared out into the darkness. A few lights could be discerned from Vancouver Island. I looked down and saw spots of foam sparkling from reflected ship light. A gentle background thumping noise permeated the night as the ship's hull pounded through the gentle waves.

We held hands as we returned to the cabin, then discarded clothes and climbed between the sheets. Suddenly I found a soft body snuggling against mine. A warm surge shot though me, and something in my lower quarters started to enlarge.

"What's that poking me?" Marion asked with a giggle.

"I'll be darned. You seem to have inspired a little-used part of my anatomy."

"I wouldn't say that it was little used."

"I certainly don't remember the last time it came alive like this."

Our two old bodies engaged, and we built up as much friction as any of those twentysomethings who had been on treadmills earlier could have mustered.

Afterwards, I lay there spent, marveling at my strange life and the blessing of having Marion there with me. I could have been an abandoned street person like Lumpy or Curly, but instead I had a wife keeping me warm as we sailed the oceans of the world.

CHAPTER 6

My eyes popped open, and I discovered I was in a little room that was gently swaying. Next to me rested the form of a woman with silver gray hair cascading over the pillow. I knew immediately I was on the Scandinavian Sea Lines *Sunshine* sailing to Alaska with my wife Marion. And I had short-term memory loss and wasn't supposed to remember things from the day before. But I recalled yesterday as clear as a polished set of crystal. What was happening? Had the sea air cured my crappy mental peculiarity?

I stretched. So this was what it was like for normal people to wake up in the morning. I thought of a nice hot cup of java and some vittles but felt contented in knowing where I was and why I was here.

Marion stirred and propped herself up on her elbows. "Are you up already?" she asked, eyes hardly open.

"Yup. And something amazing happened. I can remember yesterday."

She sat up, and I admired how attractive she was even in her sleepy and disheveled state.

"You're a fine-looking woman."

She rubbed her eyes. "I don't think this is my best appearance of the day."

I whistled. "You look darn good to me. I still can't believe my memory is clicking on all cylinders."

Marion chuckled. "This happens once in a while, Paul."

"What's the secret? Was it the change of venue or the rocking ship shaking things up?"

"Oh, it was shaking things up all right." She giggled.

"There's some classified information here that you're keeping from me."

"It's something we did last night."

"Let's see. Eating at the Captain's table, strolling on deck, the hypnotist show. . . . Is this a delayed reaction from being hypnotized?"

"No, it's something we did when we returned to the cabin last night."

"All we did was crawl into bed and then . . ."

"That's right."

"You mean our little romp upon the mattress?"

"Exactly."

My yap must have dropped open because Marion said, "Close your mouth before you catch mosquitoes."

"I can't believe that our intimacy would shake up the old brain cells."

"It's one of your interesting idiosyncrasies."

"In that case I wish my old body were up to a repeat performance."

"We'll see. Maybe the right circumstances will present themselves again soon."

"Wow. Something to look forward to. How long will this new mental acuity last?"

"You fade overnight. Tomorrow you won't remember things from the short-term past anymore."

"Too bad. Last night was a night to remember."

Marion dropped back down and rested her head on the pillow. "I'm not ready to get up. Are you going to sleep some more as well?"

"No. I'm wide awake now. I think I'll explore a little and take my morning constitutional."

"You have your walk, and when you return, I'll be ready to dress."

"I suppose as a newlywed I should stay with you."

"Go walk. You'd only thrash around."

"Maybe something else might happen."

"Not after last night but maybe soon."

"Okay. I have something to anticipate."

Marion buried herself in the covers, and I put on my sweat-suit, donned my dark glasses and grabbed a baseball hat that read, "Geezer and proud of it." I wondered if that had been a wedding present or something I'd collected in my deep dark past.

Remembering my way around the ship from the day before, I climbed the stairs to deck thirteen and emerged into the bright sunlight. Off to starboard I could see some emerald green islands. I leaned over the railing and tried to spot a whale. After ten minutes of squinting and only seeing whitecaps, I abandoned that exercise and decided to really exercise. I revved up my engine and started off at a brisk pace clockwise around the walking and jogging track. On my first revolution, I passed six eager walkers and two joggers heading the other way. Then I reversed my direction and encountered another two walkers and a jogger. They all seemed in good shape and two to five decades younger than me. It was up to me to uphold the honor of the octogenarians. On the next pass I heard footsteps behind me, and a man in his sixties pulled up alongside. He was pant-ing. "I wanted to catch up to you, but you've been moving at a pretty brisk clip," he said.

"At my age once I get going, there's only full speed ahead and a dead stop, the emphasis on dead."

He chuckled. "I'm more into starting slowly and then build-ing up speed after a few laps. This your first cruise?"

I turned toward him and noticed that he was approximately my height with a tan face and wore a floppy white hat.

"First time on a ship since the Navy during World War Two."

"All right. A swabby. I was in the Air Force during Vietnam."

"You see much action?"

"I was a navigator on transport duty between the States and Saigon. How about you?"

"Logistics. I supported Operation Overlord by providing supplies to the troops landing on Utah Beach in Normandy."

"No kidding. That must have been quite an operation."

"I didn't see any action, but I sure pushed a lot of paper."

"So we both had our experience behind the lines. By the way, my name is Andrew Black." He held out a large paw and I clasped it.

"Paul Jacobson here. You been on a cruise before?"

"Yes siree. This is my third. My wife and I did the Caribbean and Hawaii."

"Since I'm a newcomer, tell me how this whole cruise scene works. What should I be sure to do and what should I avoid?"

Andrew bit his lip. "Let's see. First of all, it's very easy to overeat on these cruises. I try to limit myself to a light breakfast and lunch and then usually have a good dinner. I supplement that with my morning walks as well. Still, I'll put on five pounds by the end of the trip."

"You look pretty fit."

"Yeah, I work at it. You seem in good shape as well."

"Physically I'm doing great for an old fart, but I have short-term memory loss."

"That's too bad. How does it affect you?"

"I remember things fine during the day. I still have my photographic memory. But overnight someone removes the batteries and the day before goes blank."

"How do you cope with that?"

"My wife reminds me of things, and she's given me a journal to record my life events in. So all I have to remember is to write in it every night before I go to sleep. Then the next morning I can reacquaint myself with what's transpired."

He shook his head. "I can't imagine what that's like."

"Things could be worse. I'm healthy otherwise. Now back to cruise advice."

"Let's see. There are specialty dining rooms on the ship. My wife and I usually try dinner at one of these during the week, although the regular dining rooms are superb."

"We had an excellent dinner last night."

He stared over at me. "I thought you couldn't remember things from the day before."

"Touché. Nothing wrong with your memory. Once in a blue moon my brain cells get jogged and I can remember. Last night was one of those rare occasions."

"You need to find a way to jog it every night," Andrew said.

"I wish it were that simple. How about excursions?"

"We sign up for shore excursions on most stops, but sometimes we just wander around on our own. That's the beauty of cruises. You can be with other people when you want or you can go off on your own when you choose."

"My wife and I signed up for the spa. Do you do that?"

He smiled. "Yes, indeed. That's one of the best services. It isn't crowded and particularly up here with the cool outside air, it gives me a chance to swim some laps in the pool."

"I hate swimming, but I like the idea of a hot tub. Nothing like a good soak for the old bones."

"And be sure to take in the evening shows. Tonight the ensemble is doing a collection of Broadway show tunes."

"Last night we went to the hypnotist show. He called all the newlyweds up on stage, and I was his first victim."

"That's why you look familiar. I saw the show. He tried to

have you remember from the day before, and you couldn't."

"Evidence of my normal overnight memory."

"So I'm walking with a celebrity." He chuckled. "I'd never go up on the stage like that."

"I'll probably never do it again either."

"We should get together for dinner with our wives. Do you have any plans tonight?"

"None whatsoever. I'm just working on finding my sea legs and learning which end of the ship is which."

"Let's meet at the Regal Room restaurant at seven. We're in room 10590. Give a call if you're delayed."

"I'll remember that." I tapped the side of my head. "As long as I don't take a nap before I write it down. Marion and I are in room 10610 so we're practically neighbors."

He looked at me askance. "I'm glad you remember your room number."

"That's my super memory when I don't fall asleep."

"Now one last recommendation for you. On Friday night at midnight, they have a chocolate buffet. You like chocolate?"

"In any shape or form."

"Then this is a must-attend event. The whole dining room is full of different kinds of chocolate: cake, cookies, pastry, ice cream. Plus they display chocolate sculptures."

"If I can stay awake that late, Marion and I will have to sample some goodies."

Andrew indicted that he had completed his laps and excused himself until we would reconvene for dinner.

I continued for a few more rounds, pausing several times to look unsuccessfully for whales.

When I returned to the cabin, Marion was up.

"I met a nice gentleman who invited us to join him and his wife for dinner tonight."

"Our second dinner invitation in two nights."

"Yeah. We're becoming quite the party animals. What do you want to do today?"

"Breakfast and then the spa."

After Marion had finished beautifying, we proceeded to the Orlean Room for a sit-down breakfast. A pleasant woman with a Swedish accent insisted that we squirt goo on our hands to stave off unwanted viruses before we entered the restaurant. Then we were seated at a table for two.

"My new buddy Andrew gave me a rundown of how a cruise works. The secret is pigging out in moderation and taking in the chocolate buffet at midnight on Friday."

"That will be a challenge on this cruise—eating in moderation with all the choices."

"And we'll have to stay active between meals, taking advantage of excursions, walks and exploring the ship."

After I finished off my Eggs Benedict, we returned to our stateroom to collect swimsuits.

Marion extracted a beach bag from the drawer and dropped in a book. "Paul, you might want to bring something to read while we're in the spa."

"Okay, I'll take this short story collection." I picked up the O. Henry book that rested on my nightstand.

Marion laughed. "You and your short stories. That was sure a clever idea that your granddaughter came up with."

I scratched my head. "I hate to be dense, but I don't recall what Jennifer did."

"It's simple. You used to try reading novels but found it very frustrating because you'd forget from the day before and have to start over every day. Jennifer suggested you read short stories. That way you can enjoy a whole story at each reading."

"And it doesn't even matter if I reread the same story. Except for special mornings like today, I wouldn't remember it. I obviously have a very bright granddaughter. She must take after my new wife."

"Oh, she takes after you. You're pretty good at figuring out things like murders."

"Well, other than the hypnotist helping me remember the red bandanna on the body in Seattle, I haven't done much to assist Detective Bearhurst."

"That just may be the clue he needs."

"We'll see. Let's go experience this spa."

After a brief hike, we turned in our key cards for locker keys. Inside a shiny clean locker room, I shed my clothes, donned my swim trunks and grabbed a towel. I found two open lounge chairs facing the ship's wake and reserved them for Marion and me.

When my bride emerged in her swimming frock, she informed me she wanted to swim a few laps in the pool.

"I hate swimming pools, but for you I'll give it a try," I said.

It was warm and shallow. I waded around, took two tentative strokes, came up spluttering and decided I would walk the pool instead. Water was sloshing back and forth forming small waves.

"You could almost body surf in here," I said to Marion when she came up for air after her laps.

We climbed out and next tried a pool that had contoured rollers you could lie on with water bubbling up around.

"This is more my speed," I said. "I can lie down in hot water and not sink."

"Oh, Paul. If you worked at it you could swim."

"I've tried, but I'm a natural rock, not a fish."

It was so relaxing that I almost fell asleep, catching myself so I wouldn't do my memory reset trick.

Marion wanted to stay on the rollers, but I was ready to move on so I entered the Jacuzzi, which was the hottest of the three bodies of water. A large man rested there with a smile on his face.

"Enjoying the spa?" I asked him.

"Yeah, bruddah. Dis da best. I could sit here all day long."

"You from Hawaii, by any chance?" I asked.

"Yeah, Maui."

"What's a Hawaiian doing way up north in Alaska?"

"My wife always wanted to see the forty-ninth state." He chuckled. "When I was a kid there was a state fair in Hawaii called the Forty-ninth State Fair. But Alaska won out to become the forty-ninth state, and Hawaii settled for the fiftieth. I need to check out the competition."

Marion joined us and I introduced her to the man who said his name was Kimo.

"He's from Hawaii," I informed her.

"We used to live in Hawaii. Paul and I met at a retirement home in Kaneohe."

"No kidding."

After a short soak, Marion told me we should dry off before our hot stone massage appointment in thirty minutes.

My Hawaiian companion said, "Sound like you're gonna be turned into a luau. Best kind of pork is cooked with hot rocks."

"I hope the stones aren't that hot," I said. "I don't fancy being roasted with an apple in my mouth."

Marion and I excused ourselves and wandered over to the lounge chairs to dry off. Marion had picked up two white robes, which we put on over our swim gear. Then we sat down to admire the view.

"I keep looking for whales," I said, "but haven't spotted one yet."

"I'm sure you will. These waters are full of them."

I scanned the wake for a few minutes, not seeing so much as a fin. Then I read an O. Henry short story, titled "After Twenty

Years," about a man named Silky Bob who gets arrested. I hoped that wasn't an omen of what would happen to me.

The background music that played was interspersed with the sound of chirping birds. Along with the humidity in the room, I felt like I was in a tropical rain forest afloat.

I had to be careful not to doze off. This cruise was way too relaxing so far. No hassle, no fuss, just eating and being pampered. What a life for an old geezer like me.

Marion roused me from my reverie by indicating it was time to go play with the hot stones.

"You're quite the slave driver," I said. "Here I am relaxing, and you're forcing me to go have a massage."

"You be careful or I'll tell the massage therapist to overheat the rocks for you."

"Or if I complain too much, there's another solution. I could just see one of those stones being stuck in someone's mouth."

A woman on the next lounge chair looked up from her book toward me.

As we headed toward the hallway I said, "I don't know about this hot rock treatment. Kimo warned me not to turn into a luau pig."

"Don't be a sissy. It will loosen your muscles and help relieve stress."

"I'm already stress-free. I don't need some sumo wrestler pounding my back with hot stones."

"It will probably be an attractive young woman."

"Well, in that case . . ."

Marion swatted me with her book.

"What's the dress code for a massage?" I asked.

"You can go in your swimsuit and robe."

We moseyed up to the appointment desk and checked in. True to Marion's promise, a young woman with long black hair and striking blue eyes introduced herself as Inese and escorted me to a room. She told me to remove my robe and lie down on my stomach. As I listened to the tropical birds chirping, she began placing hot stones along my side, bolstered by towels. Then she placed one in the center of my back.

"Yow!" I shouted.

"I'm sorry. That one must have been too hot."

"So Inese, how'd you decide to pursue this line of work?"

"I was trained in Latvia," she said in her precise, accented English. "I wanted to travel and a job with Scandinavian Sea Lines presented itself."

I leaned up on my elbows and looked at her. "You weren't running away from anything, were you?"

Her eyes grew wide. "Why would you ask that?"

"Calm yourself. I'm just a snoopy old goat. It was an innocent question. Has traveling met your expectations?"

She sighed. "Not really. We work continuously. Each cruise is Sunday to Sunday and then the next one begins. I do get some time off to go ashore. I've seen each of the towns where we stop."

"Do you have a chance to make many friends on the ship?"

"Not many. There's a waiter named Erik. We take some hikes together when we both are able to go ashore at the same time."

"So you have a boyfriend."

"He's just a friend."

I plopped back down, and Inese massaged my shoulder blades and neck muscles. "This ship must have other routes when the Alaskan summer season is over."

"Yes. The rest of the year it sails in Hawaii."

"So you are able to see different parts of the world."

"I've completed one season in Hawaii, and this is my second season in Alaska. I plan to transfer to a ship in the Caribbean this coming winter."

"And then?"

"I'll have saved up some money. I'd like to start my own massage business."

"No plans to return to Latvia?"

I felt her hands tense on my back. "No. I think I'd like to live somewhere else."

She pummeled a few more muscles on my back.

"Now if you'll excuse me for a few minutes, I need to replace the stones with fresh hot ones."

"Just not too hot."

"All right. I'll be careful."

She disappeared into the adjoining room and shut the door.

I was left alone with the chirping birds. I tried to decide if I were in a tropical jungle or being confined in a bird cage with crazed parakeets.

This massage was a mixed bag. My muscles felt more relaxed, but the hot stones didn't do that much for me. Seemed to be more of a gimmick.

Inese didn't return as promptly as she promised, so I closed my eyes and pictured a large hawk circling, ready to pick off small chirping birds. After almost nodding off, I sat up.

Where was Inese? It couldn't take this long to retrieve some hot stones. I swung my legs off the massage table and looked around the room. Pictures of tropical settings: a beach, a mountain scene and a path through a jungle, probably lined with loquacious parrots. Between the chirping and no Inese, I was starting to get irritated. Finally, I stood up and approached the door where Inese had disappeared. I opened it and peeked in.

Inese lay twisted on the floor.

CHAPTER 7

I braced myself against the doorway. My heart beat faster than a jackhammer. I stumbled back and thrust open the main door. A dozen rapid steps took me to the reception desk. "Call for help. Inese is injured."

One woman reached for the phone. The other raced out from behind the desk. "What happened to her?"

"She's lying on the floor."

"I know CPR. Show me where she is."

We charged back to the room, and I opened the door.

The woman bent down to examine Inese. Then she screamed.

"What's the matter?" I asked.

She stood up, shaking. "She's dead. Someone stuffed a hot stone in her mouth."

My knees felt weak. Why would someone do that to this nice young woman? And how did someone sneak into the side room without anyone noticing? She obviously had an enemy on the ship.

A nurse arrived to examine Inese, followed in short order by a doctor and Norbert Grudion.

Grudion took charge immediately. "I want this room sealed off. Who found the body?"

"I did," I said with a gulp.

"Mr. Jacobson. In the thick of the fray again. Tell me what happened."

"Inese was giving me a hot stone massage. She said she

needed to retrieve more hot stones and disappeared into the side room. When she never returned, I investigated and found her body on the floor."

"Yah, did you see anyone else?"

"No. No one else came in the room."

He began questioning the spa staff and asked to see the log of who had signed in.

Another man arrived wearing a dark suit and Grudion told him to check every room in the spa and get names of the occupants. "Yah, and don't let anyone in or out of the spa until I tell you," he informed the two receptionists.

Shortly, Marion appeared in her white robe. "What's all the commotion?"

"I feel awful," I said. "Someone murdered the nice young woman who was giving me a massage."

Marion's hand flew to her mouth.

Grudion came up to us. "Mr. and Mrs. Jacobson. Please return to your cabin. I need to interview other bystanders, and then I will come to your stateroom to speak with you."

I nodded. We went into our respective locker rooms to change.

I met Marion out in the reception area. As we prepared to depart, one of the receptionists said, "We've been told to ask everyone to stay here."

"Mr. Grudion told us to return to our cabin," I said.

Grudion stuck his head around the corner. "Yah, that's correct. They can leave, but no one else yet."

As we walked along the corridor, Marion said, "This sure puts a damper on our morning."

"I'll say. And now Grudion will be all over my ass like hair on a wet dog."

"You have such colorful expressions, Paul."

"That's me, one heck of a colorful guy."

"So you never finished your massage."

"I think I'm done with massages for two lifetimes. And I didn't even have a chance to give the massage therapist a tip."

Back at our place we sat out on the balcony, watching the open ocean. I felt sad over what had happened to Inese and attempted to distract myself by trying to spot whales. No luck. As I continued to watch the whale-less ocean, I reaffirmed my belief: I liked hot tubs, but you'd never get me in big expanses of water like the Pacific.

I felt all jumbled up inside. A massage that was supposed to be relaxing had ended up in disaster. How did something like that happen? Who would commit such a heinous crime? And with me being in proximity, I knew I'd have to face the music with Grudion. I thought back over the image of Inese on the floor. I needed to learn more about people on this ship.

My musings were interrupted by a knock on the door, and I opened it to find Norbert Grudion with set lips complimenting his red hair.

"Come on in," I said.

He stepped into our room. "Mr. Jacobson, you reported finding Inese Zarins's body. Do you know the cause of her death?"

"Only what I was told about a stone being stuffed in her mouth."

"An autopsy will determine for sure, but it appears that she died from asphyxiation. You were the last person to see her alive. Did you hear or notice anything that I should know?"

"No. All I could hear were chirping birds."

He furrowed his brow. "No scream?"

"No. Nothing."

"That's very interesting. Someone in an adjoining room reported hearing a scream."

I thought back. "Well, it could have been me. I let out a yowl when one of the stones was too hot."

"Humph. And another thing. One witness reported you

speaking earlier in the morning of stuffing a stone in someone's mouth."

"Just a minute, Mr. Grudion," Marion said. "Paul was kidding around. I heard that remark."

"Yah, it's awfully suspicious that Mr. Jacobson makes that statement and within an hour someone is found dead with a stone in her mouth."

"It's a goddamn coincidence, nothing more."

"Acting a little heated, Mr. Jacobson?"

"Hell yes. I don't like being accused of things I didn't do."

He pulled out his notepad and looked at it. "Finding a dead body in Seattle under suspicious circumstances. Pushing a woman down the stairs during the lifeboat drill. And now the last person seen with another murder victim. I'd say there's a pattern here, Mr. Jacobson. Are there any new details you'd care to share with me?"

I thought for a moment. "We've been over the stairway incident. There are several things regarding Inese that you should check out. She has a boyfriend named Erik who is a waiter on this ship. You should speak with him."

Grudion wrote a note. "Yah, I will. What else?"

Marion cleared her throat. "There's one piece of information I can contribute. During my massage I asked my massage therapist, a young woman named Ingrid, if the staff worked well together. She replied that they did on the whole, but one of the massage therapists was a little snobbish and they had some arguments. You might check to see if that has anything to do with Inese."

He wrote another note.

"The only other thing I can contribute is that Inese mentioned she was from Latvia. I asked her more and she seemed very evasive. Worth investigating."

Another note. At least Grudion was paying attention.

"Anything else, Mr. Jacobson?"

"I think you've wrung the stone dry."

"Bad analogy, Mr. Jacobson. We'll be speaking again." With that he departed, leaving Marion and me staring at each other.

Then Marion said, "Cheer up. I know you're innocent."

"We know it, but Grudion doesn't act convinced. It's also scary that there's a murderer loose on this ship."

Marion put her hand to her mouth. "That is a disturbing thought. Still, we can't let this spoil our cruise."

I let out a deep sigh. "I suppose you're right, although it's hard for me to think of doing anything right now after finding that poor woman murdered."

"You can't sit here and fret. I'll figure out something to distract you." Marion picked up the ship's newsletter. "Here's something. If we hurry, we can catch the bingo game in the theater."

"That sounds safe. Should be only old goats like us attending."

But I was wrong on the attendance speculation. The darn place was crammed full of crazed cruisers of all ages. Young twentysomethings were jumping up and down and waving to buy cards as well as middle-aged men with stomachs escaping their Hawaiian shirts. I guessed they'd forgotten they were heading to Alaska and not Maui. Then there were the white-hairs like Marion and me. I felt like someone might rip the buttons off my shirt to use for bingo tokens. We purchased two cards apiece and settled into seats next to a group of young kids in their sixties who wore matching shirts that read, "Oldsters from Reno."

I struck up a conversation with the woman next to me. "Your group doesn't look that old to me."

She laughed. "It's all relative. We started wearing these shirts around town to bug our grown kids and it caught on."

"So being from Reno, all of you are probably well-tuned gamblers."

"Absolutely. We're going to kick butt in bingo and in the casino on this trip."

The master of ceremonies came to the microphone and welcomed everyone to the first bingo game of the cruise.

The audience whooped, led by the Oldsters from Reno who all stood up and waved.

After a few dumb jokes, he explained that he was Cruise Director Ned Farley from Australia.

This brought on cat calls of "Bring on the barbie, mate" and "Kangaroo Ned."

He explained that his mission in life was to make sure we had a good time.

An old broad in the first row jumped up, wiggled her hips and shouted, "I'm ready for a good time, Ned."

Ned stepped back in mock shock. "Please, madam, not in front of the children."

He introduced his assistant, the lovely Danielle from the Netherlands, and the lovely Danielle proceeded to pull bingo numbers out of a large machine that dispensed dancing tokens.

I started poorly. The first three numbers called didn't match anything on my cards. Then I got on a roll with two matches on one card and three on the other. I had just reached three in a row on one card when someone jumped up and yelled, "Bingo!"

"Bull pucky. I was just starting to make progress."

"With a crowd this large it will be difficult to win," Marion said.

One of the oldsters leaned toward us. "Don't worry, honey. One of us in this row will win."

And sure enough in the fourth game a woman three seats away jumped up with the winning combination. The group broke out into a cheer, "Reno, Reno, Reno . . ."

I thought I had died and gone to a Nevada crematorium.

We continued playing and my luck didn't change. I never got closer than three lined up before some yahoo jumped up, yelling bingo. Oh well. Unlucky at Bingo, lucky at love. I had my bride and my health, except for those fleeting brain cells.

"Where would you like to go for lunch?" Marion asked after our ignominious defeat at the hands of the Bingo gods.

"How about a nice picnic in the woods."

She tried to swat me, but the old man was too fast for her. In other words, I ducked.

"Let's try one of the main dining rooms," I said once I had danced out of striking range.

"I'm surprised you want to have a sit-down meal in the middle of the day."

"I have my reasons." I gave her my most mysterious smile and wiggled my eyebrows.

We discovered that only one of the two main restaurants was open for lunch and waited in a short line before reaching the receptionist.

"We'd like to sit at one of Erik's tables," I informed the young woman with hair in a neat bun.

"That can be arranged. One moment."

"So that was your ulterior motive."

"Yes. I thought it would be worthwhile meeting Inese's boyfriend."

"What if he hasn't heard yet? I'd hate for us to be the first to inform him."

"We'll take it slowly and see what he knows and find out what he tells us."

We were seated at a table for two and shortly a handsome young man appeared. I checked out his name tag and verified the name Erik from Estonia.

He asked for our drink order, we requested iced teas, and he scurried away.

"If you weren't here, I'd have to flirt with him," Marion said.

"Don't let me stop you. We need to milk him for any information."

We scrutinized the menu and when Erik returned with our drinks, Marion ordered a cobb salad and I chose broiled salmon.

After he had written down our orders, I began the inquisition. "So tell me Erik, what does a young fella like you do for a social life on this ship?"

He gave us a pleasant smile. "Not much. I work breakfast, lunch and dinner seven days a week."

"Don't you have some shore time?"

"Yes. Every cruise there is one day when I'm able to go ashore."

"There seem to be many attractive young ladies on the crew. You must have met some of them."

"One of the girls in the spa likes to join me for hikes."

I winked at him. "Sounds serious."

"Oh, no. We're just friends."

He left to place our orders.

"He obviously hasn't heard about Inese yet, Paul."

"No. Or he's a good actor. His account coincides with what Inese told me."

When our meals arrived I began the interrogation again.

"So, Erik, you mentioned that you sometimes went hiking with one of the girls in the spa. That wouldn't by any chance be Inese?"

His eyes widened. "Why, yes. How did you know that?"

"She gave me a massage earlier. Have you seen her today?"

He looked over his shoulder, then back at me. "No. I probably won't until Wednesday when we both go ashore in Skagway."

"Estonia and Latvia are neighboring countries, aren't they?"

"Yes, why do you ask?"

"Just curious."

He left, and Marion and I began masticating, me on the fish and her on the salad.

"I think you should back off, Paul. The young man obviously doesn't know of Inese's death."

"You're right. I'll behave."

We each ordered tapioca pudding for dessert and then thanked Erik for his attentive service.

Back in our room I asked Marion what she would like to do for our afternoon at sea. She picked up the ship newsletter and scanned through it. "Here are some choices: a ping-pong tournament, an art auction, bridge, a shuffleboard tournament and a blackjack tournament in the casino."

"Sounds like lots of options for my competitive spirit. I didn't hear whale watching."

"We can do that too."

"Okay. What if we enjoy the fresh air on our balcony for a while and then check out the shuffleboard. I can take out my aggression by smacking a puck into someone else's."

"Your anger management system?"

"Yeah. Something like that."

We put on jackets and sat outside watching the ocean.

"Look, a fin," Marion cried out.

I jerked my head toward where she pointed.

"Oh, now it's disappeared," she said.

"Damn. I still haven't spotted a whale."

"Keep looking over there." She pointed again. "It might breach again."

I peeled my trusty eyes, but it did no more good than peeling an orange. Nothing. Nada. Nyet. No useless whales. They were all in hiding and teasing me by appearing only to Marion.

After a half hour of frustration, we headed up to lucky deck thirteen to participate in the shuffleboard event. The smarmy cruise director stood with a microphone. "All right, ladies and gentlemen. This is a mixed doubles event. Choose your partner."

Marion snuggled up against me. "I choose you."

"Good. We'll whip some butt against these young whippersnappers."

Marion and I took our turn and did quite well. I couldn't place the puck worth a tinker's damn, but I did blast our opponents' disks to kingdom come several times.

Afterwards we each received a certificate of participation.

"This can go right up there with my college degree and the first dollar I earned in my auto parts store those many years ago."

"And how about our marriage certificate?"

"Nah. Doesn't come close to comparing with that."

Marion wanted to wander through the shops, so I excused myself and said I'd meet her back in the cabin before dinner.

I had my own wandering to do. I headed to the spa but had something else in mind rather than soaking. When I arrived there, I asked to speak to the spa supervisor and was informed that Madeline Bouchon would be with me momentarily.

As promised, a tall, striking woman with glitter on her nails approached me and introduced herself.

"Is there a private place where we can speak?" I asked.

"Yes. Come to my office."

I followed her as high heels clacked on the inlaid marble floor. She ushered me into a small office, closed the door and then sat down behind an uncluttered desk.

"What may I do for you?" she asked.

"I appreciate you seeing me. I'm here because of the unfortunate incident regarding Inese Zarins."

Her full-lipped smile sagged. "We're all saddened by what happened to Inese."

"It appears that she may have had some enemy on the ship. I figured you might have witnessed something that would lead to finding the killer."

"Inese wasn't the most popular person among her co-workers, but there was nothing that would have led to her death."

"Why wasn't she popular?"

Madeline opened a hand toward me. "Her demeanor. Most of the girls like to talk to each other. Inese was standoffish and didn't socialize."

"Any particular confrontations with people?"

"No. Just the undercurrent as if she felt superior and it was beneath her to spend time with the other staff members."

"I understand she befriended a waiter named Erik."

Madeline's head jerked. "She never spoke of him to me."

"Do you know Erik?"

"Yes. One of the other massage therapists, Renee, has hinted that she had her eye on Erik."

"Is Renee around now?"

"No. She worked the early shift. She'll be here tomorrow morning at seven."

"Can you think of anyone who might have had a grudge against Inese?"

"No. No one. But I'm curious. Why are you asking these questions?"

I thought for a moment about being evasive and then decided, what the heck, I'd tell the truth. "I was her customer when she died."

Madeline stood up. "You're that man. Norbert Grudion says you could be the murderer."

CHAPTER 8

"Just a minute," I said to Madeline, the spa supervisor. "I happened to be there when someone killed Inese, and that's why I'm trying to get to the bottom of this situation. I had nothing to do with her death but want to clear myself of any false accusations."

"I shouldn't be talking to you. I'll have to report this to Norbert."

"Do whatever you feel you need to, but be assured I did nothing to harm Inese."

I found myself summarily escorted out of the office.

Having done myself more harm than good, I returned to the cabin to await Marion. While stewing over my predicament, the phone rang. I answered it to hear the voice of my walking companion from the morning, Andrew Black.

"I'm calling to confirm that we're meeting for dinner tonight."

"Absolutely. My bride and I are anticipating it, and I'm looking forward to meeting your wife."

"Good. We also want to get acquainted with Marion. We'll see you at seven o'clock outside the Regal Room."

"We'll be there with bells on."

Marion returned and we spruced up for our dinner date. I forced a tie around my neck for "formal" night.

"I don't know if this is good for a guy my age. This neck contraption is cutting off my circulation. I might keel over into the soup from lack of oxygen."

Marion gave me a stare that made me feel like she had thrown a dart at me. "Don't be a sissy."

"I know. Real men gasp but don't complain about wearing ties."

We met Andrew and his wife Helen at the appropriate time. Helen was a short brunette who greeted us with a warm smile and a tinge of a southern accent.

"I don't think you were raised in Omaha," I said.

She laughed. "Biloxi."

The hostess led us to a table with a view out the stern, and a young waiter named Ciro from Spain helped us with our napkins.

"I have the best people on the ship to serve tonight," Ciro said with a smile that lit up the room.

"I don't know about that, but you may have one of the oldest in me," I said.

He opened his mouth wide and stepped back, feigning shock. "Not you, sir. You don't look any older than my father and he's forty-two."

"He must have aged quickly."

"No, the mountain air of the Pyrenees has kept him most youthful."

"You'll have to bottle some of it for me," I replied. "In the meantime you can bring us all drinks from the ship's fountain of youth."

He took our drink orders and dashed off.

"So how did you two meet?" Marion asked Helen.

"I moved into Yankee territory and met Andrew in Chicago."

"And I was the luckiest man in the world to be in Marshall Fields on that Saturday when I accidentally bumped into this gorgeous woman."

"You met her in the store?" Marion asked.

"No. I knocked her over. I was in a rush and wasn't paying

attention. I mowed her down, knocking packages everywhere. The only recourse was to buy her a cup of coffee. We were married three months later."

"The impetuousness of youth," I said. "Marion and I had a courtship that spanned three states and part of the Pacific Ocean. I'll let her recount it since with my short-term memory loss I only know what she's told me."

"Paul and I met in Hawaii in a retirement home. Then I moved back to the mainland. While he was living with his son in Colorado, I visited him twice. On the second occasion he proposed to me. Then we were married in Venice Beach, California, where we now reside. We're newlyweds of one month."

"That calls for a toast," Andrew said. He signaled Ciro and ordered a bottle of champagne.

When the bubbly arrived, we all raised our glasses.

"To romance, friendship and long life," Andrew said.

"I'll drink to that," I said. "All noble attributes."

We all recounted our life histories and enjoyed a robust meal. As I patted a full stomach, I felt a tap on my shoulder. I turned to see Erik standing there, a scowl on his face. He pointed a finger at me. "I need to speak with you."

I shrugged. "Go ahead."

He looked across our table. "I'd prefer to step over to the side so we can talk in private."

I figured I might learn something. "Why not?" I stood and faced my companions. "Excuse me for a moment." Then I followed Erik over to a corner of the room.

In a soft but firm voice he said, "I just heard that Inese was killed today. You were questioning me at lunch when you knew all about it. I even discovered that you're a suspect in her murder."

"Hold your horses," I said. "I didn't feel it appropriate to break the news to you. I had nothing to do with her death, but I'm trying to find out what happened since I'm being unjustly suspected by the security man on this ship."

He continued to glare at me. "If I find out you had anything to do with her death, you'll be sorry." He turned and stalked away.

I returned to the table.

"What was that all about?" Andrew asked.

I explained finding Inese's body in the spa room that morning, being on Grudion's suspect list, speaking with Erik at lunch to try to gain some information to clear my name and now hearing that Erik was upset with me.

"That's awful that a young woman died on our ship," Helen said.

"You can imagine how devastated we were," Marion added.

"She was a nice woman." I shook my head. "I was shocked to find her dead on the floor."

"I can understand why you want to clear your name," Andrew said. "I once had false accusations levied against me. It's not a pleasant situation."

"How'd you resolve it?" Marion asked.

"Just like Paul is doing. I had to find evidence pointing to the real culprit. Even then there were people who never quite trusted me again."

"This is a pisser, pardon the French," I said. "I have the security officer breathing down my neck, an irate boyfriend threatening me, and I didn't do anything more than have a massage. I may have to limit any future back rubs to what Marion might be willing to give me."

"I may be able to help you," Andrew said, "with proving your innocence, not with a massage."

"Any assistance would be gratefully accepted."

"I have some contacts that should prove useful."

At that moment Ciro returned. "You all look hungry. It's time for dessert."

I licked my lips. "Yes, bring us one of everything."

"Your wish is my command." He darted off.

"Wait a minute. I thought I was kidding."

"Ciro has a good sense of humor," Marion said. "We'll see what he does."

And he did all right. In ten minutes Ciro and two waitresses returned and began piling desserts on our table. We had ice cream, sherbet, strawberry shortcake, German chocolate cake, Boston crème pie, rice pudding, a cheese plate and a fruit selection.

"You've taught me a lesson," I said, shaking a finger at Ciro.

"Enjoy." He gave us a huge smile and pranced away.

After we demolished a good portion of the sweets, Andrew looked at his watch. "We have half an hour before the show starts. Are you up for some Broadway entertainment?"

We all readily agreed. As we stood up to leave, I noticed a jacket hanging on a chair of an empty table next to us.

"Did you see who was sitting here?" I asked.

Helen, Andrew and Marion shook their heads.

"Looks like someone forgot a coat," I said, sauntering over to inspect it. I picked it up and searched the pockets for some identification, finding nothing but a balled-up tissue.

Just then a man came charging up. "What are you doing with my jacket?" He grabbed it away from me and started patting the pockets.

"My wallet's gone. What did you do with my wallet?"

I stared at the squat, balding man. "I did nothing. I was only trying to find the owner of the jacket."

He thrust an index finger at me. "I saw you going through the pockets. You stole my wallet."

"Nothing of the sort. I was looking for identification to locate the owner."

Andrew jumped in. "That's correct. Paul was being helpful, not stealing anything of yours."

The man's eyebrows pinched together. "I'm reporting this. What's your name?"

"It's Paul Jacobson, and I've done nothing wrong."

"You're trying to rip off one of the Oldsters from Reno."

"You one of the bingo maniacs?"

"Don't insult my favorite pastime."

He turned abruptly and stomped off. I saw him stop at the reception desk, point toward me and shake a finger at the receptionist.

"Very intense fellow," I said.

"Don't worry about it. I'm sure he'll come to his senses."

Marion linked her arm with mine, and we headed off to the theater to be sung and danced to. The enthusiastic performance made me feel old, but I was entitled to that feeling since I was old.

After the show, Andrew, who seemed to only be gaining energy as I waned, suggested a trip to the casino.

Along the hallway we were almost mowed down by a group of twentysomethings in weird hats.

"What the hell's going on?" I asked politely.

"Come join the party, old man," one of them said, blowing a tin horn.

"You act like it's New Year's Eve," I said.

"That's right. We're the pub crawlers celebrating New Year's Eve in August." He tossed a handful of confetti at me and disappeared around the corner.

"Now I feel really old," I said.

"Cheer up," Andrew said. "You can win big in the casino."

But once we entered the land of slot machines and game tables, I continued my winning streak from the bingo game: the

87

machines ate all my money and spit nothing back.

"I'm ready to wander back to the cabin," I informed Marion.

"You go ahead. I'll be along in a while. I'm on a hot streak."

"I'm glad someone in the family is winning."

I thanked Andrew and Helen for an enjoyable evening and returned to my stateroom where I stepped out on the balcony to watch the white foam illuminated by reflected light from the ship. No midnight whales.

My stomach knotted up at the memory of Inese's twisted body on the spa room floor and the resulting accusations. I had to do something. Maybe Andrew could help. And tomorrow I'd be up against my biggest problem. I'd have forgotten everything from today. Then I remembered what Marion had given me. A journal. I reviewed the activities of the day in my mind, realizing that I needed to speak with a massage therapist named Renee in the morning. Then I sat down at the small cabin desk and documented what had transpired.

With no Marion back by the time I had finished, I lay down on the bed to await her return.

I felt a shaking at my shoulder. My eyes popped open. Where was I?

"Paul, are you awake?"

A woman who looked vaguely familiar stood over me.

"You're . . . you're . . ." I couldn't find the name.

"Marion."

"That's right. Where are we?"

"We're on an Alaskan cruise. You nodded off. Did you know your head is in a pool of chocolate?"

I felt the pillow and my hand encountered brown goo.

Marion laughed. "You fell asleep on the chocolate the maid left when she turned down the bed. It melted."

"I've always been a hothead, but never like this." I proceeded into the bathroom to scrub off.

"I see you've been writing in your journal," Marion said.

A distant memory of writing something came back to me. Now that I was wide awake, I added a few scribblings about attack-chocolate in my journal, left a reminder note and retired for the night.

I stretched as I woke up, one arm bumping into a silver-haired woman lying next to me in bed. Who was she and where was I? I surveyed a cramped, tiny room. I plunked my feet down on the floor and padded to the curtains and peeked out. Holy crap. An expanse of ocean filled my view. I was on a ship. My last ship adventure occurred returning on a destroyer from the European theater after World War II. What was I doing out here in the middle of some ocean now?

I turned back toward the bed and noticed a piece of paper on the nightstand. It read: "Read this first thing, you old goat. You're on your honeymoon cruise to Alaska with your new wife Marion. Don't get all worked up just because your short-term memory is in the crapper."

It appeared to be my handwriting. So I had left myself a love note to explain which end was up. I let out a deep sigh. New adventures for an old fart.

Marion stirred. "Paul?"

"Yeah, I'm up."

"I want to sleep a little longer."

"I found a note telling me that we're married."

"That's right. Read your journal and it will fill you in on the details. We can catch up further when I'm up."

She turned over and buried her face in the pillow.

How about that? I'd gotten myself hitched again. I picked up the journal, went to the small desk, turned on the desk light and proceeded to read of the life and times of Paul Jacobson of the errant brain matter.

When I had finished, I shook my head in wonder. On a honeymoon cruise and being accused of two murders. A homeless man in Seattle and a massage therapist on the ship. An old guy like me couldn't have done all these things.

From my reading I ascertained that one other item required my attention. I needed to speak with the massage therapist named Renee who was supposed to be on duty that morning. It was a long shot, but maybe Inese had been involved in some sort of love triangle.

With the help of a pleasant young woman who was pushing a cart along the corridor, I found the spa and asked for Renee.

"I'm sorry, she's with a client right now," the receptionist informed me as she inspected a bright red fingernail.

"When might I catch her for a moment?"

The woman now inspected all the fingernails on her right hand. "I'd say in thirty minutes."

I thanked her and decided to take a stroll. Following my routine of the previous day as described in my diary, I headed to deck thirteen and began walking along the track.

I shivered in the cool air and looked up at wisps of clouds overhead. Off to the starboard appeared an emerald green coastline. I had never been to Alaska before, that I could remember, so this would be a whole new experience for me.

On my second pass around the deck, I heard a voice call out behind me, "Paul, slow down so I can catch up to you."

A man in a sweatsuit came trotting up beside me. "Whew. You walk a mean pace."

"Once my legs shift into gear, they have one speed. . . . I hate to be impolite, but you know me. Since I can't remember yesterday from split pea soup, who are you?"

He chuckled. "We met on this track yesterday morning and had dinner together last night. I'm Andrew Black."

The name clicked from my journal. "That's right. We even went to a shipboard Broadway show with our wives last night."

"Memory coming back?"

"No. It's gone forever, but I wrote a journal entry last night and read it this morning."

"That's a good way to augment your memory."

"My bride will help me catch up more, but she's sleeping in."

"Helen is doing the same. Whereas we male types are too hyper and have to burn off some energy."

"Yeah. A good walk boosts my circulation. I only wish it could stimulate my brain cells."

We completed another lap, and Andrew cleared his throat. "Last night at dinner I told you I might be able to help you with some of the problems you've encountered."

"I read that in my journal."

"That's good. Sounds like you're keeping accurate records."

I shrugged. "That's the only way I can keep a handle on this whole strange sequence of events."

"I did uncover a little information. You have moved up from being a person of interest to being a suspect in both murders."

"Great."

He patted me on the shoulder. "Don't take it personally. That's just how the police and ship security operate."

"How can I not take it personally? It's my life, or at least what's left of it anyway."

Andrew chuckled. "The good news is that you're not the only suspect in each murder, just one of the suspects in each."

"Who are my competitors?"

"A homeless man in Seattle and the waiter who accosted you last night in regards to the shipboard slaying."

I thought back to my journal. "I passed a name on to the Seattle detective. Maybe he's following up on it."

"It appears so."

"And this guy Grudion. What do I need to do to keep him off my back?"

"Just cooperate fully. The truth will come out."

"I sure hope so. Say, how were you able to find out this information?"

"I have a confession to make. I used to do some work for Scandinavian Sea Lines. I'm an attorney."

"Horse pucky. I've always hated lawyers, and here one is being kind to me."

He laughed. "Cheer up. There are lots of lawyers who help people."

"That's not been my experience."

"You obviously had a negative run-in with a member of my profession."

"Many years ago when I ran my own business. The bugger filed a frivolous suit and tried to take my business away from me."

"But it sounds like he didn't succeed."

"After two years of court appearances, the thing finally was thrown out."

"See, justice prevailed."

"Yeah, but it set me back twenty thousand dollars. Took me three years to recoup the money wasted on defending the lawsuit. All because some ambulance chaser had the bright idea of trying to scam me."

"I'll keep checking in on your situation. I spoke with Grudion this morning, and I assured him of your solid character."

"But you hardly know me."

"I had a chance to see you in operation last evening. I'm a good judge of character."

"Well, I'm a character all right. And I appreciate the vote of confidence. If you can only convince Grudion now."

"I'll work on it."

We said our goodbyes. I thanked him again for his concern and moseyed back to the spa to find Renee. The same receptionist womaned the desk.

"I'm back looking for Renee," I said, "and you have a chip missing on your right index nail."

Her eyes widened in panic, but upon checking, she discovered everything was in order. Rather than being mad, she let out a sigh of relief. "You fooled me there." She actually looked at me this time. "You can wait in the first room on the left." She pointed, and I followed her directions and entered a small cubbyhole with a massage table in the middle. I inspected the place and imagined that this must have resembled the room where I received the ill-fated hot stone massage. From overhead the irritating bird-chirping music permeated the air.

My thoughts of Jonathan Livingston Parakeet were interrupted by an attractive young woman entering the room. She reached out a slender hand. "You want to speak with me?"

"Yes. It's in regard to a waiter named Erik."

She wrinkled her brow. "Erik?"

"I understand you mentioned him to some of your coworkers."

She laughed and flicked her wrist at me. "Oh that. We were talking about men on the staff. I just said that he was hot."

I imagined a hot stone sculpted in Erik's likeness. "Are you seeing him?"

"Goodness, no. I have a fiancé in Buenos Aires. It was only girl talk. Why are you asking?"

I didn't want to tip my hand, but I had to say something. "I had heard that Erik was seeing Inese."

Her eyes flashed. "And because of what happened to Inese you were checking on me?"

I gulped. "Just trying to learn more about Erik."

"Well, I know nothing other than having seen him from a

distance." She turned and exited the room.

I let out a sigh and followed her out. As I passed the reception area, I saw Renee speaking with Miss Fingernails. Then Renee pointed at me.

I waved and headed back to my cabin. Marion had awoken, so we headed off to have some chow.

After breakfast Marion said she wanted to visit the spa.

"I'm not sure they'll let me in after the events of yesterday I recorded in my journal."

"You're a paying customer. Until they lock you up, you're entitled to all the services of the spa."

"Thanks for putting it so gently. I just hope they don't try to stuff me in one of the lockers."

Miss Fingernails had been replaced by another young woman who gave me a locker key without any dirty looks. After changing, I entered the pool area and deposited my towel on a lounge chair while listening to the bird-chirping music. Then I headed over to the hot tub. The place was deserted except for one bald-headed guy already in the Jacuzzi.

"How are you this morning?" I asked.

No answer.

He seemed to be asleep or unconscious.

I shook his shoulder.

He slumped into the water.

My heart started racing. He'd drown. I reached under and propped him back up. His head lolled to the side.

"Help," I shouted. "I need some help."

No one was there. Then Marion appeared.

"Marion. Find someone. There's an unconscious man who I'm trying to help."

She dashed out and returned with a man and woman in white uniforms who charged over to assist me.

Between them, they lifted the man out of the hot tub and

placed him on a lounge chair.

"He's breathing," the woman said.

Just then two attendants showed up with a gurney and carted the guy away.

"Where are they taking him?" I asked.

"To the infirmary on Deck Four," the woman informed me.

So much for a calm morning of listening to chirping bird music.

The woman took down Marion and my names and then she left.

Neither Marion nor I felt inclined to stay in the spa, so we adjourned to our respective locker rooms to change and then met in the reception area to return to our cabin.

"That spa isn't the healthiest place," I said as we strolled along the corridor.

"It should be. You've just had unfortunate luck there."

"I think it's the chirping birds. They drive people to do crazy things."

Back in our stateroom, I decided it was time to look for whales again, and Marion joined me on our balcony. I scanned the horizon and leaned over the railing to look closely at the sea around us. I spotted a log and that was it.

"Not very friendly whales around here," I said.

"A watched whale never breaches," Marion replied.

"Hell, I'd settle for a peek at a fin or two."

Then I sank back in a chair and continued to peruse the horizon. No whales.

My reverie was broken by a knock on the door.

"I'll answer it," I said, rising from the contentment of my oceanview perch.

A man with bright red hair stood there.

"We didn't order room service," I said.

"We need to speak, Mr. Jacobson."

"You seem to know me, but who are you?"

He whipped out an identification card to show me.

"Oh, Mr. Grudion. The ship dick."

"I beg your pardon."

"It's slang talk for cop. Come on in."

He entered.

"May I offer you something out of our mini-bar?"

"No thank you. We have several items to discuss."

"Fire away."

"Yah, Mr. Jacobson, I received a call earlier that a man matching your description was asking pointed questions of one of the massage therapists in the spa."

I gave Grudion my most sincere smile. "Nothing more than trying to check on one of the suspects. I thought there might be some romantic entanglement that led to Inese's murder. That turned out to be a dead end."

"Poor choice of words, Mr. Jacobson. I also received a complaint from Mr. Julian Armour that you stole his wallet."

"I don't know the name, but there was a man at dinner who was all worked up when I tried to return a jacket that had been left in the restaurant."

"I thought you had memory problems, Mr. Jacobson."

"I do. But I read pretty well and keep a journal of what happens to me." I tapped the side of my noggin. "That's my memory-assistance device."

He stared at me, and I felt like two laser beams were trying to penetrate my skull.

"Then this morning I had a report of you being at the scene of an unconscious man in the Jacuzzi in the spa."

"That's correct. Some guy passed out in the hot tub."

"Do you know who that was?"

"I have no clue. Some man who I tried to keep from drowning."

96

"Keep from drowning or trying to drown, Mr. Jacobson? That was Julian Armour."

CHAPTER 9

Crapola. I'd had an altercation with a guy in the dining room, and the next morning I found him slumping unconscious in the hot tub. How did I end up in this mess?

I took a deep breath. "I can assure you, Mr. Grudion, that I happened upon Julian Armour in the Jacuzzi and had nothing to do with him being unconscious. I called for help. I wouldn't have done that if I were trying to harm him."

"Or did the situation go beyond your control?"

"It was already beyond my control. He was unconscious when I spotted him in the hot tub. Rather than harassing me, why don't you find out what happened to Mr. Armour?"

"Yah, I will, Mr. Jacobson. When he regains consciousness, I'll interview him."

"Good. You'll find I had nothing to do with him other than trying to keep him from drowning."

"We'll see, Mr. Jacobson. We'll see."

After Grudion left, I sat out on the balcony, steaming. "I thought cruises were supposed to be relaxing. I've done nothing but have run-ins with the local constabulary since I crossed over the gangplank onto this ship."

"You just need a shore excursion, Paul. We'll be disembarking in Juneau in several hours."

"Good. I need some land without Grudion breathing down my neck."

After a fortunately uneventful lunch, we gathered our jackets and headed up to the same deck where I had walked that morning to watch our docking in Juneau.

We sailed up Gastineau Channel with green hills on both sides of the ship. I watched a waterfall cascade down a ravine and splash into the sound. Then ahead a town appeared nestled below two steeply sloping mountains. The emerald green intermixed with gray from avalanche corridors commanded a view above another cruise ship anchored in the Juneau harbor.

"We're not the only tourists today," I said.

"I understand there are half a dozen cruise ships in the Inside Passage right now."

"And here I thought we were so special."

"We are." Marion gave me a peck on the cheek. "Oh, I just remembered something. We're close enough to civilization that the cell phone reception should be acceptable. I was supposed to remind you to call your granddaughter." She reached in her purse and fiddled with a little gadget and handed it to me.

I looked at it like she had given me a piece of road kill. "What do I do with this?"

"Push the green button and speak with your family."

I punched the green button and started yapping into it as if it were a microphone.

Marion grabbed my arm. "Put it against your ear and wait until someone answers."

"Oh."

I thrust it against the side of my face and heard a buzzing-ringing sound. Then a woman's voice answered and I recognized it from my distant past as that of my daughter-in-law Allison.

"This is Paul of Alaska calling."

"How are you enjoying the cruise?"

"It's interesting, but I haven't seen any whales yet."

"Jennifer told me you found a dead body."

"Actually a couple of them."

"What?!"

"Just my propensity to attract strange events. Is my grand-daughter around?"

"Yes, but I'm not going to let you get off the phone before you tell me what happened."

I recounted my adventures and then Allison retrieved Jennifer.

When she picked up I said, "I read in my journal that you and Austin had given me some ideas on how to solve the murder in Seattle."

"Did that help?"

"Indirectly. I was hypnotized and remembered an important detail."

"Cool. What was it?"

"A red bandanna that I had seen another street person wearing that same morning."

"Ah-ha. So there was a grudge involved."

"Could be. Anyway, I phoned Detective Bearhurst and gave him the clue. He didn't sound very impressed, but he at least agreed to look into it."

"That's good, Grandpa. By the time you return to Seattle the police will have it solved."

"I hope so because I've got myself in more trouble on the ship."

"Not another dead body?"

"Yes. A strange choking murder in the spa. Then I was accused of stealing a man's wallet, found the same man unconscious in the Jacuzzi and was also accused of pushing a woman down the stairs. But I still haven't seen any of those sneaky whales."

"I can understand the whales. You've been too busy with other problems. Now tell me exactly what happened."

I went through the events as I had read them in my journal.

"So will you come bail your grandpa out of an Alaskan jail if they lock me up?"

"It won't get to that. I'll help you solve the murder. The other ones are easy. The wallet is a simple misunderstanding. The man will find it."

"I sure hope so."

"And the man unconscious in the hot tub. You were only trying to help. Too bad he was the same one who accused you of stealing his wallet."

"Yeah, that didn't look good."

"And the woman falling down the stairs was an accident."

"Unless someone intentionally bumped into me."

"But the only situation that's really serious is the dead woman in the spa."

"I'll say it's serious."

"I've been reading about crime investigation. There are three factors: means, opportunity and motive. MOM. You had the means with the hot stones and the opportunity because you were receiving a massage. But you had no motive."

"She was a nice young woman and didn't deserve to die that way or any way."

I heard Jennifer tapping on the phone. "So what we need to figure out is who else had a motive. Clearly that person snuck into the other room and used the hot stone as a murder weapon. Like the street person in Seattle, it might have been someone with a grudge."

"I nosed around the spa staff and the victim Inese wasn't very popular. I checked out one lead but it didn't pan out. Also, I can't see one of her coworkers going to the extreme of killing her."

"No, maybe not. Who else could there be? Murders are often committed by family or friends."

"I don't know about her family but she had one friend, a

waiter named Erik."

"Ah-ha. The boyfriend."

"I didn't pick up a real romantic interest, more good buddies. I've checked him out and he's a possibility."

"Okay, one suspect. Another avenue to pursue would be something about money. Greed is a prime motive."

"Thank you, Professor. I can't imagine someone working as a massage therapist on a cruise ship being rich."

"Maybe she's an heiress who has run away from home. Hiding out as a common crew member."

"Then who would know who she really is and why would they kill her?"

"Someone trying to prevent her from sharing an inheritance, Grandpa. Greed. Try this scenario. Another heir tracked her down and made it look like you were the murderer to hide his own motive. Then he will inherit more money and not have to share it with Inese."

"Seems a little far-fetched."

"You never know, Grandpa. You'll have to check out all the possibilities."

"That's what the security officer Grudion is supposed to do, but he's so busy sniffing my butt that he's probably not pursuing anyone else."

"That's why you need to keep working on it. Why don't you give me the victim's full name and I'll see if I can find anything by googling it."

"Whating it?"

"Google. I'll go check the name out on the Internet."

"Is that like a circus net?"

"Grandpa, I don't know what I'm going to do with you." I heard a disgusted sigh. "I'll use my computer to research information—to learn anything I can. What's her name?"

"Inese Zarins."

"Is this the right spelling?" Jennifer spelled it back correctly. My granddaughter was a sharp cookie.

"I'll hop right on it, Grandpa. The next time you call I'll let you know what I find out."

"Have at it."

"Will do. Now I need to finish my chores so Mom will let me go play tennis."

"Smash a few serves for me."

We parted and I handed the cell phone back to Marion, who tucked it away for the next time.

After Captain Sanderson had expertly navigated us into the dock, we disembarked with two thousand of our closest friends. When they scanned my key card as I left the ship, no bells rang to prevent me from scampering ashore. Once my feet hit solid ground, I felt I had escaped Grudion's clutches.

"So what's the agenda?" I asked Marion.

She held up two tickets. "We're scheduled to take a bus tour of Juneau and then visit the Mendenhall Glacier."

"No whales?"

"Not on this stop. We'll go on a whale-watching excursion in Ketchikan."

"Hot damn. As long as I spot at least one whale on this trip."

The small town of Juneau rested right against the base of Mount Roberts and Mount Juneau. No room for the city to expand, and visitors had to either fly or sail here as no roads led to Juneau.

We climbed up the steps and onto our own private bus—one of twenty lined up along the dock amid a mob of savage tourists. After the bus was crammed full of squirming visitors, the driver took his seat and we were underway.

"Good afternoon, folks. Welcome to the capital of Alaska. Care to venture a guess on the percentage of residents who work for the state government?"

There were a smattering of guesses.

"It's approximately seventy percent. The rest of us are in the tourist trade. And many of the shop owners only reside here during the summer before retreating to Florida during the winter."

After cruising the streets of Juneau, which didn't take very long given its small size, we hightailed it out onto a highway and entered a parking lot of a large building.

"This is the Macauley Salmon Hatchery. We'll be stopping here for a tour and you can visit the shop afterwards. Synchronize your watches. We'll depart in forty-five minutes and remember you're on bus ninety-three."

Marion and I followed the crowd, and a woman in a brown uniform began explaining the wonders of salmon and how they returned to this spot every year. We viewed a salmon ladder that zig-zagged up a hill.

Then we were led down stairs toward large vats of baby salmon.

"Please watch your step," our guide informed us.

I was reaching for the railing when someone above me bashed into me. I tripped and bumped the person below me who went sailing into the vat and landed with a loud splash.

CHAPTER 10

People gasped.

The guide jumped into the pool and brought up a spluttering woman.

After they climbed out, the soaked woman shook a finger at me. "I saw you push me in."

"Wait a minute, lady," I said. "I'm sorry you fell in. It was an accident. Someone bumped into me."

She leveled a gaze at me. "I've seen you before. You're the old man who knocked me down the stairs during the lifeboat drill." She reached over and picked up a cane.

I remembered reading that in my journal.

"Did you see who pushed me, Marion?"

"No, I was looking into the vat on the other side of the ladder."

"Something's fishy here," I said. "Twice now I've been shoved into that lady."

I asked those around me, but no one claimed to have seen what happened.

We navigated the stairs with no further mishap and entered the gift shop. On a table rested crackers with creamed salmon spread, which filled my tummy while Marion perused the gewgaws on the shelves.

I returned for a second helping of salmon pâté.

"We've seen how the salmon start out and how they end up," I said, patting my stomach.

We clambered back onto bus number ninety-three and headed to the Mendenhall Glacier, where we parked with a covey of other tour buses.

"These things congregate like flies on a succulent cow," I said to Marion.

"It is the tourist season, and we're tourists."

"Darn tourists," I grumbled.

Marion and I wandered down a path and came to a point where we had a full frontal view of the glacier. A huge bed of ice and snow flowed from mountains down to a lake filled with calved chunks of ice.

"Makes me think of a huge ice cream float," I said.

Marion had me stand close to the water and snapped a picture with her digital camera.

"Now I've been immortalized for posterity."

"Your granddaughter Jennifer will enjoy seeing a picture of you in Alaska."

"Maybe you can shoot a picture of me with a bear as well."

"If you find one, let me know."

Marion indicated she wanted to visit the gift shop.

"I wonder if they have any of that good salmon pâté here," I said.

"Why don't you come along and find out."

"I will in a little while. You go ahead. I want to explore the wonders of nature a little more."

Marion strolled back on the main path, and I navigated a less-traveled path along the edge of the lake. At first there were several other jacket-clad touristas with me, but then the crowd cleared out and I had nature all to my lonesome.

I found a spot to enjoy the view of both the glacier and a waterfall cascading down a green hillside. I noticed sections of brown where the glacier had cut away rock, but vegetation hadn't yet grown in. It was obvious that the glacier used to be much larger.

With my head filled with visions of glasses of iced tea filled with ice cubes, I moseyed back toward civilization.

As I rounded a corner in the faint trail, I saw a bush ahead thrashing. Being the inveterate snoop that I was, I peeked into the undergrowth. A brown bear was happily munching on red berries.

Uh-oh.

I backed slowly away, but the bear had spotted me. He rose up on his hind legs. Although he wasn't fully grown by bear standards, to me he appeared too large to mess around with. My heart thumped lickety-split, as I tried to decide between having a seizure or being a bear snack. Not turning my back, I continued to feel my way along the trail.

Then he started following me, not running but ambling along like he thought I had a treat for him. I kept moving and he kept up with me. Finally, I came out in a clearing near the buses. Then I broke into a run as fast as my old legs could carry me.

As I turned my head, I saw the bear loping along behind me. Then I spotted a ranger.

I waved my hands at the ranger. "Help! This bear is chasing me."

The bear came to a halt and stood up on its hind legs, sniffing.

"Sir, were you trying to feed the bear?" the female ranger inquired.

"Hell no. I just looked in the bushes and there it was."

She wagged a finger at me. "Were you harassing the bear while it was feeding for winter?"

"It harassed me."

"This time of year bears don't want to be interrupted. They're fine if you leave them alone."

By this time the bear had decided he'd had enough of tourists and ambled back into the undergrowth.

My breathing had slowed to twice normal.

"May I see some identification please?"

"What for?"

"We've had several incidents lately of people deliberately bothering bears in restricted parts of the park. You just came running out of an off-limits area."

"I never saw any signs. I was just trying to get away from the damn bear."

"Sir, are you going to be cooperative?"

I sighed, took out my wallet and showed my identification card.

She made some notes on a pad. "Where are you staying in Alaska?"

"I'm on the Scandinavian Sea Lines *Sunshine*."

She jotted again and then looked me in the eyes. "Please refrain from harassing the wildlife for the duration of your trip and follow the signs." She pointed to a large placard I had not seen that indicated a restricted area and warned people to not enter.

"Yes, ma'am."

Duly warned, I headed into the gift shop to mingle with wildlife of the human variety and to find Marion.

I spotted her by a counter where she was looking at carved animal figures.

"There you are," she said. "Enjoy the wildlife?"

"Not particularly. I got busted for giving a bear an idea for a larger meal."

Marion put her hands on her hips. "What happened now?"

I explained the whole encounter with the bear and the ranger.

She shook her head. "Maybe we better limit you to whale watching."

"Yeah. Since I haven't seen any, that will be safer."

Back on the bus, Marion struck up a conversation with a woman across the aisle while I watched to make sure no bears were following the bus.

"What excursion are you taking in Skagway?" the woman asked.

"We're going on the White Pass railway."

"We are too." I turned toward the woman and saw that her eyes lit up. "You're taking the afternoon ride, aren't you?"

"Let me check," Marion said. She rummaged through her purse, found a sheet of paper and said, "No. We're scheduled for the morning."

"You should change that to the afternoon, which is supposed to be the most spectacular time of day to see the pass."

"Is that right?" Marion said.

"Yes. We had friends who were here a month ago and raved about it."

"What do you think, Paul?"

"I can try to change the reservation when we return to the ship."

"Would you?"

"Why not?"

We stopped at a scenic spot for one last look at the glacier. No bears and no whales.

The bus returned us to downtown Juneau where we had a chance to spread around a few more tourist dollars. Marion picked out gifts for her grandson and my granddaughter, and then we wandered back to the ship.

Later Marion and I sauntered down to deck seven to visit the excursion desk to try to change the time for our train ride the next day. After waiting patiently for half a dozen other passengers to harangue the clerk, our turn came. Marion stood off to the side while I stepped up to speak with the clerk.

"I have a very simple request," I said. "I want to exchange our morning White Pass railway ride for the afternoon."

The man pursed his lips. "That's not possible."

"Why's it not possible?"

"We don't make changes twenty-four hours before the excursion begins."

I stepped back and looked around the counter. "I don't see any sign indicating that."

"It's our policy."

"Well, why don't you just check to see if there are seats available in the afternoon?"

He clicked away on his keyboard. "There are, but we don't make changes at this late date. We've already given a count to the railway."

"What if I were coming here to make new reservations for the afternoon?"

"We could accommodate that."

"Fine. Make me a new reservation for the afternoon and cancel the morning."

"That's not possible."

"You just told me that there were seats available in the afternoon."

"Don't be difficult, sir."

"Don't be difficult? What the hell are you being?"

"There are other people waiting to be helped."

"Great. Why don't you help me, and then I'll be happy to let you help them."

"I'm sorry. There's nothing I can do for you."

"I'll say. You're a pathetic, useless, bureaucratic twerp."

I felt a tap on my shoulder. I turned to see Grudion with his flaming red hair.

"Please step out of the line, Mr. Jacobson, and stop intimidating our employee."

"How about if he tries providing some service?"

"Don't be difficult, Mr. Jacobson."

"I'm tired of everyone accusing me of being difficult. I'm only trying to trade in tickets for the train ride tomorrow."

"Haven't you already caused enough problems today? After our earlier conversation, I've had two reports concerning your escapades in Juneau. First, you pushed a woman into a vat at the salmon hatchery, and then you harassed a bear at the Mendenhall Glacier."

"Word sure circulates fast up here," I said.

Grudion gave me a broad smile. "Yah, I have people watching you, Mr. Jacobson."

"Great. That's all I need. Being tailed by some Swedish gumshoe."

"And we'll be continuing to watch you, Mr. Jacobson. Although you're a customer, I don't want you endangering any other passengers or crew."

"How is Julian Armour doing?" I asked.

"He is recovering."

"That's good to hear. I hope he told you that I did nothing to harm him in the hot tub."

"I haven't had a chance to speak with him yet."

Marion came to my side. "Mr. Grudion, Paul and I want to do something to overcome these problems." She looked at me. "First of all, we'd like to speak with the woman who was bumped and fell in the pool at the salmon hatchery. Would that be possible?"

"I'm not going to divulge her name to Mr. Jacobson."

I saw where Marion was headed so I jumped in. "How about this, Mr. Grudion? I'll write her a note of apology. My wife and I would like to invite her to dinner at one of the specialty restaurants." I looked toward Marion.

She nodded her head.

"You don't have to tell us who she is, but would you give her the note and let her decide if she wants to accept my apology?"

Grudion wrinkled his brow. "Yah, I guess that would be possible."

"Good." I stepped to the desk, took a piece of stationery and dashed off a brief note. I handed it to Grudion. "This was all an accident, but I'm willing to try to improve relations between your passengers."

"We'll continue to watch you, Mr. Jacobson."

"While you're doing that see if you can scare up some whales as well."

After Grudion left, Marion said, "That was a good idea to send a note. We need to change people's perceptions."

"Darn right. I may be an old curmudgeon, but I don't intentionally push anyone down stairs and into a vat of squirming baby salmon."

Marion kissed me on the cheek. "And you're not even that much of a curmudgeon. But you certainly seem to attract trouble."

"I guess I'm making up for my earlier years when I led such a calm and mundane life."

"No dead bodies then?"

"Nope. This seems to be a new trend."

We adjourned to the balcony to survey the sound and town of Juneau. Still no whales.

My whale-less reverie was interrupted by the phone ringing. I answered it.

"Is this Mr. Paul Jacobson?"

"It is."

"My name is Mrs. Ellen Hargrave. I received a note from you that was just delivered to my cabin. You want to apologize to me for the two times you've bumped into me?"

"Thank you for calling, Mrs. Hargrave. I want to let you

know I'm sorry for the two accidents. My wife and I would like to make it up to you my taking you out to dinner at one of the specialty restaurants of your choice."

"I don't know if I can trust you, Mr. Jacobson."

I detected a hint of humor in her voice.

"I'm a harmless old fart, but I have a tendency to be in the wrong place at the wrong time. Anyway, my wife will be there to chaperone us."

"Fine. I'll bring my friend Gladys Heinz and my niece and nephew who are traveling with me. Why don't you arrange for a party of six at the Asahi Restaurant at seven P.M. tonight?"

"Okay. We'll see you there."

After we hung up, I called to make a reservation for us to eat raw fish. It would be a small price to pay for harmony among the passengers.

I felt like one of those hamsters running around in a little metal wheel: Curly the murdered street person, Inese, Julian Armour, the bear, Mrs. Hargrave. I sighed. I wanted out of the rat race, and things kept being thrown at me. I should be curled up with a pair of binoculars, watching the whales frolic. Instead, I had to deal with all these accusations. Well, I needed to start resolving these issues one at a time. First, I'd make amends to Mrs. Hargrave tonight. That would be a start. Then I had to keep my butt out of any more trouble. I'd have to stay diligent and not step in any more of the brown stuff.

At seven we arrived at the Japanese restaurant, and I recognized the portly woman in her sixties I'd seen shaking her fist at me from the salmon vat. She walked with a cane and came up to us. Accompanying her were a man and woman in their thirties who were introduced to us as Gina and Gary, and a skinny, middle-aged woman with a pug nose who indicated she was Gladys Heinz. Gina had a pleasant smile and the enthusiasm of an ageless, slender cheerleader while Gary had the sullen look of someone who would have preferred to be off with his friends bar hopping.

We were led to a round table, and Gary raced over and held out a chair. He forced a smile. "For you, Aunt Ellen."

"Why thank you, Gary."

Gary didn't bother to hold chairs for anyone else but plunked down next to his aunt and resumed his dour gaze.

Ellen Hargrave launched into background data. "Gina and Gary are my primary heirs and kindly agreed to join me on this cruise." She smiled at them.

Gina returned the smile, and Gary wrinkled his nose.

"Not too excited about tailing along with your aunt, Gary?" I said.

He flinched and gave me a pointed stare. "I have a lot going on at work."

Aunt Ellen patted him on the arm. "The stock market can survive a week without you, Gary. You're helping your old aunt."

"Right." He gritted his teeth, picked up his aunt's napkin, shook it out and handed it back to her.

"And Gladys is my oldest friend. We grew up together in Baltimore."

We ordered a menagerie of sea creatures, some raw and some stuffed in rice and seaweed. I made sure to also request a tall non-alcoholic tropical drink.

"Have you spotted any whales on this trip?" I asked.

"Oh, yes," Ellen Hargrave replied. "We've seen a dozen or so."

"I keep looking and haven't seen a single one yet."

"Both mornings I've looked out from my balcony and seen them breaching," Gladys said.

"What side of the ship are you on?" I asked.

"The right side."

"That must be it." I turned to Marion. "We're on the whale-less side."

Large platters of sashimi and sushi arrived and we all dug in.

"How did you select this particular cruise?" Marion asked.

Ellen finished a bite of squid and leaned toward Marion. "I'll let you in on a little secret. I've had a detective tracing my family, and I discovered one long-lost relative who may be working on this ship."

I noticed Gary scowling.

"One more heir?" I asked.

"Possibly. My husband Matt, may he rest in peace, left me very well off. Unfortunately, we didn't have any children. My younger brother also died. He was Gary and Gina's father. But there might be one other niece. I had another younger brother who disappeared in Europe during the sixties. He was reported to have this one daughter. She apparently changed her name, and we think she may be working on this ship."

"Any luck in finding her yet?" I asked.

Ellen bit her lip. "The ship security officer, Mr. Grudion, hasn't been very cooperative."

"What a surprise. And to me he's been the sweetest guy. I'll have to use my influence with him."

"Could you?" she asked, her eyes wide.

"I'll try. But he doesn't think much of me, although we seem to meet regularly."

I could feel that Gary was anxious to escape, but Ellen insisted on dessert, so we all placed orders. When the sweets arrived, Ellen's palaver slowed, and I noticed her head lolling to the side. Then her face went plop into her dish of ice cream.

I grabbed the waiter's sleeve. "Call your emergency number. Something's happened to Mrs. Hargrave."

Gary snarled at me, "What did you do to her this time?"

CHAPTER 11

Gina, Gary and Gladys accompanied the two attendants who carted Ellen Hargrave to the medical center. Marion and I sat in our chairs in stunned silence. We could hear people at tables around us speculating on what had happened—"heart attack," "stroke," "what a place to have this happen," "I hope it wasn't the food," and "I've lost my appetite."

I'd lost my appetite as well, but I was stuffed to the gills, so to speak. I charged the meal to my key card and, after signing, we returned to our cabin.

"Something's fishy here," I said to Marion. "I just know that Grudion is going to make a big deal of this and accuse me of something. Particularly with that young twerp Gary making snide comments."

"Gina and Gladys seem nice, but Gary is an odd duck," Marion replied.

"I'll say. I don't trust that bastard one iota."

Marion regarded me thoughtfully. "Why don't you take the initiative? Call Grudion and proactively discuss this rather than waiting for him to come to you."

I shrugged. "It couldn't hurt." I picked up the phone, asked for security and requested to be put in touch with Norbert Grudion.

"He's not available at the moment," I was informed by a clipped male voice.

"Have him contact me and preferably come to my cabin as

soon as possible."

We bundled up in jackets and sat out on our balcony. The ship had just left the Juneau dock and we watched in the light of the Alaskan evening as we sailed down the Gastineau Channel.

"Beautiful view," I said. "Too bad they don't have more whales up here."

Marion swatted me with the brochure she was reading. "There are whales all over the place. You're just not paying attention."

"I've been looking like mad. They're all avoiding me."

After continuing unsuccessfully to spot a whale, my period of relaxation was disturbed by a knock on the door. I opened it to find Grudion in his red-haired splendor standing there.

"You wanted to speak to me, Mr. Jacobson?"

"Yes, indeed. Come on in to our humble abode." I waved him inside. "Mrs. Hargrave passed out, and I want to talk to you regarding our dinner with her."

"Did you do something to her? Her nephew gave me an earful."

"And I want to talk to you about him. He seemed more interested in blaming me than showing concern for his aunt."

Grudion stared at me. "You didn't answer my question."

I sighed. "Mr. Grudion, my wife and I had a pleasant dinner with Mrs. Hargrave and her friend, nephew and niece. Then all of a sudden she didn't look well and keeled over onto the table. What does your medical crew have to say about her condition?"

"They're tending to her now. Did you put anything in her food?"

"Absolutely not. She seemed fine until dessert was served. The whole purpose of the dinner was to make amends for the previous accidents. I want to improve relations, not hinder them."

"Yah, we'll see what the doctor says."

"And I have a question for you, Mr. Grudion. Mrs. Hargrave said she was trying to find a long-lost niece who she suspected was on the crew of this ship." I wagged a finger at him. "She indicated you weren't very cooperative."

"We maintain strict privacy for our personnel."

"Come on, Mr. Grudion. If someone was looking for a relative, I'm sure you could be more accommodating."

"It's not anything that I'm going to discuss with you, Mr. Jacobson."

"Fine. When Mrs. Hargrave recovers, you can cover it with her."

"Not likely."

The guy was starting to tick me off. "Why the hell not? What's the matter with you security guys? You think everyone is plotting against you?"

"You have no understanding of the matter, so just stay out of it."

With that he turned and left the room.

Marion, who had been listening, came up to me. "Something strange is going on here."

"You've pegged that right. Mrs. Hargrave loses consciousness, and now Grudion acts like it's a terrorist plot and clamps his lips."

"Well, I hope Mrs. Hargrave is going to recover."

"I do too. Once we got past the two accidents, we were hitting it off fine. I hope she's up and around right away. Besides, I don't like the accusations from her nephew. And there's the strange way Grudion is acting." I thought for a moment. "I wonder if my buddy Andrew Black can poke at this a little."

"It's worth a try."

I picked up the phone and asked to be connected to his cabin. No answer. I left a message for him to call me.

"They're probably at the evening show. Speaking of which,

would you like to go see a comedy routine?"

"Sure. I could use a few laughs."

We headed to the auditorium and joined the mob of cruising fanatics. We squeezed into two seats next to a rowdy group of revelers who were gulping down tall tropical drinks. It helped me remember why I wanted to stay sober.

The comedian dashed onto the stage with a microphone in his hand. "Welcome to the waters of Alaska. I hope you're having a whale of a cruise."

"Don't remind me about whales," I muttered.

"Up here this time of year it stays light until eleven o'clock. That's so people can find their way back to their cabins after a few too many drinks. And when the stars finally come out in the wee hours of the morning, you know what they call the older people who stay up to watch? Star geezers."

I leaned over toward Marion. "I'll have to write that one down in my journal. Since I won't remember it, I can chuckle every time I read it."

The comedian continued with a good routine making fun of people on a cruise ship including the captain, social director, tipsy passengers and himself. My rowdy companions laughed loudest during the reference to drunken passengers. They obviously felt it referred to some other people.

As we filed out afterwards, Marion pointed out Andrew and Helen Black.

"Would you join us for a nightcap?" I shouted. "I have something to discuss with Andrew."

We adjourned to one of the bars that had soft background music rather than karaoke that would have driven me nuts.

I ordered a tropical drink without the booze to keep my wits about me.

"What's on your mind, Paul?" Andrew asked.

"My predicament keeps getting more precarious. Tonight at

dinner our tablemate Mrs. Ellen Hargrave did a nosedive right into her ice cream dish and was taken to the infirmary. Her nephew accused me of doing something to her. In addition, she said she is looking for a long-lost niece who she suspects is a member of the crew of our ship. I spoke with Grudion and he was not just uncooperative but hostile."

"Yes," Marion said. "Mr. Grudion acted very strange and wouldn't share any information with us."

Andrew smacked his lips. "Norbert Grudion is a very intense security officer, but he's one of the best in the fleet. Something unusual must be going on because he is usually more politic about problems concerning passengers."

"See what you can find out. I need to extract myself from these accusations, and he certainly isn't ready to engage in meaningful dialogue."

"Let's meet for a walk around the track at eight in the morning," Andrew said. "I'll see if I can find out anything tonight."

"All efforts will be appreciated."

When we returned to our cabin, Marion reminded me to update my journal.

I reviewed the activities of the day, which only caused my stomach to churn. My best intentions this evening had somehow gone awry. Hopefully Ellen Hargrave would recover quickly from whatever happened to her. And then there was Julian Armour. I had been around two people who ended up in sickbay. I sure hoped everyone bounced back. I also needed to keep Grudion away while I figured out the chain of unfortunate events. And then I had to do whatever I could to assist my crapola memory. I licked my lips, picked up a pen and documented the life and times of Paul Jacobson, cruiser extraordinaire.

Finally, I left a note on top to tell myself to read it in the morning and to meet Andrew for our morning stroll.

★ ★ ★ ★ ★

I awoke in a state of disorientation, wondering what planet I had plunked down on. I noticed a person of the female persuasion sleeping next to me. Who was she and why were we in bed together? Images of a midnight tryst danced in my addled brain.

I turned my attention to the room. My domain sported off-white walls with reddish-brown veneer. Across the room a modern painting of a canoe, grass shack and palm tree met my eyes. I squinted. Was I in a Hawaiian Motel Five-and-a-Half? Vertical-striped curtains with all the colors of the rainbow covered what must have been a large window, given the light seeping in from the sides. In one corner of the room a small television set was mounted above a telephone and a small table of the same reddish-brown wood, accompanied by one chair. This place was either built for midgets or I had ended up in the economy section. In another corner of the room a mounted table surface contained a coffee pot and cups. Mr. Coffee was waiting to feed my caffeine need. Underneath, a red stool rested. I patted the bed my companion and I had slept in. It was strange. It appeared to be two identical single beds brought together and made up as a double bed. This whole place reminded me of a cramped hotel room.

Just then I spotted a note, which read, "Read this before you pee, you old fart. You have an appointment with Andrew Black at eight A.M. on the jogging track on deck thirteen."

I wondered what that was all about. Who was Andrew Black and why would I go to a jogging track? I hadn't run in years. I settled down to read the diary and it all made sense in an absurd sort of way.

I followed the directions, wondering how I would spot this Andrew Black. Fortunately, a man came up to me. "Paul, you're right on time."

"Are you Andrew?"

He chuckled. "That's right. Your short-term memory problem. You don't recognize me."

"I read a note, but I wouldn't know you from Shamu the whale."

Andrew patted his stomach. "I'm a little skinnier than Shamu."

"I read in my journal that you were going to check with Grudion. Any results?"

"Yes and no. I did speak with him, but he was very close-mouthed. It has something to do with the murder investigation concerning the massage therapist in the spa."

"So he won't talk about Mrs. Hargrave's niece because of Inese's death. Does he think Inese is the missing niece?"

"It's possible, but I couldn't dredge up anything useful from him."

"That puts a whole new light on things. Could Inese's murder be linked to Mrs. Hargrave?" Then it struck me. "And that's one more circumstantial link that Grudion has against me. I'm there when Inese is murdered. I'm associated with three incidents with Ellen Hargrave. And then last night I asked Grudion why he's not helping Ellen." I squeezed my hands to the side of my head. "I can't remember seaweed from squid except for what's written in my journal, but none of this looks good for me."

"It certainly makes it apparent why Grudion is suspicious of you. But obviously there is another explanation."

"I have no motive for harming Inese or Ellen. But someone else does."

As we circled the deck I ruminated on this while admiring the green mountains and snow-capped peaks surrounding the port of Skagway. "If there's snow up there in August, think what it's like during winter."

"I don't imagine there are many people here during the

winter," Andrew said. "I understand the population is only eight hundred people. With our ship and three others in port, we account for ten times the permanent population."

"Darn tourists." I looked at my watch. "I better retrieve my bride so we can catch a bite to eat before our train ride."

"Enjoy your trip. I'm going to take a few more laps around the deck."

Back in the stateroom, Marion was up and around, making her final preparations, so I decided to check on Ellen Hargrave.

I called, asked to be connected to her room and a woman's voice answered.

"Is this Ellen Hargrave?"

"Speaking."

"This is Paul Jacobson. I was worried about you. I'm glad you're out of the medical center."

"Thanks for your concern. Apparently there was a problem with some medication I've been taking. I'm planning to stay on the ship today to rest."

"We're taking a train ride, but I'll check in with you when we return."

"If I'm feeling better I'd love to see you and Marion this evening."

"We'll give you a full report on our excursion. Marion sends her best."

After I hung up, I turned to Marion. "That's a relief. Ellen is doing better and isn't accusing me of anything."

"That is good news. Now if her nephew Gary will stop blaming you, that will help."

"I don't know about him. From what I read, he seems to be an obnoxious little snot."

Marion chuckled. "He's not that bad, but he does act strange. He vacillates between appearing like he wants to be somewhere else and then acting overly solicitous of his aunt."

"Well, he should protect her from people bashing into me rather than accusing me of being the problem. On another subject, I read in my journal that Jennifer is checking out the name Zarins for me. I should give her a call to see if she's made any progress."

Marion fished the cell phone out of her purse, set it up for me and I pushed the green button.

"Jacobson residence," said a girl's voice.

"Well, hello. This is the senior member of the Jacobsons."

"Hi, Grandpa. Are you staying out of any more trouble?"

"No. In Juneau I bumped into the same woman I had in the lifeboat drill and knocked her into a vat of baby salmon."

"Grandpa, how could that happen again to the same person?"

"This is the second time someone bashed into me causing a chain reaction."

"You're not going to make many friends if that keeps happening."

"You're right, kiddo. I tried to make it up to the woman, Ellen Hargrave. Marion and I took her and her entourage out to dinner last night. Unfortunately, she fainted and her nephew accused me of poisoning her."

"How do you end up in these fixes?"

"I'm just lucky. She did call this morning, and it appears she had a problem with her medicine and isn't holding me responsible."

"That's good. Speaking of medicine, have you been good and taken your pills?"

"Unfortunately, yes. Marion keeps cramming them down my throat."

"Do what she says."

"Yes, ma'am. And I had one other adventure that you will appreciate."

"You saw some whales?"

"No. I was chased by a bear."

"I'm glad it didn't catch you."

"So am I. But the ranger accused me of harassing wildlife."

"I'm sure that was just to scare you so you'd be more careful."

"It will if I remember to read my journal or avoid going back there again."

"Grandpa, you be nice to animals and people."

"I have made a new friend. Andrew Black. He and I walk along the jogging track in the mornings. Of all things he's a darn lawyer."

"In spite of your dislike for attorneys, you seem to make friends with them. Meyer Ohana was a lawyer and your best friend in Hawaii."

"Yes, I read that I gave him a call a few days ago. So, did you find anything for me in researching the name Inese Zarins?"

"Couldn't find any Inese Zarins, but I came across lots of Zarins including a trombone player, an eastern European businessman, a playwright and a professor of theology, to name a few."

"That doesn't help much." Then I remembered something else from my journal. "Wait, here's a tidbit for you. Inese said she was from Latvia. See if you can find any Latvian connections to the name."

"When I'm on the computer this afternoon, I'll check it out. Any other clues on your end?"

"No. Same old, same old. The ship's security guy, Grudion, keeps bugging me."

"You have to find some way to enlist him as an ally."

"Fat chance. He's too busy trying to lay any misdemeanors or felonies on me."

"Keep at it, Grandpa, and I'll continue to research Zarins in Latvia."

I signed off and with my phone responsibilities completed for the morning, we headed up to graze at the breakfast buffet and then disembarked to catch the train that was waiting for us a short distance along the wharf.

"Look at this service," I said as we clambered aboard. "We don't even have to walk into town."

A conductor presented us each with a small blue bottle that read "White Pass and Yukon Route Demineralized Drinking Water."

I inspected the bottle. The label on the bottle indicated that it contained 250 milliliters of pure drinking water. Embossed in the plastic surface was the image of a train engine.

"Perfect size for carrying in a jacket pocket."

The train chugged through town, passed a roundhouse where other engines stood and began climbing an incline through a valley. The view was stupendous: lush green, jagged cuts above the treeline with pockets of snow, deep gorges with water cascading down, a tall abandoned trestle spanning a canyon. At one spot we could see back down the valley to the town of Skagway with the fleet of cruise ships docked there.

"We're up in this mountain wilderness with a trainload of whiny tourists," I said.

Marion smiled at me. "Including you."

"I'm not a tourist. I'm a geezer."

Marion snapped pictures like mad with her digital camera as we continued up the mountainside.

I thought back to the last time I'd been on a train. With my warped mental acuity I couldn't dredge up anything in the last half dozen years, but one image came to mind. My first wife Rhonda and I had taken the Zepher through the Rockies and sat in an observation car looking out a clear dome at the wonders of Mother Nature. Our son Denny was with us, and he raced back and forth along the aisle pointing at one rock formation after another. We even saw an eagle soaring above us.

I shook my head. Amazing how the brain works. I could still recall the details of that day forty years ago when yesterday had disappeared into the dustbin of my mind.

We rounded a turn, and again I had a view down the long valley to the sound where the town of Skagway and the large ships rested. I liked the mountains and was glad I wasn't out in the ocean. This cruise was okay as long as I remained inside a large ship, but the ocean still gave me the willies.

"Look, there's Julian Armour, the man who was unconscious in the hot tub," Marion said.

CHAPTER 12

A man with a shirt that read "Oldsters from Reno" was walking down the aisle toward us, holding a camera.

"Are you feeling better?" Marion asked.

He stopped and then saw me sitting next to Marion and pointed. "No thanks to him."

"Just a minute, Julian," Marion said. "Paul found you and called for help."

He wrinkled his forehead. "I don't know. First he takes my wallet, and then he does something to me in the Jacuzzi."

"Hold it a damn minute," I said. "I did nothing of the sort. I'm sure you'll find your wallet, and in the spa, I was only trying to help."

"That's right, Julian. Paul didn't mean any harm."

He at least looked doubtful this time.

"Let's let bygones be bygones," I said.

"We'll see," he replied and continued to the back of the car. I watched as he went out the door and stood on the back platform, snapping pictures. On his way back he stopped to talk to a couple sitting in front of us. I overheard him say, "I'm still thirsty, but I finished that little blue bottle of water they gave us, and we didn't bring anything else."

A thought occurred to me where I might contribute to cruise harmony.

"Julian," I called out.

He turned. "Yeah?"

128

I stood up and handed him my blue water bottle. "I haven't opened it yet. Why don't you take it?"

Julian raised his eyebrows. "You sure?"

"Yes. I'm not thirsty so you can have it."

"That's mighty kind of you. Maybe you're not such a jerk after all."

I smiled. "That's what my bride tells me."

He faced forward and returned to his seat.

I leaned into the aisle and watched as he twisted the top off the blue bottle, chugging it down. He turned around and waved to me. Maybe I had turned around a problematic situation.

Marion and I continued to admire the scenery. From her window seat she periodically pointed out a rock formation, craggy peak or steep ravine. This would be fantastic country to hike through, and my old legs could withstand several miles of it, but this train ride provided the panorama of views so much more extensive than I could cover on my own. Here was Alaska in all its glory: the forests, streams, wildlife and mountains hampered by only a few pesky tourists crammed in our little railroad car.

My reverie was broken when I noticed Julian Armour sprinting up the aisle like he was attempting to break the hundred-yard dash for the over-fifty senior masters road racers. He sailed past me, and I spun around in my seat to see where he was headed. He reached for the handle on the door of the one restroom in our car. Someone else was obviously inside because the door didn't open.

I continued to gawk as Julian released the handle and then pushed through the back door of the railroad car to reach the back platform where he had taken pictures earlier. He leaned over the railing.

I was close enough to see that he was retching over the side like a seasick sailor. I could understand that happening on a ship, but on a train?

Turned around in this awkward position, my neck hurt, but I watched as Julian stood up for a moment and then leaned over again for a repeat performance. Poor Julian. I'd hate to be puking my guts out on the railroad tracks.

Finally, he stood erect and wiped his mouth on his sleeve.

I decided I didn't want to be sitting next to him, but maybe his seat companion would be more tolerant.

He swayed on the platform. I didn't know if the jerky train caused his motion or if he was still feeling under the weather.

Then he staggered back inside. Rather than immediately heading back to his seat, he stopped beside me.

He pointed a stubby index finger at me. "What are you staring at, and what did you do to me?"

I flinched. "Huh?"

"You gave me a bottle of water."

"That's right."

"What did you put in it? Were you trying to poison me?"

"What are you talking about?"

"I drank the water you gave me and started feeling funny. Than all of a sudden I was sick to my stomach."

"You guzzled it pretty quickly. Maybe your stomach just protested to that."

"You . . . you . . . you are a menace. I know you made me sick."

Marion leaned across me. "Julian, Paul didn't do anything to the water. He was given the bottle when we got on the train and hadn't opened it before he gave it to you."

"He did something to the water. I know it."

He stumbled off and returned to his seat.

"I'll never win with that guy," I said.

Marion patted my arm. "You tried."

At the top of the pass, the engineer announced that the

engine would be disconnected and make a circuit on a parallel and connecting set of tracks to go to the opposite end of the train for our return journey. We were in the last car so we watched as the engine eventually passed by us on the other set of tracks in front of an icy lake. It disappeared around a corner and soon reappeared, backing up to re-engage.

After re-coupling, we headed back down toward Skagway. Half an hour later, the engineer announced a bear sighting off to the right side. We all swarmed to that side of the train and sure enough a big brown furry object was disappearing into the undergrowth. Marion raised her camera and pushed the button. Afterward, she brought the image up and proudly showed me the picture of a bear butt.

"I wonder how this compares to the one that chased you at Mendenall Glacier?"

"Couldn't say, but I think the other end of the bear was after me that time."

We safely completed our journey and exited at the train depot in downtown (as opposed to suburban) Skagway. While Marion used the restroom, I waited in the lobby and watched a model train circle above a coffee shop. The walls were lined with pictures of trestle construction, a turn-of-the-previous-century hotel, trains, boats, float planes and prospectors carrying supplies on sleds. I felt like Paul of the Yukon.

"Let's do some shopping," Marion announced when she returned. She grabbed my arm and practically dragged me out to the boardwalk. The town was in fine fiddle with mobs of tourists dashing around with shopping bags and backpacks. We meandered through several stores, and I noticed a similarity of souvenirs in each shop. Although a few curios appeared to be native-made, when I looked at labels, there were the invariable knickknacks from China.

When my shopping tolerance gave out, I let Marion continue

while I sat on a bench to watch the mob scene of scurrying humans, buses, trains and helicopters. The temperature was in the fifties and people were outfitted in every combination of shorts, jeans, jackets and T-shirts. The buildings had fresh coats of paint, brightly decorated in yellow with green trim, reddish brown with yellow trim, rust with olive trim and navy blue with yellow trim. I guessed in the middle of twenty feet of winter snow you could pick out the right second story by the color combination.

A man plopped down next to me on the bench. "Phew," he said. "I can't keep up with my wife when shopping."

"I know what you mean," I replied. "I ran out of gas after three stores, but Marion is still going strong." As he leaned toward me, I noticed his shirt read "Oldster from Reno" and remembered something from my journal. "I sat next to some folks from your group at a bingo game."

He chuckled. "There are fifty of us on this cruise. We're everywhere."

"Do you travel in a herd like this often?"

"Once a year we have a major expedition. Last year we went to Hawaii and the year before the Caribbean."

"So Alaska is the recipient of your presence and tourist dollars this summer."

"Yup. And we're taking the forth-ninth state by storm."

"Do you know Julian Armour?" I asked.

"Yes, indeed. He's one of our ringleaders."

I didn't mention that I thought Julian should be left in a cage rather than allowed into a ring.

He spotted some other members of his group and charged off to join them.

I continued to reconnoiter the street scene, glad that I had the reprieve from shopping. I watched a small boy with a huge smile on his face hug a stuffed moose. Ah, the wonders of youth, when a stuffed animal could provide so much pleasure. Kind of like when I enjoyed a morning because I knew who I was and what was going on. Maybe I could have a custom-made stuffed moose with a recording inside that played when I pushed its stomach, "You're Paul Jacobson and you remember squat overnight unless you've had a little hanky-panky with your wife Marion the night before. Stay away from dead bodies."

Other people collected stamps, coins or model trains. I seemed to be collecting crime accusations. But the bright sunny Alaskan summer day was too nice to allow me to feel sorry for myself. I had to count my blessings. How many old farts my age could still be wandering around on two solid legs, newly married to a young thing in her seventies and being chased by a bear at a glacier? I had to be grateful for my life, however much was left of it. Time to suck it up and get on with figuring out who had killed Inese. I decided to check in again with Ellen Hargrave when we returned to the ship. I had to understand more regarding this long-lost niece and whether it was Inese.

Marion appeared, having sprouted numerous shopping bags from both arms.

"Did you buy out the whole town?" I asked.

"I found presents for everyone," she replied with a smug smile.

"I'm glad you took care of that. We have a perfect division of labor. I provide the Social Security check and you spend it."

"I bring in my fair share as well," she said with a pout.

"I'm not complaining. I'm delighted that I don't have to take care of shopping details."

I unloaded some of the bags so Marion could stand up straight again, and we headed back to the ship. As we approached our home-away-from-home, Marion accosted a fellow traveler and asked her to take a picture of us. After displaying my pearly whites, Marion showed me the picture. There were our smiley mugs in front of a huge white object that resembled a face with its two sets of windows that looked like horizontal eyes, a bow for a nose, a red-painted design above water line that reminded me of lips and antennae for hair. Behind rose the peaks across the bay. With this last souvenir of Skagway, we picked up our parcels and re-embarked.

Once back in our snug little cabin, I placed a call to Ellen Hargrave.

"How are you feeling?" I asked.

"I seem to be fully recovered."

"Good. Can you join us for a nightcap after the show tonight?"

"I'll meet you in the Rendezvous Lounge."

"I've been wondering about this long-lost niece of yours. What exactly have you learned?"

"Not very much. As I mentioned before, she grew up in Europe."

"Do you know precisely where?"

"Some city in Latvia."

CHAPTER 13

My heart started thumping like I was being chased by that bear again at hearing that Mrs. Hargrave's long-lost niece had lived in Latvia. "And what led you to the discovery that she was working on our ship?"

"The detective I hired tracked down a childhood friend who had received a phone call saying she was working on the Scandinavian Sea Lines *Sunshine*."

"Then she should be easy to identify."

Ellen shook her head. "Apparently she changed her name, because no one I've spoken to knows an Ann Hargrave on this ship."

"And the childhood friend didn't know her new name?" I asked.

"Apparently Ann didn't divulge it to her . . . Whoops. I have to run to meet Gladys and my niece and nephew. We can continue our discussion tonight."

I immediately called Andrew. "A new piece of information from Ellen Hargrave. Her long-lost niece came from Latvia. It's very possible that the niece was Inese, who also came from Latvia."

"Wow. That is an interesting coincidence. Let me make some more inquiries. Do you and Marion want to meet for dinner tonight?"

"Sure. I'll fill you in on the bear butt we saw today."

"That sounds interesting."

"It was."

On our way to dinner, I decided to do a little detecting on my own. I noticed that the crew members wore name badges with their name and country. There was still a possibility that there might be another woman in the crew from Latvia, so I surreptitiously stared at each woman's name badge I passed. I squinted at one well-endowed maid and made out the name of Angelina from Hungary.

She came to a stop and gave me a strange look.

As we continued on, Marion elbowed me in the ribs. "That's not like you to blatantly stare at a woman's breasts, Paul."

My cheeks turned warm. "Oops. I was checking out her name tag. I'm trying to see if there are any other female crew members from Latvia."

She rolled her eyes. "I don't think that's a good idea. You may get slapped next time."

At dinner we met Andrew and Helen in the waiting area. As a hostess led us to a table, I checked her out, so to speak, and spotted a country of origin of Brazil. She didn't catch me ogling her.

Over lamb chops, Andrew filled me in on the latest. "The important thing I learned is that only one woman on the crew is from Latvia, the murder victim Inese."

Marion smiled. "That will save you from a sexual harassment charge, Paul."

Andrew looked perplexed. "What do you mean?"

I grimaced. "I started looking at name tags of female crew members earlier to see if I could find any listing Latvia. I can't help it that they wear their nameplates on their breasts."

Andrew chuckled. "Paul, you find the most interesting ways to get into trouble."

"Yeah, my next thought was to break into the quartermaster's office to steal a crew list."

"Fortunately, you won't have to do that."

I sighed. "So odds are Inese is the long-lost niece, but before Ellen Hargrave could hook up with her, someone stuffed a hot stone into her mouth to choke her to death."

Marion looked thoughtful and then said, "If Andrew could track down that Inese was the only crew member from Latvia, someone else could have done the same."

"I don't know," Andrew said. "That information is pretty closely held. I had to call in a favor to find it out."

"Still, someone must have learned it," Marion said.

"And the people least excited about Ellen finding a new heiress would be Gary and Gina," I added.

"You're right," Marion said. "When that topic came up at dinner last night, Gary in particular didn't look pleased."

"Maybe I should have a heart-to-heart chat with Gary," I said.

"I don't know if that would be a good idea," Andrew said. "He'd only deny any accusation. We need some proof."

"I wonder if Grudion and his security people found any fingerprints on the hot stone or anything else in the room where Inese was killed."

"I'll suggest Grudion check out Gary and Gina," Andrew said.

"Good idea. He'll listen to you more than to me."

With that decided, I relaxed and enjoyed the crème brûlée.

"Do you realize our cruise is half over?" Marion said.

"I was just starting to get my sea legs. That means I have only a few more days to clear this whole mess up."

"We'll keep helping you, Paul," Andrew said.

"And I appreciate that. In any case, I'll have to face Detective Bearhurst of Seattle's finest when I return."

"Maybe he's made some progress on that other murder."

"I sure hope so. I wouldn't want him and Grudion fighting

over who had the pleasure of drawing and quartering me."

We all adjourned for the show.

"What do we have on tap tonight?" I asked.

"It's a magic show." Marion squeezed my arm. "Maybe you'll be invited on stage again."

"I think I'll settle for being the audience, but maybe the magician can make my troubles disappear."

Frederick the Magnificent was good. He made a rabbit, a cage of doves and his lovely assistant Madeline all disappear. In addition, he levitated Madeline, which was especially amazing since the ship was rocking at the time.

It was a good thing I wasn't invited on stage since he probably would have made me disappear through a hole in the floor where I would have slid into the brig.

Frederick ended with a routine where he invited three male passengers up on stage, wowed them with a sleight of hand card trick and then showed them that he had also lifted their wallets. They all checked their billfolds and found a coupon for a free drink in one of the lounges.

"Not bad," Andrew said.

"And I still have this guy Julian Armour accusing me of stealing his wallet."

"Except you're not that good, Paul. You only picked up his coat to return it."

I looked at my watch. "Time to meet Ellen Hargrave. Andrew and Helen, do you want to join us?"

Andrew looked toward Helen, and she said, "No thanks. I'd like to go out on deck for some fresh air and then retire."

"Okay," Andrew said. "Paul, will I see you on the walking track in the morning?"

"As long as I'm still alive, I'll be there."

Marion swatted me. "Don't even say such a thing."

"Hey, at my age, I have to be realistic."

We waved goodbye and headed to the Rendezvous Lounge.

"Since I can't remember Ellen Hargrave from a hole in the wall, do you see her here?"

Marion looked around the room. "No. She hasn't arrived."

We found a table and shortly a portly woman using a cane waddled in.

Marion waved to her, and she came over to join us.

"We're so glad you're feeling better," Marion said.

"Yes. That put a scare in me. I take medication for high blood pressure and somehow the medicine got switched. The doctor said if I hadn't been treated immediately, it could have been fatal."

I had a bad feeling. "How did you discover that the medicine was switched?"

"After I came to, the doctor asked what medication I took. I had wrapped a pill up in a tissue and put it in my pocket to take again after dessert."

"Why didn't you just bring the whole bottle with you?" Marion asked.

Ellen gave an indulgent smile. "I didn't want to take my purse so I just slipped one pill and my key card in my pocket. When the doctor saw the pill I showed him, he turned red and said it was medicine to increase not lower blood pressure."

I put my hands on the table and leaned toward her. "Mrs. Hargrave, I think someone switched your medicine on purpose. Did you leave your medicine unattended at any time before dinner yesterday?"

"No. It was with me or in my cabin."

"Was anyone in your cabin with you?"

"Besides the steward and maid staff, only Gary and Gina."

I looked toward Marion. She nodded. I took a deep breath and then returned my gaze to Ellen Hargrave. "I hate to say this, but Gary or Gina might have switched your medicine."

Her eyes grew large, and she put her hand to her mouth. "Please, Mr. Jacobson. My nephew and niece wouldn't have done anything like that."

"Is there any chance that they might be jealous because you're now looking for this long-lost niece?"

She pursed her lips. "Well . . . they haven't been as excited as I have been about the endeavor, if that is what you mean."

"Exactly. They may see this as a threat to their inheritance."

She gave me a dismissive wave. "They'll inherit a large sum with or without a third heir."

"I don't know. Some people don't look that kindly on having their share reduced. They might even take steps to prevent you from finding this other niece."

"Oh, posh. Gary and Gina would never do that."

I looked again toward Marion, who only shrugged her shoulders. I had given it my best shot, but Ellen Hargrave wasn't open to the suggestion that her relatives might not be nice people. And besides, I didn't know if one or both of them were causing all these problems.

Our drinks arrived, and I sipped my tall glass of various fruit juices without rum.

"I'm looking forward to seeing Glacier Bay tomorrow," Marion said. "Sailing by the glaciers is supposed to be very spectacular."

"I'd like to see a map of the area," I said.

"I have a very detailed map," Ellen said. "It shows how some of the glaciers have retreated since the eighteenth century."

"Kind of like how my memory has retreated."

After we finished our drinks and kibitzed a little more, Ellen said, "This has been a pleasant interlude, but I'm tired and ready to retire to my cabin."

"I think I'll stop at the casino," Marion said with a glint in her eyes.

"My bride has found the magic touch with the slot machines. She's going to pay for our whole trip."

"The trip was free, Paul."

"See. Even if she loses, she's paid for the trip."

I offered to walk Ellen back to her cabin. She held my arm in one of her hands and her cane in the other.

At the door to room 11580 Ellen said, "Why don't you come in for a moment, and I'll show you that map of Glacier Bay."

"Your nephew and niece nearby?"

"They have the room next door." She inserted her key card.

When we entered, a maid was turning down the bed and placing chocolate on the pillow.

"Oh, Anita. You're leaving me a little treat."

The woman turned and smiled. "You surprised me. I'm sorry I'm so late tonight, but one of the other girls is sick and I had to cover both of our rooms."

"Mr. Jacobson and I were just going to look at a map of Glacier Bay so you can continue."

I noticed Anita's tag that listed France as her country. "Bonjour, mademoiselle." I gave my most distinguished bow.

Anita smiled. "Bonjour, monsieur. I will be done soon."

Ellen retrieved the map, and I plunked down in a chair to scan it. Lines indicated where the glaciers had taken up most of the bay in the late eighteenth and nineteenth century but now had retreated to form pockets in the inlets.

"It's supposed to be spectacular even if it's much smaller than centuries ago," I said.

"There are actually a few places that are growing, if you look carefully."

I squinted and sure enough, several spots showed lines that had expanded some during the twentieth century. "Still doesn't make up for the huge losses in the main part of the bay."

"You're not one of those global warming fanatics, are you,

Mr. Jacobson?"

"What do you mean?"

"Do you think ice is disappearing around the world because of carbon dioxide emission heating the planet?"

"I think the evidence is pretty clear here. Look at all this lost ice."

"Posh. That's just the normal cycle. Throughout history there have been ice ages and then ice retreats."

"Give me a break. This is no small change." I thrust my finger at the map.

"Mr. Jacobson, you're getting hot under the collar."

"Damn right. You must be one of those people who don't want to accept facts. Just look at this map."

"Please, watch your language."

"I'm done," Anita said, looking wildly about and edging toward the cabin door. She scuttled out and closed the door.

"Now look what you've done," Ellen said. "You've scared Anita."

I took a deep breath. "I'm sorry. I tend to get carried away." I refolded the map and stood up. "Thanks for the use of the map. Just remember not to fall asleep on your bed until you've eaten or removed the chocolates."

"Oh?"

"Yeah. I read in my journal how I inadvertently had a chocolate rather than mud bath."

"I'll remember that."

"Good night. I'll rejoin my bride in the casino now."

I left and wended my way to the bright lights and clinking sounds of the gambling hall. I traded in a twenty-spot of my hard-earned cash for quarters. In five minutes, eighty quarters had disappeared. I had won only five along the way to my financial demise.

Deciding that was enough fun for one evening, I moseyed

over to watch Marion who held a container full of silver.

"How's it going?" I asked.

She was concentrating so hard, she hadn't noticed me sneaking up on her. "Oh, Paul, when did you arrive?"

"Just now, after wasting a little money."

"I'm winning." Her Cheshire cat grin appeared. "But I don't want you watching over my shoulder. You'll bring me bad luck."

"I don't want to interfere with your streak. I'll meet you back in the cabin."

She gave me a half-hearted wave and continued to feed quarters into the machine. The only difference was that after two quarters, her machine spat out forty quarters.

"I'll be horn-swoggled. These machines never do that for me."

"You just need to have the touch, Paul."

"Which apparently I don't."

I decided to make one pass outside on the promenade deck to view the scenery of the extended Alaskan dusk. Even at this late hour it was still light. Little islands peeked out of the water as we passed a coastline of rich forests.

Then with my addled brain full of images of the wonders of nature, I headed back to our stateroom to document my adventures and to eat chocolate before I fell asleep on it.

The next morning I awoke to the sound of someone pounding on a door. My eyes scanned an unfamiliar little room, and I discovered a woman lying next to me in bed. Where was I, and who was she?

The pounding continued.

My companion didn't budge so I lifted the covers, plunked my feet onto the floor and padded over to open the door.

A red-haired man in a white uniform stood there, a scowl on his face.

"I don't remember calling a paramedic," I said.

"Mr. Jacobson, I need to ask you to join me in the captain's quarters."

I scratched my head. "Who the heck are you and what captain are you referring to? I'm not in the navy anymore."

"This concerns what you did last night."

"That will be a short conversation. We can do it right here. Last night is a blank. Now if you'll excuse me, I need to find out who the woman in my room is."

I started to close the door, but he inserted a large polished black shoe in the way. "Not so fast, Mr. Jacobson. This is a serious matter."

"I'll say. I still don't know who you are."

A heard a rustling behind me. "Paul, let me speak to Mr. Grudion."

I turned around to see the woman sitting up in bed. She was fully clad in a flannel nightgown.

"Mr. Grudion, Paul can't remember anything from yesterday. If you give him a chance to read his journal, he will be more useful in answering any questions you have."

"What journal?" I asked.

She pointed to a stack of paper on the nightstand.

Grudion stepped inside and stood with his arms crossed.

I picked up the papers and began to read. I'm sure my eyes widened as I discovered I was married to this woman named Marion who had been sleeping with me, that the red-haired intruder was head of security on the Scandinavian Sea Line's *Sunshine* taking my bride and me on an Alaskan cruise and that I had been linked to two murders and several other incidents.

"This is a hell of a way for an old fart to wake up."

"Are you ready to put on your clothes and join me?" Grudion asked.

"I suppose so. You serving breakfast?"

144

"Mr. Jacobson, this is not a laughing matter."

"I have no clue what kind of matter it is, but I know I'm hungry. Give me a minute to find some clothes."

I searched through the miniscule closet, extracted a pair of pants and a shirt, retrieved underwear, undershirt and socks from a drawer and slipped into this tiny bathroom to change. Good thing I didn't have arthritis or I never would have been able to negotiate the tight space. Once presentable, I emerged and found some tennis shoes to put on.

"Mr. Grudion, do you want me to join you as well?" Marion asked.

"Not at this time, Mrs. Jacobson. I need to speak with your husband first, and then I'll talk to you later."

"Why all the mystery?" I asked. "You sound like you're planning to interrogate me."

"Exactly, Mr. Jacobson."

"Have it your own way. It'll be a short interview. All I know is what I just read in my diary."

"Then we'll see what you have to say from that."

Grudion held the door open for me and then followed me out.

"Go toward the central elevator," he said.

"I'd be happy to, but I don't know where it is."

"Yah, to the right."

"Why all the interest in me?"

He harrumphed but said no more. We entered an elevator, which we had to ourselves, and ascended to the fourteenth deck.

"So we're up in the high-rent district," I said as we exited.

"Second door on the right."

We entered a spacious cabin with walnut wood paneling, marble counters and a large window overlooking water and emerald green shoreline. Two men in full dress whites sat in

145

chairs. Grudion pointed to a seat for me and then joined the other two.

Not one smile appeared on the three faces. The man who appeared to be the captain from the epaulettes on his shoulders had a distinguished short white beard and intense blue eyes. The other man's square jaw and steel eyes gave no hint of warmth.

"Let the inquisition begin," I said.

"Mr. Jacobson, this is a very serious matter," Captain Whitebeard said. "I met you the first night of the cruise when you joined me for dinner."

"I don't remember that, but I read about it in my journal. To set the record straight for all you fine gentlemen, I'm at a significant disadvantage. I have short-term memory loss and can't recall anything concerning this cruise before this morning. I'll help any way I can from what I kept in my diary."

The captain continued. "First Officer Henricks, Mr. Grudion and I need to ask you some questions."

"Fire away."

"First, what did you do last night after dinner?"

"I can't say for sure, but I'd be happy to share what I wrote in my journal. I went to the magic show with my wife and Andrew and Helen Black. Then my wife and I joined Mrs. Ellen Hargrave in the Rendezvous Lounge. Afterward, I accompanied Mrs. Hargrave back to her room before joining my wife in the casino. Then I retired for the night."

"Did you go into Mrs. Hargrave's suite?"

"Yes. To look at a map of Glacier Bay."

"What time was that?"

"I don't remember, but it must have been within an hour of the time the show ended."

I noticed Grudion was jotting notes on a pad of paper.

"After leaving Mrs. Hargrave's room, who can vouch for your

whereabouts?"

"My wife saw me in the casino and I apparently went to sleep before she returned. Why all the questions?"

The captain cleared his throat. "When the maid entered Mrs. Hargrave's cabin this morning, Mrs. Hargrave had disappeared. There was blood on the balcony railing, and you were the last person reported to be with her."

CHAPTER 14

I gulped at the news of Mrs. Hargrave's disappearance. It suddenly dawned on me what deep doo-doo I had stepped in. I had read that the maid had seen me in Mrs. Hargrave's cabin the night before.

"She was in fine fiddle when I left her cabin. In fact, Anita was turning down the bed."

"I thought you had a memory problem, Mr. Jacobson," Grudion said, a cruel smile crossing his lips.

"I do." I tapped my temple. "But I read pretty good, and that was in my journal."

The captain stared at me. "Anita reported seeing both of you in the cabin, but then she left. That corroborates you were the last person known to be with Mrs. Hargrave."

Crap. Things were stacking up against me. "Someone else obviously came on the scene after I left. Wasn't anyone else spotted in the hallway or didn't other passengers hear any commotion?"

"There were raised voices overheard."

"There you go." I opened my hands toward my inquisitors. "And besides, I had no motive."

Grudion stared at me intently. "Actually, you did have a motive. Anita reported that you and Mrs. Hargrave were arguing when she left the cabin. Your voices were also heard by a passenger in the corridor. So, Mr. Jacobson, you argued with Mrs. Hargrave, were there alone with her and had the means to kill her. Would you like to make a statement?"

"Yes. I didn't do anything to Mrs. Hargrave." I thought over what I had documented in my diary. "But I'd suggest checking with her nephew and niece, Gary and Gina. They might have visited her after I left."

"We have. They both state they didn't see their aunt last night."

"Talk to them again," I said. "I suspect they're jealous that Mrs. Hargrave was seeking a long-lost niece who would decrease their inheritance."

"We've been over this before," Grudion said, pointing a finger at me. "I think you killed Mrs. Hargrave. You attempted to injure her twice before, tried to kill her by switching her medicine and this time you succeeded."

"Wait a Goddamn minute. I have no reason to do anything to Mrs. Hargrave. She's a nice lady. Whereas Gary and Gina both gain an inheritance if she's dead. Plus they're motivated to make it happen before she splits her loot with a third relative."

"I don't know if you committed a crime from anger or if you're a serial killer, Mr. Jacobson." Grudion narrowed his gaze at me. "I had that report concerning the death of a homeless man in Seattle before you boarded the ship."

"No. I'm not any type of killer. I'm just an old fart who somehow got in the middle of all of this."

"You had access to Mrs. Hargrave, an opportunity to kill her and motive—anger over an argument." Grudion ticked off three fingers.

"Gentlemen, I want to solve this as much as you do. But you have to keep searching because if you only focus on me, the real killer will escape."

Grudion grimaced. "I need to interview your wife."

"Am I free to leave?"

Grudion looked toward the other two. "You have nowhere to

go since the ship is sailing all day today. Just don't return to your cabin until I've had a chance to speak with your wife."

I remembered reading that Andrew Black had invited me to join him for a walk this morning. "Fine. I'll be on the walking track."

I departed, descended the stairs one flight and went outside to see the beauty of Alaska in the bright morning sun.

My stomach was churning as if I were seasick. How did I end up in this predicament? What could I do? Maybe Andrew Black could provide some advice and council. I would have to locate him.

I strolled the wrong way on the track and in half a lap, a man stopped me.

"Paul, you made it."

"Are you Andrew Black?" I asked.

"The same." He chuckled. "You remembered to come even if you didn't recognize me."

"I figured if you were here, you'd eventually accost me."

"So, Paul, how are you this fine morning?"

"Not so good. Mrs. Hargrave has disappeared and the ship Gestapo are blaming me."

"That's absurd."

"You and I know it but tell that to Grudion."

"I'll have to speak with him again."

"Just be careful. He's apt to accuse you of being my accomplice."

"I'll take my chances. Now tell me exactly what happened."

I summarized that the maid found blood but no Mrs. Hargrave and how I had been in the wrong place at the wrong time last night with my hair-trigger temper.

"You get mad often?" Andrew asked.

"Only when arguing about glaciers."

After we had completed our laps, we parted, and Andrew

promised to call me after he tracked down Grudion. When I returned to the cabin, Marion was out on the balcony watching the coastline.

"I just saw a whale, Paul."

"What! Without me?"

"You'll see one eventually."

"I don't know. They've been consistently avoiding me so far. How was your discussion with Grudion?"

"He thinks you did something to Mrs. Hargrave, but I assured him that you wouldn't have harmed her."

"Thanks for the endorsement, but I'm sure he didn't believe you."

"He was skeptical, but I made sure he heard my reasoning. And I asked him a question."

"Oh?"

"Yes. I inquired if he had found Mrs. Hargrave's cane in her room."

"And the answer was?"

"At first he didn't want to tell me anything, but finally he admitted that they had found no cane."

"Interesting."

"I think so. I would have expected the cane to be lying somewhere in her cabin."

"Unless someone pitched it over the side with her."

"Anyway, on a more pleasant note, we're approaching the glacier. Come see."

And sure enough, the ship was sailing slowly alongside a humongous chunk of ice.

I sat down with Marion. "Tell me more of your tête-à-tête with Grudion."

"He asked me what time I had seen you in the casino. Fortunately, I had checked my watch so I was able to be accurate."

"I thought you were too wrapped up in winning quarters to notice the time of day."

"I dropped a quarter and that was when I happened to look at my watch. Then he asked what time I returned to the stateroom afterwards. I was less exact on that."

"Did he say he was coming to clamp me in irons?"

"No, but you obviously are his prime suspect."

"I should charge him with geezer discrimination."

"You don't like all the attention?"

"From you, yes, but not from him."

I looked out at the scenery. Through a valley of jet-black rock sprinkled with specks of ice flowed a huge jagged mound of white. Even in the now overcast sky, parts of the ice flow appeared turquoise. At the water's edge pillars of ancient ice rose as high as our tenth deck suite. Chunks of ice floated in the water. I stood up and leaned over the railing. No dead bodies floated there, only a seagull on a small iceberg. Returning to my chair, I watched as Marion snapped a picture of the scene.

"Do you suppose we'll see ice calving?" I asked.

"I hope so. I want a picture if it happens."

The ship was moving extremely slowly to give us a good long view.

"There's a precarious outcropping of ice that's ready to break off." I pointed.

We waited.

Nothing happened.

Then cracking sounds rang out, and chunks started to fall.

"Camera ready," I shouted.

Louder cracking and then a whole side of ice came crashing down to splash into the sound. A wave flowed out to shake the ice cubes floating in the water.

"That was spectacular," Marion said. "I took the picture just in time."

Additional pieces began to break off. As we sailed by, we saw half a dozen major sections of ice crash into the water.

"Reminds me I need to use the restroom," I said.

When I returned, Marion immediately accosted me. "Now, Paul. There's something you need to do."

"I know. Find a whale."

"No. You have to take your pills."

"But I hate pills."

"Your doctor's orders are to take these twice a day." Marion headed inside, reached in a drawer, extracted a container and handed me three horse pills.

"You've got to be kidding. I can't swallow these rocks."

She glared at me. "Don't give me any guff. Fill a glass with water and be cooperative."

"Yes, ma'am."

Somehow I managed to swallow them. "It's a good thing I can't remember overnight. I'd hate to know each morning that I had to go through this."

"That's what I'm here for. To enforce that you take your medication."

"I hope that's not your only role."

"My other job is to remind you to come watch the glacier."

We returned to the balcony to see chunks of ice still falling. I enjoyed the view as we sailed toward another glacier, this one blanketed in black.

"Looks like it's covered with soot," Marion said.

"It must have picked up a little debris along the way. Kind of like my mental faculties."

Marion reached over and gave me a hug. "You do fine except for your one little flaw."

"Are you referring to my memory or my temper?"

At that moment someone knocked on the door. I opened it

153

to find a waiter holding a breakfast tray.

"I ordered room service while you were off with Grudion," Marion said.

We feasted while the ship completed a half circle of the bay and headed back whence we had come.

"All this cold water and ice makes me ready to sit in the hot tub," I said. "You want to join me?"

"Sure. That's the warmest place on the ship."

We gathered our swim gear, trudged to the spa, changed and soon were soaking in the 104-degree warmth.

"I'm glad you're here to protect me, Marion. I read in my journal that the last time I came to the Jacuzzi on my own, a guy passed out and I was accused of hurting him."

"I'll be happy to be your bodyguard."

"And I'll be happy to reciprocate by guarding your body every chance I get."

Duly prunized, we donned our white robes and lay down on lounge chairs to look out the back windows. The overcast had changed into a light drizzle and rain drops coursed down the slanted window.

We passed another glacier and I relaxed in the warmth of the spa, watching the ice outside and listening to the chirps of tropical birds. For the first time in my life I had the desire to buy a shotgun and hunt fowl.

"Sure a lot of cold water out there," I said. "It pleases me that we're bundled up in here."

"Think of the Inuit in their kayaks paddling through icy waters."

"No thanks. I don't even like warm oceans. I couldn't imagine being close to cold water."

I almost dozed off, but caught myself in time. When my stomach rumbled, I decided it needed to be filled with something from the ample food store on the ship.

"I haven't eaten in at least an hour. You up for a snack?"

"There's an ice cream stand on deck twelve. Grab a bite, and I'll meet you back in our cabin."

After changing, I followed Marion's directions and found a window where a cheerless young woman was dispensing peach, chocolate and peppermint ice cream cones.

I ordered chocolate. After the first lick, it started dripping.

"May I have a napkin?"

"I'm sorry. We can't use paper napkins while we're in Glacier Bay National Park."

"Are you kidding me?"

"Sir, those are the rules."

"So your customers have to suffer with dripping chins because there's a ban here on paper napkins?"

"That's right."

I was pretty heated now. "One of these damn nonexistent whales that I haven't seen might choke on a flimsy napkin?"

"Don't be difficult, sir. There are other people waiting."

I turned around and saw a group of fidgety teens chewing gum and standing on one foot and then the other like they needed to find a restroom.

I shook my head. "Pissant rules." Then I stomped away, wiping my mouth with the back of my left hand. I hadn't taken more than half a dozen steps before I felt a tap on my shoulder.

"Harassing our employees again?"

Grudion stood there, his bright red hair flapping in the breeze.

"You have some mighty peculiar rules on this ship."

"Questioning the wisdom of the Unites States National Park Service?"

"I'll question any dumb rules irrespective of who issues or enforces them."

"Mr. Jacobson, you're a regular vigilante."

"Yeah, I'm right up there with Jesse James, Zorro and the

Lone Ranger. Are you following me, Mr. Grudion?"

A thin smile appeared. "Yah, I'm keeping an eye on the one-man crime wave on this ship. I can't have you causing any more problems."

"Fine. You keep watching me. You'll see I'm a fine upstanding citizen."

"Who has a temper and takes it out on other people. How violent are you, Mr. Jacobson?"

"I've been known to tear junk mail into shreds, kick cans I find lying on the sidewalk and even make faces at people I don't like." I gave him the Jacobson glare.

"Do you get angry enough to lodge a hot stone in a massage therapist's throat, kill a homeless man, push Mrs. Hargrave over the side and try to drown a man in the Jacuzzi?"

"I plead guilty to verbal running-off-at-the-mouth but that's all. Mr. Grudion, I do get pissed off at times and may open my yap when I shouldn't, but I've done nothing to injure anyone. You need to keep looking for Inese's murderer and to find out what happened to Mrs. Hargrave. I think the two are linked, and a good investigator like you should be able to discover what's happening. I'd start with Mrs. Hargrave's nephew and niece. If you insist on following me around, it's your choice, but you're barking up the wrong spruce tree."

He stared at me like he was trying to decode a strange language printed on my forehead. Then he pointed an index finger at me. "No more trouble from you for the rest of the cruise. We'll settle all this when we dock in Seattle."

"I can hardly wait."

"Yah, and I'll continue to keep my eye on you."

I shrugged. "I can't stop you wasting your time, but you must have more productive things to do than watch my back-side."

I turned and headed back to my cabin. As I walked through

the corridor, I had the distinct impression that he was following me. He'd have to see with his own two eyes that I was a harmless old fart. Other than that, I didn't know what else I could do to change Grudion's opinion of me.

Marion had already returned to the stateroom. "What happened to you?" she asked. "Did you get lost?"

"No. I had a little close encounter of the third kind with the napkin police and then a chat with my good buddy Grudion."

She raised an eyebrow. "I think there's a story here."

I explained my latest adventures.

"You certainly have a way of discovering interesting anomalies."

"That's me. Grudion thinks I argue with everyone and cause all the problems on the ship." I looked at Marion. "Do I have that terrible a temper?"

She patted my arm. "Let's just say you don't hold back your feelings when something you don't like happens."

"Hell. I can't be that bad."

"See. Your natural reaction is an expletive."

"I'll be damned."

"Maybe I should put some duct tape over your mouth to keep you out of trouble."

"Nah. I'd probably kick a wall instead. I suppose that's why I've lived so long. I get pissed off and express myself rather than holding it in and developing an ulcer or having a heart attack."

"And I'm grateful for that."

"Me too. But I need to watch myself so my yap doesn't cause me more trouble with Grudion. I'm still convinced that something is going on with Gary and Gina. I just haven't been able to convince Grudion to start looking at them."

"Maybe Andrew will discover something."

"I hope so. I'll give him a call."

I picked up the phone and asked to be connected to the Black residence, but no one answered, so I left a message for Andrew to call me.

"What's on our social agenda now?" I asked.

"I'd like to go to a naturalist talk that's scheduled in twenty minutes."

"Lead on."

We joined a hundred or so other folks in the auditorium and learned that Glacier Bay became a national park and preserve on December 2, 1980. We were informed that five species of Pacific salmon swam under our keel, that king, Tanner and Dungenes crabs crawled the sea floor and that the elusive whales were easy to spot. Yeah, right.

I raised my hand. "What's the species of bird that chirps in the spa?"

The speaker gave me a dirty look. "That music features the Brazilian parakeet."

Marion gave me a much-deserved elbow.

Upon returning to our cabin, the light on the phone was flashing. I retrieved a message from Andrew and gave him a call.

"Any good news for me?" I asked.

"Not particularly. Grudion is convinced you pushed Mrs. Hargrave over her balcony. He just doesn't have any confirming proof."

"And there's no reason he would since I didn't do it."

"But I'm afraid the only thing that will turn Grudion around is finding who actually committed the crime."

"Possibly the same person who killed Inese. I think the two incidents are linked."

"Could be, but there are no definite suspects besides you."

I thought over what I had read in my journal. "Several possibilities. With Inese it could be the sort-of boyfriend Erik or the team of Gary and Gina, avoiding sharing their inheritance. With

Ellen Hargrave the most likely are Gary and Gina who both benefit from her demise. Have you located any new poop about those two?"

"Actually one thing. Gary has a prior assault charge. There was a plea deal and he walked away with probation."

"Interesting. Maybe he has a bad temper like me. Anything on Gina?"

"No. She's clean."

"You should also know that Grudion is following me."

"Not surprising. He's convinced you're a villain, and he doesn't want any more deaths or disappearances on this cruise."

"But how's he going to find the real killer or killers when he's wasting time with me?"

"That's a problem."

"I have to figure out a way to redirect him toward the right target."

"Good luck."

After hanging up, I contemplated my predicament. I felt like a bug under a microscope. But rather than feeling sorry for myself, I had to do something. If Grudion was on my fanny, I'd have to lead him to the real culprits. If I could shake up the hornets' nest, he'd see the stingers.

With an hour before our next feeding frenzy, I decided to try a few things on my own. Marion wanted to rest so I left the cabin and headed to the main dining room.

There was no one at the reception desk so I stepped inside the room and scanned the group of white-clad men and women scurrying around setting up for dinner. One waiter came up to me. "I'm sorry, sir, but we're not open yet."

"I know. I'm looking for Erik. Any idea where his station is?"

He pointed to the far corner. "Over there by the coffee machine."

I ambled over and spotted a man smoothing out a tablecloth

and adding salt and pepper shakers along with a container of packaged sugars.

"Erik, may I have a moment of your time?"

He looked up and then scowled. "You again."

"Hey, is that any way to address one of your favorite customers? I've been wondering about Inese. Did she ever mention a Mrs. Ellen Hargrave from the United States to you?"

"No. Why would she?"

"Mrs. Hargrave might have been a long-lost aunt."

"I doubt that."

CHAPTER 15

I stared at Erik. "Why are you so certain that Inese couldn't be Mrs. Hargrave's relative?"

His eyes darted from side to side. "She . . . uh . . . knew who her family was."

"Okay, Erik. Give me the straight scoop. You know something here."

He looked over his shoulder like Grudion had been following him instead of me. Then in a hushed tone he said, "Inese comes from a very close family. She has no relatives in America."

"Maybe there are some you're not aware of."

"No. The family is all in Latvia. Now leave me alone. I have a job to do."

As I walked away, I pondered the conversation. Something strange was going on here. Erik knew a lot more than he was letting on. Still, his adamant statement regarding Inese's background seemed to support that she wasn't Ellen Hargrave's long-lost niece. So that meant someone else on the ship was. It also raised questions concerning the link between Inese's murder and Mrs. Hargrave's disappearance. Two random killings? Seemed odd during one cruise. My tummy didn't think these were unrelated. There had to be a connection. My addled brain just hadn't put the pieces together yet.

My next stop was Gary and Gina's cabin. I had written Ellen Hargrave's stateroom number in my journal, and Ellen had indicated that her niece and nephew shared a room to the side of hers. So I had two choices. After an eeny, meeny, miny, moe, I selected the one to the left. Even though it had a "Do Not Disturb" sign, I knocked.

A woman answered the door, looked startled and slammed the door in my face. I heard some sounds, and then she re-appeared and swiftly stepped outside.

"Mr. Jacobson. What are you doing here?"

"You seem to know me, but because of my short-term memory loss I don't recognize you. I'm looking for Gina and Gary Hargrave."

She continued to protect the door. "I'm Gladys Heinz, Ellen Hargrave's friend. We met at dinner the night before last."

"I'm concerned about what happened to Ellen and need to speak with Gary and Gina."

"We all are concerned about Ellen. Gary and Gina's room is two doors down." She pointed past Ellen's room and quickly disappeared back into her room.

Strange woman, but, hey, this ship seemed to be full of strange people and even stranger goings-on.

I knocked on the door to the other side of Ellen Hargrave's room. This time a young woman answered.

"Gina, may I speak with you for a moment?"

She looked wildly around. "This isn't a good time."

"Is Gary in?"

"No. He'll be back shortly."

"I can wait."

"No." She didn't invite me in, but she didn't slam the door in my face either.

I decided to take my best shot. "Did you ever meet a massage therapist on this ship named Inese?"

"I . . . well . . . no."

"She was from Latvia and your aunt was seeking a niece from Latvia."

Gina stared at me with large round eyes and her mouth opened, like someone suffocating and gasping for air. She couldn't or wouldn't speak.

"Any chance Gary might have tracked her down?"

Sparks flashed in her eyes. "No. Gary wouldn't have spent any time with her."

Something wasn't right here. "Maybe Gary suspected Inese was the long-lost niece and he did something to protect your inheritance."

"No." Then the door slammed in my face.

Okay. Erik, Gladys and Gina were all acting weird. I was getting closer, but the pieces weren't all there yet. I had stirred things up a little. I'd have to see what would pop out.

I shouted down the corridor. "Grudion, if you're here, check out Gina, Gary, Gladys and Erik. There's something suspicious going on."

No answer.

I knew Grudion or one of his minions was out there.

With my mission accomplished, I decided to take a short stroll on the promenade deck. I felt like a bug on a pin with one of those scientists examining it. If only I could convince Grudion to do something more constructive than tailing me.

In the meantime I had to figure this all out. Behind door one was Erik the antagonistic waiter. Behind door two was the Gary and Gina show. Erik and Gary were both squirrelly enough, but had either of them committed crimes? And Gina seemed nice, but was she really a money-grubbing heiress behind the veneer?

I'd keep after it and see what clues I could collect. But first I needed to return to home base to prepare for the next feast.

After Marion and I had duly stuffed our faces, we proceeded to a musical show, the evening's entertainment. As a group of only slightly post-pubescent wenches paraded across the stage to the sound of Rogers and Hammerstein music while trying to wash that guy right out of their hair, I could only think of Grudion, Erik, Gladys, Gary and Gina standing in front of a police line-up. It would be healthy for Grudion to see how it felt from the other side.

The song and dance troop put on a fine performance, and as we exited, Marion hugged my arm, obviously having enjoyed the show as well.

We hadn't proceeded more than fifty feet along the corridor when suddenly a young man planted himself right in front of me.

"What were you doing harassing my sister this afternoon?"

Uh-oh. I squinted at the face I didn't recognize but decided it had to be Gary. "Just asking a few polite questions."

He wagged an index finger at me. "Don't bother my sister. If you want to accost someone, see me."

"You weren't there. But, okay, since you're here now, did you stuff a hot stone down Inese's throat and push your aunt off a balcony?"

He started spluttering. "No . . . no . . . of course not."

Now I pointed a finger at him. "I think you found out Inese was from Latvia and decided she must be the long-lost niece your aunt was searching for. You eliminated her and then decided to speed up your inheritance by the disappearance of your aunt."

Gary opened his mouth and then thought better of what he was going to say. He paused for a moment, then said, "Stay away from my sister." He turned and merged with the receding crowd.

"That was an interesting response," Marion said.

"Yeah. I apparently hit a nerve. So now I have a complete set. Grudion, Erik the waiter, Gina, Gary and Julian Armour are all pissed off at me. Are you still on my side?"

I received a peck on the cheek. "For the duration."

"Well, stay tuned. All of my nosing around should lead to something soon."

"Just be careful."

We retired to our cabin, found no lurking intruders, consumed our pillow chocolates and then I sat down to document the life and times of Paul Jacobson, inadvertent criminal suspect.

I awoke to sunlight streaming through the opening between two curtains and was informed by a young chick in her seventies lying next to me that I was on a honeymoon cruise and that my aging body now resided in the port of Ketchikan. When the shock didn't stop my old ticker, I lay in bed and read a manuscript on the nightstand, learning that I had been very busy stirring up trouble lately.

I staggered out of bed and parted the curtains to look out at a small town nestled against a hillside. Amid evergreen trees, Victorian houses peppered the landscape and sent plumes of smoke up brick chimneys.

"Looks like a cozy place," I said.

"Probably pretty cold in winter."

"I wonder when we arrived here."

"The ship newsletter from last night indicated that we docked at six A.M."

I twisted my arm to check the wristwatch that had slept with me and my bride. Seven-thirty. "I guess we missed all the docking excitement. What's on the agenda today?"

"After we eat, we can disembark. Our tour starts at ten."

"And what are we touring?"

"First a rain forest and then a boat ride. You wanted to see some whales."

"Darn right. And from what I've read, the whales have been hiding from me the whole cruise."

"Well, this is your big day. I'm sure we'll spot them when we're out in the smaller boat."

"Is that a promise?"

"There's no sure thing, but everyone I've ever talked to who has been on a whale-watching boat this time of year in Alaska has seen whales. Now before all of that, you should give Jennifer a call."

"That's right. My journal had a note that she was checking out Inese's family name for me."

After Marion helped me with the cell phone gadget, Jennifer answered. "Are you and Mr. Grudion getting along better?"

"No. He's now after me for the disappearance of a passenger."

"Oh, Grandpa. What now?"

"Another unfortunate coincidence. There's this woman named Ellen Hargrave who I've been accused of knocking down twice. At least they haven't accused me of knocking her up."

"Grandpa, stay focused."

"Yes, ma'am." I proceeded to tell her all the latest trouble I had gotten into.

"Grandpa, are you having any fun on this trip?"

"Sure. Although I still haven't seen any whales, I did see a bear butt from the train."

"Not to change the subject, but I have some information for you."

"Fire away."

"With further research on the name Zarins in Latvia, I discovered several references to Karlis Zarins, a crime boss. Could Inese be part of a mob family?"

"She seemed too nice for that."

"Still, it's a possibility. Maybe she was the victim of a turf war between crime lords or retribution or a power struggle . . ."

"Hold your horses, young lady. I'm trying to digest this. Gary and Gina seem better prospects to have knocked off Inese to eliminate a competitor for their inheritance, and they might have dispatched Ellen to speed up the inheritance process. This Karlis Zarins wouldn't have any reason to do anything to Ellen Hargrave."

"It is complicated. You'll have to do some investigating on your own to tie it all together."

"It's like a plate of spaghetti right now."

"I predict you'll figure it all out by the end of the cruise."

I wanted to believe my intelligent granddaughter but wasn't one hundred percent convinced. My stomach churned with all the accusations hanging over my head. A geezer like me was supposed to be sipping tropical drinks with my aging body on a deck chair, watching whales doing triple flips in front of me, not finding dead massage therapists and dealing with rich women disappearing. But rather than wallowing in the muck, I needed to suck it up and get on with my life, however much of it was still left.

"We'll see. In the meantime keep your computer humming to try to learn anything new. I'm going to look at trees and finally see the phantom whales of Alaska."

"Just don't harass any of the sea creatures, Grandpa."

"No. I leave the harassment to Grudion. When will I next see you?"

"I don't know. Mom and Dad haven't planned any trips to Southern California yet. Too bad you and Marion aren't stopping here on your way back home."

"We should have brought you along on the cruise. With your private investigation skills, you would have tracked down some whales for me by now."

"Today's your big day, Grandpa. I'm sure you'll see oodles of whales."

"I'll settle for a measly one."

"Are you really going out in a whale-watching boat?"

"That's what Marion tells me."

"But you hate the ocean."

"I do. I'm fine when there's a huge cruise ship between me and the water."

"But now you'll be out in a tiny boat."

"Damn. I hadn't thought of that."

"You'll have to be brave."

"I don't know what the world is coming to. Suffering from being around lawyers, having to take pills and being close to the ocean. For an old poop, I still have a number of indignities to put up with."

"You can't fool me, Grandpa. You enjoy complaining."

"You pegged me again, Jennifer. I can't fool you."

"Nothing escapes Jennifer Jacobson, private investigator."

"Now don't let it go to your head. Humility is a virtue."

"I know. When I'm playing tennis, every time I think I'm hot stuff, I lose to a player who's not as good as me. Then I discover I haven't been practicing hard enough."

"That's right. You can't take success for granted."

"So, Grandpa, you figure out all the shipboard crimes, and I'll keep working on my tennis game and checking the Internet for new leads."

"It's a deal."

"Say hello to the whales for me."

We signed off, and I sat there trying to imagine this twelve-year-old girl. The image of her at six still stuck in my jumbled-up mind. It was amazing the way my crazy brain operated. Perfect memory of this morning and things in the distant past. But yesterday. Forget it, which I did. As elusive as the whales.

Marion shook me out of my reverie, and we dressed before foraging in the cafeteria. I made sure I was well nourished with scrambled eggs, bacon, pancakes, orange juice, coffee and a sweet roll. "Now I'm ready to take on the world," I said, having to stifle a burp.

We passed through security, and no one tried to clap me in irons. On the dock a guy in a duck costume accosted us and pointed toward a booth that read, "Duck Tour." If it had said whale tour, I might have paid attention.

Marion led me onto a bus, and shortly we left the town of brightly colored blue, brown and red houses. After a short drive we reached a forest. I could tell by all the trees. The guide showed us deep marks on a tree where a bear had scratched.

"You know all about bears from being chased at Mendenhall Glacier," Marion said.

"This one must have been much larger. Look how high up those marks go."

Then Marion took a picture of me in an opening in a tree that provided a good-sized cave. Above our heads I heard a buzzing sound and looked up to see a man with a helmet on fly by. "Do you have superman wannabes in this forest?" I asked the guide.

"No. That's a zip-line. People can also take a tour through the forest canopy."

"I think I'll just stick to ground level," I said.

We approached a stream and saw an eagle sitting on a rock watching for the right salmon to swim by. Marion snapped another picture.

"We'll have lots of photographs so we can remember the trip," she said.

"And for me it will be something new every time I see the pictures."

"I'll have to remind you how much fun you had."

"Like finding dead bodies and having the ship detective trail me around?"

"Of course. You'll look back at all that and laugh."

"Yeah, right."

After we had communed with the trees and wildlife, the guide led us through an old sawmill that was being reconstructed, and finally we visited a pen where a group of mottled reindeer grazed.

As we rode the bus back to the port area for the next leg of our tour, the important one of going out in a small boat to hopefully spot a pod of whales, I noticed that Marion had turned a shade of green.

"Are you feeling all right?"

"No. Something from breakfast must be disagreeing with me."

As the bus pulled up, I said, "Maybe we should just head back to our room."

"I think I'll do that, but you go ahead with the rest of the tour."

"Are you sure?"

"Yes." She handed me the ticket stub. "Go to the end of the dock. There will be a group of zodiac boats picking you and the others up."

I escorted Marion up the gangway and watched as she staggered aboard the ship. Then I joined the crowd congregated at the end of the dock. I was the last one in line. I gulped as I looked at the small inflated boats. I had to go out in the ocean in one of these? The ocean scared the piss out of me, and I wanted something more substantial between my butt and the water. The sacrifices made to see whales.

A young man dressed in weather gear tapped me on the shoulder. "This way, Mr. Jacobson." He pointed toward one of the zodiacs, and I gingerly climbed in, holding on to a loop of rope for dear life. Once inside I continued to clutch the rope, leaned over the side to admire some eclectic flotsam in the harbor and was almost knocked over as the boat shot away from the dock.

I steadied myself and looked within the boat. There were only three of us. The man who had ushered me in sat in the stern driving us and another man in his sixties rested across from me smoking a cigar.

"What the . . ." I stammered. "Where are the others?"

The man with the cigar tapped an ash over the side and stared at me. I noticed steely gray eyes above pockmarked cheeks. A shiver ran down my spine.

"We're going on a private little cruise, Mr. Jacobson," the man said, tossing his cigar away.

Chapter 16

"And how do you both know my name?" I asked the older man in the zodiac.

Now a thin smile appeared on his pock-marked face. "You're a very well-known person, Mr. Jacobson. I've received many reports about you," he said in accented English.

"Who the hell are you, and why would you be interested in me?"

"I'm Inese's father, Karlis Zarins."

I gasped, remembering what Jennifer had told me. "From Latvia?"

"Yes. And I want to have a very frank conversation with you. I expect straight answers. People who are thrown into these waters don't survive long."

I looked around. None of the other zodiacs was in sight, and I could only see one other boat far behind us. Other than that all that was visible was verdant coastline and several small islands.

"I have a hunch I'm not going to see any whales today."

My companion didn't answer.

My old thumper was pounding lickety-split as I assessed my predicament. I could feel a cold sweat against my skin under my shirt and windbreaker as the cool breeze shot past. My stomach tightened at the thought of the cold water. I couldn't swim worth crap even in warm water. How would I deal with a maniac father? All I could do was level with him and hope for the best.

"Look, Mr. Zarins, let me explain something,"

"Yes?" He stared at me.

"I know you're upset with the loss of your daughter. I'm trying to find who killed her as well. I can assure you I had nothing to do with her death."

He extracted a new cigar from his pocket, took his time lighting it with a match cupped in his hand to protect the flame. Then he tossed the spent match overboard and turned his gaze to me. "I think you killed her."

I sighed. "There's a fact you should know about me. I have short-term memory loss, but I keep a journal of what happens every day. On the morning of your daughter's murder, my wife and I went to the spa. Your daughter was assigned to give me a hot stone massage. She left the room and didn't return. I went to investigate and found her dead on the floor. Someone had suffocated her by stuffing a hot stone down her throat."

"Erik says he suspects you're the one who did it."

I flinched. "You've talked to Erik? He's one that I thought could be involved."

Zarins laughed. "Funny man. Erik works for me. I hired him to keep an eye on Inese."

"Apparently he didn't do a very good job."

Zarins's eyes flared, and he raised a hand as if he were going to whap me but thought better of it.

"No. He didn't. But he's now highly motivated to help me punish the murderer."

"And I'll help any way I can. Just rest assured that I didn't do anything to Inese." Then a thought struck me. "If Erik wasn't involved, there is one other possible explanation that you should be aware of."

"Go on."

"I'll share everything I know, but I'm a little uncomfortable being out in all this cold water. Do you suppose we could find some dry land, and I'll divulge what I think happened?"

He laughed again. "I like that. Trying to negotiate from a position of weakness." He pointed to a small island, nothing more than a spit of sand, rocks and a few trees. "Valdis, take us in there."

Valdis brought the zodiac up and let it float into the island. Zarins stepped out and stretched his arms. I followed.

"Okay. Sit there and talk." He directed me toward a rounded rock and I plunked my butt down.

I took a deep breath and began. "In addition to your daughter's death, there has been a disappearance of a woman named Ellen Hargrave. She was traveling with a nephew and niece, Gary and Gina. You should know that the ship detective, Grudion, has been all over my ass accusing me of doing something to Mrs. Hargrave."

"What does that have to do with my daughter's death?"

"Here's the link. Mrs. Hargrave was looking for a long-lost niece. An investigator she had hired traced this niece to the crew of the Scandinavian Sea Lines *Sunshine*. Mrs. Hargrave said her long-lost niece was from Latvia. The only crew member listed from Latvia was Inese."

"And where is this Mrs. Hargrave from?"

"The United States."

"Obviously a mistake. We have no relatives in America."

"Exactly. So I think someone was trying to get rid of Mrs. Hargrave's niece and drew the wrong conclusion that Inese was that niece."

Zarins watched me carefully. "You either have something or have concocted an elaborate subterfuge."

I stared back. "Mr. Zarins, you sure speak excellent English for someone from Latvia."

He laughed. "In my business I deal with many British and Americans. It's essential that I communicate clearly with them."

"What is your line of work?"

"I'm in the import-export business."

From the side Valdis snickered.

Zarins gave him a menacing look and then turned back toward me. "So if I follow your train of thought, Mr. Jacobson, who do you think killed my daughter?"

"I'll be happy to share my suspicions if you promise not to export them away until I'm sure they did it."

He smiled. "Touché. Go on."

"I'm suspicious of Mrs. Hargrave's nephew and niece, Gary and Gina. They may have decided to eliminate who they thought was the other niece in order to keep the inheritance from being diluted. Then that person may have pushed Mrs. Hargrave overboard to speed up the inheritance process."

"Possible. But Erik thinks you killed Inese."

"But I have no motive. I'm an old fart on a honeymoon cruise with my new bride."

He raised his eyebrows. "You just got married?"

"Yes. Second time around."

"What happened to your first wife?"

"She died of cancer."

He was silent for a moment. "Go on with your explanation."

"I have no vendetta against anyone. I've been a law-abiding citizen all my life and certainly have no desire to end up in jail or cold Alaskan waters because I bumped off a nice young woman."

He regarded me thoughtfully. "Erik's conclusion was based on you nosing around."

"That's because the ship's detective was accusing me of the crime as well. I've been trying to clear my name and along the way find out who the real killer is."

"I'm not convinced."

"If you give me a chance, I think I'll be able to prove it by the end of the cruise. I set things in motion with Erik, Gary and Gina that I think will flush out the guilty party. Since Erik works for you, that leaves Gary or Gina."

Zarins pulled another cigar out of his pocked, rolled it between his fingers a moment, then returned it to his pocket.

"I'm a fair man, Mr. Jacobson. I'm not going to kill you yet." He turned to Valdis. "Get word to Erik to check out this Gary and Gina." Then he turned back to me. "But I'm not ready to let you go either."

"What does that mean?"

"I'm going to leave you here. That way if Gary or Gina aren't the murderers, I'll know where to find you."

"But I'll be shivering on this little rock. I'm only wearing a windbreaker."

"No storms are forecast for the next three days. You'll survive. If you're right, I'll let the authorities know where you are. If not, I'll be back to take care of things personally." He pushed his open jacket aside so I could see the pistol stuck in his belt.

"Damn. I'm sure glad I didn't have to import anything from you when I was in the auto parts business."

"I do auto parts." His nostrils flared. "But I also do body parts."

With that he stood up and motioned Valdis toward the zodiac. Without so much as another threat, Zarins climbed in, and as soon as Valdis had started the engine, the zodiac zipped away, leaving me alone on my island paradise. I took a quick tour. I resided on a rough circle one hundred feet in diameter. All around was a rocky beach with a central highlands raised up to five feet above the high water line. A dozen fir trees mixed with grass. I could huddle in the trees when it got dark, but there wasn't much protection if the wind came up.

I watched the zodiac disappear in the distance and only spotted one other boat, but it was too far off to signal. Now what were my alternatives? I felt like a shipwrecked mariner. In World War Two I had been a sailor, the desk jockey variety, handling supply logistics for Operation Overlord. Now I was a castaway on this little speck of an island. I felt deserted and alone. But I needed to suck it up and get the mental juices flowing to figure out a solution to my predicament. I surveyed the water around me. I noticed two other equally small islands. A mile or so away appeared a substantial peninsula that either was part of a large island or the mainland. I had no clue regarding the geography and which way was what. My choices were to sit tight or try to reach that large body of land. And I couldn't swim more than two strokes. I put a finger in the water. Brrr. I'd never last in that even if I had a way to swim to the land I'd spotted.

I thought over what I had read years ago. When stranded in the wilderness it was better to stay put rather than trying to wander off. As if I could wander anyway. No one from the tour would know I had disappeared. When I didn't return, Marion would alert the authorities, but no one would know where to search. I could wave to anyone flying overhead, but this didn't seem to be in the flight path of anything other than geese.

How could I clear my name if I couldn't return to the ship? How could I survive overnight on this little clump of rocks and trees? How did I end up in this mess, anyway? For an old fart my age, you'd think I would have known better. Here I was on a relaxing honeymoon cruise, and all I'd done was find a dead body, been accused of pushing a woman over the side and now ended up marooned because a Latvian Mafioso had it in for me.

What kind of justice was that? I took another spin around my new home, looking for anything useful that might have floated up on the rocky beach. I found a clam shell, the remains of a cereal box and various drift sticks. I would need to start a fire. That would keep me warm at night and might attract attention.

Too bad I didn't smoke. Then I'd have matches. If I'd smoked, I probably wouldn't have lasted this long anyway.

I regarded the highlands. Plenty of kindling. Where were my Boy Scout fire-starting skills when I needed them?

I scanned the ocean again. That one boat I'd seen earlier was still there. It seemed to be a little closer. I scrambled up on the grass that represented the highest section of my island and waved my arms.

The boat was too far away, I was sure, to see anything. Unless someone happened to be looking through binoculars at exactly the right moment. I continued to frantically gesture.

Then I spotted something shiny on the ground. I reached down and picked up a quarter. I turned it over. 1953. A good year. My first wife, Rhonda, and I took a trip up the coast from Los Angeles to San Francisco that year. We had a great meal at Fisherman's Wharf. I wondered if that was the last time someone had visited this remote island.

CHAPTER 17

I pocketed the quarter. If I survived, I'd drop it in a slot machine at the ship's casino to see if it was really a lucky quarter.

Then a disturbing thought struck me. If I fell asleep, my memory would do the Jacobson reset, and I'd remember nothing of Zarins or how I'd ended up here. I slapped my cheek. I'd have to stay awake.

A light breeze rippled past, kissing my cheeks with a reminder of a cold night to come. I zipped up my jacket all the way and paced around my small domain. I'd hate to be here if a storm passed through and waves started pummeling the island. Still, the trees and grass had survived so the island probably hadn't been inundated with salt water. I could always climb a tree. I surveyed my forest and selected a strong tree in the highlands (five feet versus two feet above high tide) that I could scale a few feet if needed. At least there were no bears to escape from. I wondered if bears swam out to these little islands. That would be just great if some furry monster decided to visit and check me out for dinner. I had to get a grip.

Looking out in the water, I spotted no whales, but no sharks either. Just that one lonesome boat. It was getting closer. I did my waving routine again. I felt I should have a pair of pom-poms, and then I could do a cheerleader routine.

What the heck. I couldn't remember squat, but my weird brain could still dredge up absurd images.

Maybe Shamu the whale would rescue me, and I could ride

on his back to shore. Wherever the mainland was. I hadn't paid attention exactly to the route we'd taken.

Crapola. Other tourists were out watching whales, and here I was, Robinson Crusoe of the Yukon.

Looking up again I could see the boat was actually pointed toward me. Maybe it would keep coming! I began waving frantically again. Then I had a thought. I unzipped my jacket, slipped it off, grabbed a sleeve and waved it in the air like one of those ribbon-dancing routines at the Olympics. I was competing in the survival Olympics.

I kept it up until my arm tired. The exercise helped, but I was getting cold, so I put the jacket back on. I could now make out a white Chris-Craft. My heart beat faster as I saw white water parting at the boat's bow.

Someone on the boat must have seen me, as it headed smack toward me. Who would my rescuers be? I hoped they had a thermos of hot coffee.

I performed a few jumping jacks to stay warm and attract attention. That would be a sight. An eighty-five-year-old geezer doing jumping jacks. Still, I could move pretty well for an old fart even if I had a brain that held memories like the Maginot Line contained the Germans.

I could hear the boat's engines cutting back, and it coasted near shore. I watched as a dingy was lowered. I felt a little dingy myself.

Then a man climbed into the dingy and rowed toward me. As he reached the pebbly beach, I noticed a Scandinavian Sea Line logo on his outfit and a head of flaming red hair. This could only be one person. Grudion.

"I'm damn glad to see you," I said. "And I never thought I'd say that."

"Here all alone, Mr. Jacobson?"

"Hell yes. I was kidnapped and left on this desolate place by

Inese Zarins's father. Did you realize she was the daughter of a Latvian gangster?"

Grudion blinked. "I'm obviously missing something here."

"Let me explain. I planned to take a nice calm whale-watching tour. When I entered the zodiac, it shot off and I was the only tourist in the boat. The driver was someone named Valdis in the employ of a Mr. Zarins. Zarins questioned me about Inese's murder. He had enough doubt that he didn't kill me on the spot, but he left me on this deserted island."

Grudion held up his hand. "Slow down. You're saying this little side journey wasn't something you planned?"

"No way. I was abducted."

He regarded me thoughtfully. "Interesting. When we were following you, I wondered why you went off in a different direction from the other tourists. It took me a while to catch up to you."

"And I'm glad you did." Then a realization struck me. "We need to return to the ship ASAP. I told Zarins my suspicion regarding Gary and Gina Hargrave. They might be guilty as sin, but they also face danger from an irate father who has no qualms about killing people."

He signaled me toward the dingy. "Yah, let's head back to the ship. I'll radio ahead to alert one of my people."

I clambered in the tiny boat, and Grudion rowed us out to the Chris-Craft. I climbed the ladder with him following me. Once the dingy was raised, we took off.

Grudion picked up a microphone and started speaking in Swedish. He apparently didn't want me to understand his conversation.

When he finished, he turned toward me. "I'm not sure I believe all of your story, but I'm not taking any chances."

"You should also interrogate a waiter named Erik. He's doubling as a spy for Zarins."

"You're full of fascinating information, Mr. Jacobson."

"I aim to please. Does this help take me off the most-wanted list?"

"We'll see. There are still more things to check out."

"You do your investigation, and you'll see that everything I've told you is accurate."

Back in Ketchikan I thanked Grudion and headed up the gangplank to find my bride. She was lying in bed, reading the ship newsletter.

I sat down beside her. "How are you feeling?"

"Much better. I took some Tums and my stomach settled down, which is a good thing because tonight is the chocolate lovers' feast."

"What's that?"

"At midnight the main dining room opens for a meal of every imaginable type of chocolate—cake, pie, ice cream, cookies, candy."

"I'm up for that. After my adventure I have a big appetite.'

"Adventure? Did you see lots of whales?"

"No. I was kidnapped by Inese's father."

Marion put her hand to her mouth. "What happened?"

I recounted the saga of Paul Jacobson, kidnap and maroon victim.

Marion shook her head. "You certainly have a way of attracting peculiar people."

"Except for you. You're my one tie to reality."

Marion sat up and gave me a hug. All was right in the universe.

Sort of.

I moseyed out and sat on the balcony to let my emotions settle after the encounter with Karlis Zarins and the rescue from the tiny spit of sand and rock. I felt like a wet dish rag. I was getting too old to be cavorting around in zodiac boats, hob-nobbing with the criminal element and trying to figure out who did what to whom and why. Still I had to be thankful that I wouldn't be spending the night on that pathetic excuse for an island. I sighed.

It must have been louder than I thought because Marion stuck her head out the balcony door. "What's wrong, Paul?"

"Just contemplating my life, the universe and everything."

"If you reach any conclusions, let me know."

"You'll be the first to hear any wisdom I might spout."

She ducked back inside, and I returned my gaze to the hillside. I surveyed a gaggle of multi-story homes clumped together like cattle huddled in a storm. One dark green structure had a second-story porch facing the harbor. I spotted a man in a red flannel shirt standing there. I waved, but he must have been too far away to see me. He probably was sick and tired of huge cruise ships obstructing his view of the sound. How would I like living up here? This time of year would be fine, but I'd freeze my butt off in the winter. No thanks. I'd stick with the tourist routine for visiting Alaska and leave it at that. But the guy on the balcony didn't have to deal with obsessive ship security officers and people dropping dead from weird murders. He could have been contemplating his salmon dinner and preparing to store wood for winter.

But enough of my reverie, I still had to figure out this whole piss pot full of unexplained events so Grudion wouldn't lock me up and Zarins wouldn't feed me to the whales.

I decided to call Andrew Black, so I re-entered the cabin and reached for the phone.

"Paul, it's good to hear from you."

"I'll say. I almost ended up on a different kind of cruise." I explained my recent exploits.

"You certainly find yourself in some strange predicaments."

"That's what my bride says as well. I have a favor to ask."

He chuckled. "Here we go again. Okay, Paul, what is it?"

"Could you use your sources to check on this Zarins guy? I'd like to verify what I'm up against."

"Sure. I'll see what I can find. You and Marion want to meet us for dinner?"

"Provided I'm not turned into Latvian stew by then."

When we arrived in the dining room, I asked if Erik was on duty.

The receptionist wrinkled her brow. "No. He didn't show up tonight."

"Is that unusual that a waiter misses without notifying anyone?"

She twitched and looked over her shoulder. "All I know is that he isn't here."

Uh-oh. Either Erik had jumped ship like a fleeing rat or Zarins had taken out his displeasure on one of his minions.

Andrew and Helen appeared, and we were seated at a cozy table for four with a view out the stern. The ship was cruising at full speed at dusk as we had a long way to go to reach our next destination, Victoria, as my own personal cruise director, Marion, had informed me. Good thing she read the ship's news and had a solid memory.

We were handed sparkling white cloth napkins by a skinny waiter with a thin moustache who reminded me of a bulimic Errol Flynn. He did a little trick of spinning a plate on the back end of a fork, we all applauded, and he bowed. After I had ordered a shrimp cocktail, clam chowder and sea bass, I felt I had wrought revenge on the ocean I had been stranded in.

Andrew cleared his throat. "Paul, I have some disconcerting news for you."

The beat of my old ticker raised a notch.

"You going to let me know why I haven't seen any whales?"

"No. But I have a rundown on one Karlis Zarins."

"My new mafia buddy. I'm expecting the worst, so fire away."

He toyed with a corner of the tablecloth and then looked up, wrinkles lining his forehead. "The man is evil and dangerous."

"Tell me something I don't already know. Give me the background."

"He was raised in Russia and immigrated to Latvia after the communist breakup. He is the leading crime lord in Latvia, reported to have personally killed a dozen men."

"At least it's not thirteen."

Andrew frowned. "I'm not sure you realize how serious this is."

I shuddered, thinking back to standing with Zarins on the deserted Alaskan island. "I've seen the man's eyes. I know what he is. I guess I'm lucky to still be breathing. He had no qualms about leaving me to freeze my butt off on that little spit of rock, so it wouldn't have been any skin off his back to kill me instead."

"I'm sure Grudion already did this as well, but I alerted Interpol that he has been seen in Alaska and might show up in Victoria tomorrow."

"Are the Mounted Police ready to track him down?"

"Yes. Zarins is suspected of eliminating two Canadian nationals. He probably has traveled on to Victoria. I'm expecting that he will make some move when we dock there tomorrow. Unless he found a way to sneak aboard our ship."

That didn't give me a comfortable feeling. "How could he accomplish that with Grudion's security system?"

"He'd have to obtain a stolen ID and doctor it somehow. I'm sure he's an expert at that sort of subterfuge."

"I'd hate to think he's skulking around the ship."

"You shouldn't have too much to worry about. Gary and Gina are the ones who will have a problem."

"And they don't even know he exists. I wonder if I should warn them or let it play out. I still think one or both of them could be murderers."

"Fit right in with Zarins, eh?"

"You sound so Canadian, Andrew."

He shrugged. "I have to prepare for visiting Victoria tomorrow."

Helen said, "Someone should alert the security office that Zarins might be on the ship."

"I think I've worn out my welcome with Grudion," Andrew said. "He knows I'm your friend, Paul."

"I suppose it's my responsibility," I said, "although every time I speak with him I feel like a San Quentin escapee. Still, he may be more interested in what I have to say after our little boat trip together this afternoon."

"He'll eventually come around," Marion said, giving my arm a squeeze. "So tomorrow should be an interesting day. We have Zarins, Gina and Gary, Erik possibly in hiding, Grudion and various law enforcement officers converging on peaceful Victoria."

"Paul, you may want to consider staying on the ship," Helen said.

"No way. I want to see this all out. Besides, my bride told me this afternoon that she's looking forward to seeing the Butchart Gardens."

Andrew placed a hand on my arm. "Just be careful. You're dealing with a very dangerous man."

"Whoever killed Inese has more to worry about than I do."

Once I had demolished my ocean feast plus a fruit tart, I asked what was on the agenda for the evening.

"The song and dance troop members are putting on a performance," Helen said.

"How are you feeling?" I asked Marion.

"I'm fine and would like to see the show. Then, of course, there's the chocolate feast later."

"I'll be ready for that," I said. "But first I better have a little chat with my favorite security officer."

"Let's stop by the casino," Marion said with a glint in her eyes. "I haven't won anything yet today."

"I'm for that," Helen replied. "You gentlemen want to accompany us?"

"You go ahead, Andrew. I'm going to stop in the little boys' room and then call Grudion."

They took off, the ladies moving so fast that I thought Zarins was on their tails. I shook my head. That bride of mine sure liked to play the slots.

I entered the powder room and did my business, thankful that for an old fart my plumbing still worked as it was supposed to. As I washed my hands I saw the door open. I flinched, thinking of Zarins but then was relieved, for the second time in five minutes. It was Grudion entering.

"Following me again, Mr. Grudion?"

He smiled. "Yah, I wanted to make sure you didn't get flushed away."

"Nah. My face doesn't even flush when someone tells a dirty joke, but I will be flush when my bride wins in the casino, probably having a royal flush."

He stared at me like I was a whale turd.

"Okay. You don't appreciate my warped sense of humor. I do have something I want to mention to you. At dinner we were speculating in regard to one Latvian criminal named Karlis Zarins and came up with the hypothesis that he might be on the ship."

"Impossible. Our security system wouldn't allow it."

I wagged a finger at him. "Don't get too cocky. Someone like

Zarins probably has a lot of resources at his disposal. I wouldn't put it past him to find a way to compromise the system and invade your little boat."

"Ship."

At first I thought he had made an expletive but then realized it was just his accent. "So my friends and I want to make sure you watch out for him here as well as in Victoria tomorrow. Have you spoken with Gary and Gina Hargrave?"

"Yes. They continue to claim they had nothing to do with Inese Zarins's death or the disappearance of their aunt."

"But a good law enforcement type like you can see through that, right?"

He regarded me thoughtfully. "Just like you're always protesting your innocence?"

"The difference being that I am innocent, at least of the crimes."

"What's that supposed to mean?"

"An old fart like me is no longer innocent to the vagaries of personalities and the evil deeds possible from certain elements of humanity. Be prepared for Zarins and keep your eyes on Gary and Gina."

With that I sauntered out of the bathroom and headed to the casino.

I found Andrew at a slot machine between the two ladies. They were cramming quarters in like they were feeding starving sharks. Andrew appeared to be like me. The machine happily ate his quarters without so much as a clink whereas on both sides of him the air was filled with the constant clanking of coins being returned.

I remembered the quarter I had found on the desolate island and retrieved it from my pants. "Okay, Andrew, step aside for a moment. I have a lucky quarter to insert."

"Gladly. I'm not winning anything here. You sure you want to try this machine?"

"Absolutely. It's right between these two lovely and lucky ladies, so what more could I ask for in finding a winning combination?"

Andrew stepped away, and I eyed the face of the machine with the three rollers and disks displaying "7," a sprig of cherries and a rectangle indicating "triple." I flexed my fingers and then dropped my lucky quarter in the slot. I gave the arm a yank and waited for the spinning sound to be followed by quarters cascading out the return slot.

Instead, I heard a clank and felt the arm jam as if it had hit a brick wall. A red light started flashing on top of the machine and a siren screeched.

All the commotion in the casino came to a stop as if everyone had suddenly become frozen. Then all eyes turned toward me.

"What?" I said, holding my palms up.

A husky young man in ship's uniform who looked like he had just escaped from a weight room came sprinting up to me.

"Something's wrong with your machine." I pointed to the jammed quarter eater.

"Sir, what did you put in the machine?"

"A damn quarter."

"We'll see." He raised a key that was attached by an elastic cord to his belt and opened the slot machine. He pushed a button and the flashing light and siren cut off as quickly as they had started. He tinkered inside and extracted the quarter, holding it by its rim.

"Is this your quarter?"

"I suppose so, let me look at the date." I reached for it.

"Don't touch it! Just look."

"Yes, sir." I saluted him. "Kind of touchy, aren't you?"

He turned it so the date showed. 1953. "Yup. That's the coin I found on a little island today."

He dropped it in a plastic bag and deposited it in his shirt pocket.

"Hey, what are you doing with my lucky quarter? And how come your machine gypped me out of my winnings?"

The casino had returned to normal except for Andrew, Marion and Helen who were all watching me as the hulk closed the machine.

Rather than answering my question the weightlifter said, "Please come with me, sir."

"What for?"

He grabbed my arm and propelled me forward. "I need you to be cooperative, sir."

"I'll be happy to cooperate if you tell me what you're all worked up about and where we're going."

"You need to come with me to the casino office."

"You going to show me where you keep all the money?"

"No. We're going to wait for ship security. They'll want to talk to you regarding the counterfeit coin you put in the slot machine."

CHAPTER 18

Here I was getting in trouble again just because the quarter I had found on the little island was counterfeit. I knew it was too good to be true to have found a quarter out on that pebbly beach.

I turned back toward Marion as my new companion hustled me away.

She had a frown accompanied by a wrinkled brow.

"Don't worry. I'll go with Rambo here and catch up with you later. Keep winning in my absence."

Big Guy force-marched me toward a door. He thrust it open for me and propelled me down a short hallway and into a well-lit office.

I looked around, spotting canisters of poker chips and containers of quarters.

"So this is the money room," I said, stepping over to examine a counter lined with packets of bills.

"Don't touch anything. Sit in that chair." My companion pointed toward an institutional chair resting next to a wooden table.

"Okay. No reason to get heated."

I sat down, and moments later Grudion marched into the room.

"Mr. Jacobson, your crime wave continues."

"What the hell is that supposed to mean?"

"Passing counterfeit quarters. Is there anything you're not into?"

"Yeah. I don't do drugs. Except for the pills my wife is always forcing down my throat."

"Mr. Grudion, there is some suspicious residue on the counterfeit quarter," the bruiser said.

"Really? We'll test it for chemicals as well as fingerprints."

"Well, you'll find my fingerprints on it. I found it on that island where you picked me up today."

"Do tell. A counterfeit quarter just lying there?"

"Yeah." Then it struck me. "It wasn't buried or anything but resting on top of the beach. And it was in good condition, not weathered. I bet either Zarins or his bodyguard Valdis dropped it."

"Interesting theory. We'll see if any prints besides yours turn up. Now I'd like to ask you for your fingerprints for comparison."

"Sure." I held out my hands half expecting Grudion to clamp on handcuffs.

Grudion extracted a kit and proceeded to ink my fingers and press them on a card. Then he handed me a packet of dry washes, and I cleaned off my fingers. "Not bad service here." I admired my sparkling fingers. "Now may I return to my wife and friends?"

Grudion regarded me thoughtfully. "Yah. I know this may be difficult for you, but please stay out of trouble on the remainder of the cruise."

"I can't make any promises with all the stuff going on around your ship, Grudion. With murderers and crime lords running loose, I'm the least of your worries."

"I don't know. It all seems to revolve around you, Mr. Jacobson."

"Hey, I'm only an old fart who seems to attract the wrong

sort of people, like lint on a pair of polyester pants in a low-humidity climate."

He shook his head.

"I know, go and sin no more. Grudion, we'll see if this all resolves itself in Victoria tomorrow."

"I can hardly wait."

Muscles escorted me back to the casino floor and shut the door behind me. I wandered over to the machine that had abused me and found Andrew watching the ladies plunk quarters into slots.

"These women are amazing," Andrew said. "Both of them are winning. I finally gave up."

"At least you didn't get busted by the local gendarmes."

"What happened with your little escapade?"

"The quarter I found on the island tuned out to be counterfeit. The strange part is I wouldn't have expected anyone to have wasted time making counterfeit quarters. Can't be much profit in it."

"You make a good point. It's typically twenty-dollar bills that are counterfeited. For a dollar of product cost the bad guys can make nineteen dollars' profit. If you can produce quarters for five cents each, you only return twenty cents per coin."

"My thoughts exactly," I said. "Why would a crime family bother with quarters?"

"Another of life's unexplained mysteries, such as why there are always snowstorms on a day of an important meeting."

"I've solved that one. I live in Venice, California."

He wagged a finger at me. "You be careful. It did snow in Los Angeles in 1964 and there was snow in Malibu in January 2007."

"I think I can live with that every forty years or so, especially since I won't be alive and kicking that much longer anyway."

"I don't know, Paul. Except for your involvement in crime,

you'll live to be a ripe old age."

"I'm already ripe and going to seed."

We waited until the ladies decided they had cleaned out the casino of enough money and lugged their bins of quarters to the cashier.

When they returned, Andrew asked, "What were the evening winnings, ladies?"

Helen held up a handful of bills. "Seventy-eight dollars."

Marion smiled. "One hundred-four dollars and fifty cents."

"I'll be darned. You probably earned enough to treat me to a brain transplant."

"But think of all the fun you'd miss if you could remember like other people." Marion gave me a kiss on the cheek.

"Right. As if I'd miss starting over every morning."

"We can start our romance over every day."

"As long as I have you and my journal to remind me."

When I survived until eleven forty-five without falling asleep, Andrew, Helen, Marion and I ambled down to the main dining room to find hundreds of our new acquaintances already in line.

"Popular event," I said.

"If you're on a cruise, you can't miss the midnight chocolate event," Marion said.

"These people have been in training all week." I pointed toward a group of supersized people in front of us. "Makes me appreciate my stomach." I patted it, feeling a little extra padding from all the good food that week.

At exactly the stroke of midnight, the doors opened and the feeding frenzy began. When we finally reached the beginning of the tables full of desserts, I reached for a chocolate éclair but before my hand could close on it, a rotund woman draped in what looked like pink curtains snatched it away. I was about to protest, but she shoved her way toward a piece of chocolate cake, which she grabbed before another woman could reach for it. I guarded my space like a dog protecting a prize bone and extracted another éclair.

"Don't get any chocolate on your fingers or someone might chew them off," I told Marion.

She smiled. "There certainly are a lot of enthusiastic people here."

"You'd think they never saw chocolate before. The temperature in this room will probably rise ten degrees with all these people running around berserk on chocolate highs."

We filled our plates and a waiter led us to a table for four.

"Phew. I'm glad to be out of that line," Andrew said.

"If you get hungry, you can always go back for seconds," Helen said.

"I think this is enough to keep me awake all night," Andrew replied.

I heard a shout at the next table and looked over to see a boisterous group, including a man and woman stuffing chocolate cake in each others' mouths. The woman's hat read, "Oldsters from Reno."

I remembered reading in my journal that we had encountered this group earlier in the cruise. I listened to their whooping and hollering. Then one of the men, wearing a straw hat, wove his way over to our table.

"Les hear more 'thusiasm from this table." He hiccupped.

I regarded him. "Your group seems to enjoy doing things together."

He leaned over and draped a soggy arm around my shoulder. "Thas right. We're the worl' renown Oldsters from Reno."

"You don't look that old to me."

He flinched and stepped back like I had insulted him. "Hey. We're old . . . old . . . old." He poked a finger into my chest.

"You're just a drunk young whippersnapper as far as I'm concerned."

"Are you insulting me and the grand city of Reno?"

He leaned toward me but slipped and his head hit the table, his straw hat flying off and plopping into Marion's chocolate ice cream. He collapsed and disappeared below table level.

A woman came running over. "What did you do to Julian?"

"I didn't do anything to him. He was drunk and hit his head." I peered over the edge of the table to see Julian lying on the floor unconscious with a big lopsided grin on his face.

The woman put her hands on her hips and snarled at me. "What do you mean drunk? Julian only had four drinks."

"If you mean those tropical drinks with pink umbrellas, I think he had more than his fill."

She patted Julian's cheek but he didn't come around.

Grudion and two other men pushed their way through a crowd of chocoholics. The two men lifted Julian and carried him away with his wife trailing behind. She turned and shouted at me. "Why'd you have to hurt him? He was so excited about the chocolate buffet."

Grudion regarded me. "Causing more problems after our last talk, Mr. Jacobson?"

I shrugged. "Just a guy who couldn't hold his liquor very well."

One of the other oldsters approached our table and shook his fist at me. "This man was arguing with Julian. I think he knocked Julian out."

"Wait a goddamn minute. Julian did it to himself."

"That's right," Andrew said. "Julian was intoxicated, slipped and hit his head on the table."

"You calling me a liar?" the man said to Andrew.

"Gentlemen. Everyone calm down." Grudion stepped between the man and Andrew. Grudion escorted the man back

to his table and spoke quietly with the people there. Then Grudion returned to our table.

"Now if you will stop harassing other people, Mr. Jacobson,
all will be fine."

I opened my mouth to defend my honor but then thought
better of it. Grudion never believed anything I said anyway.

"Do you know who that man is?" Grudion asked me.

"Never seen him before," I said.

"Actually you have. You were accused of stealing his wallet,
and then there was the matter of what you did to him in the hot
tub."

I thought back to what I had read in my journal. "He's that
guy?"

"The very one."

"He sure gets in a lot of trouble."

"I think you're the one who gets in trouble, Mr. Jacobson."
Please don't disturb any more paying customers." With that
Grudion departed.

"Hey, I'm a paying customer too," I shouted to the back of
Grudion.

"Actually, you're not," Marion said. "The trip was free."

After the commotion and my heart rate had settled down,
Andrew said, "You seem to always be in the center of a fracas,
Paul."

"Yeah. I attract these weirdos like flies on a piece of rancid
meat. When I get hauled in on this latest charge at least you can
testify on my behalf."

"I'll be happy to. You've done nothing wrong."

"If only Grudion shared your belief."

Marion fished the hat out of her ice cream and set it aside.

We finished our chocolate without any more incidents.

The oldsters got up and, with a final round of glares in my
direction, departed.

I sighed. "I've made another set of friends. Now in addition to Latvian hit men, murderers and the ship's detective, I'll have Oldsters from Reno stalking me."

Once I was sure the Oldsters from Reno had departed, we got up to leave. As we exited the dining room, I looked to both sides to make sure no one was waiting for me with a tire iron in hand.

"Anyone up for a nightcap?" Andrew asked.

"I think I've had enough excitement for one day," I said.

Marion nodded in agreement.

"Let's meet for a morning walk," I said to Andrew.

"If you think you'll be rested by then."

"I'll walk you into the deck, you young punk."

We said our goodbyes, Andrew and I shaking hands and the ladies exchanging hugs and congratulating themselves on their winnings.

As we strolled back to our stateroom, Marion and I held hands.

"They're such nice people," she said.

"They sure are. Amid all the problems I've encountered on this cruise, they're the one bright light."

"Nothing else has piqued your interest?" She gave me a wink.

"Well, there are the whales, but they're in hiding. And I did find a beautiful woman in my cabin."

Marion snuggled close against me.

In the lower reaches of my anatomy I felt a change.

"I'll be damned. Something's happening to my old body."

We were at our door. Marion put her arms around me, kissed me and pressed tight against me. "I sure hope so."

I fumbled with the key card, getting it oriented wrong in my haste. I took a deep breath and redirected the card. A green light flashed, and I pushed the door open.

Our room was bathed in filtered light from a tiny night lamp.

I kicked the door shut, and we embraced and began pawing each other like two randy teenagers.

I came up for air and the next thing I knew, our clothes were flying around like palm branches in a Florida hurricane.

As we were about to jump into bed, Marion said, "Don't forget the chocolate mints."

"Oh yeah. I've had enough chocolate but no sense having a chocolate bath."

I grabbed the chocolates on the pillow and flung them onto the nightstand. Then we hit the sheets and began exploring the most interesting parts of each other's bodies.

"Wow, you're a hot woman."

"I haven't heard that in twenty years—since menopause."

We engaged and things became hotter. Marion held me tight and I revved up the old body like "the little engine that could."

After some excited moaning and groaning, the engine let off its steam and we lay there panting in each other's arms.

"What a woman you are." I kissed Marion again.

"You're not so bad yourself."

I lay there contented and then drifted off to sleep.

I awoke with a start. I knew where I was and remembered the passionate exchange of the night before. The wonder of my weird brain with the pipes unclogged as a result of a little post-midnight cavorting.

After visiting the very little boys' room, I sat down to document my adventures from the day before in my journal, for once remembering everything clearly.

When I had finished my missive, my stomach felt unsettled and not just because I was hungry. What a bunch of predicaments I had managed to plunk my aging butt into. How would I extricate myself from all the crud? In addition to the unsolved murders, I kept running afoul of this jerk Julian Armour.

Everywhere I turned, he and I seemed to have unpleasant encounters. First, he'd accused me of stealing his wallet. Next, I found him unconscious in the hot tub, but rather than thanking me for shouting for help, he was pissed off and claimed that I did something to him. Then I had tried to be nice to him on the train by giving him a bottle of water, but he promptly puked his guts out and blamed it on me. And the little incident at the chocolate feast. That guy Julian Armour was a walking time bomb. I'd just have to stay out of his way for the rest of the trip. That would be healthiest for both of us.

I decided to take my morning constitutional and see if Andrew was on the jogging track. Marion stirred from under the covers.

"Going somewhere, Paul?"

"I'll take my walk around the deck and revel in being able to remember yesterday."

"I remember last night very well."

"You have a very positive effect on this old mind and body."

"There was nothing old about your body last night. I'll get up in a few minutes and we can have breakfast when you return."

I headed up to the walking deck to see if I could find Andrew and, sure enough on the second pass, I spotted him up ahead looking over the railing.

"Admiring the ocean?" I asked.

"I saw two whales breach."

"No kidding. Where?"

He pointed.

I squinted and waited in eager anticipation of finally seeing a whale.

Five minutes passed and nothing appeared.

"I think they'll have to come up soon," Andrew said.

"They're hiding from me again."

After another five minutes we gave up and decided to take our walk.

"What's on your agenda today, Paul?"

"My bride and I are touring Butchart Gardens to see all the posies."

Andrew chuckled. "We're doing the same. It's supposed to be quite a place."

"You've never been there before?"

"No. First time. Helen and I have traveled to more tropical climes but haven't visited the Northwest other than Seattle and Portland."

"My first time in Victoria as well . . . as far as I can remember."

"Say, speaking of your memory, you spotted me right off this morning."

"Yup. My brain cells were supercharged last night."

"Sounds like a story there."

"Just a little quirk of my addled cranium. So today's also my big day to see if I can resolve the Zarins, Gary and Gina show. There should be some fireworks."

"Don't get burned."

"That's the darn problem. All this is converging on poor little Victoria, but I haven't pieced it all together yet. And Grudion is still off following me rather than trying to nail one of these other jerks."

"Everything seems to happen around you, Paul, so maybe that isn't a bad strategy for Grudion."

"Yeah. I'm like the carcass attracting all the vultures."

"I wouldn't put it quite that way."

We completed our laps and then Andrew said he needed to get back to Helen.

I took one last look out to sea to verify that the whales were still laughing at me and then returned to my cabin.

I let myself in. "I'm starving," I shouted. "Are you ready for breakfast?"

No answer.

"Marion?"

Still no answer.

She wasn't in the cabin. I opened the sliding door and peered out on the balcony. She wasn't there either.

After coming back in from the fresh air, it struck me. The room smelled from a strange aroma.

Then I noticed a sheet of paper on the bed.

I picked it up and read: "If you want to see your wife alive, stay out of what doesn't involve you."

CHAPTER 19

My chest tightened as fear gripped me. One of the slimeballs had kidnapped Marion. What had I got my sorry behind and Marion's attractive one into?

I now recognized the aroma wafting through the room—chloroform. I suspected one of the bad guys had knocked Marion out and dragged her away.

Think, Jacobson.

All kinds of names swirled in my recalcitrant brain: Zarins, Valdis, Gina, Gary, Ellen Hargrave, Inese, Erik, the Oldsters from Reno . . . Grudion.

Grudion was probably following me, but I didn't want to shout in the hallway as it might alert whoever had kidnapped Marion and put her life at risk.

What to do?

I picked up the phone.

"I have a security emergency. Please have Mr. Grudion come to Paul Jacobson's room."

I waited and within five minutes a knock sounded on my door. Obviously, he was lurking close by and one of his people had reached him.

Opening the door, I pulled Grudion in and then shut the door behind him.

He dusted himself off. "Yes, Mr. Jacobson?"

"Someone abducted my wife." I pointed to the note still lying on the bed.

He leaned over and read it. "Don't touch it. I'll have it checked for fingerprints."

"I'm sure whoever did it didn't leave any."

"Maybe I'll find your fingerprints, Mr. Jacobson. Is this a stunt of yours?"

"Just a Goddamn minute. My wife's disappeared. Don't start accusing me."

Grudion leveled a gaze at me. "Just checking."

I felt like I had been captured by the Scandinavian Gestapo.

"Also, notice the smell in here, Detective?"

He sniffed. "Chloroform."

"Exactly."

He reached for his cell phone and began jabbering in Swedish.

He snapped it shut and turned toward me. "We have an alert out for your wife. Care to speculate on who might have done this?"

"Half the ship and an irate Latvian crime lord come to mind. Grudion, if you were following me, didn't you see anything?"

"No. I was watching you up on the jogging track."

I punched my right fist into my left hand. "I thought so. Then you know I didn't do this."

He shrugged. "You could have done it during the night."

I pointed a finger at him. "But I suspect you've been watching my room."

He gave me a sheepish smile. "Let's say that no one reported seeing you leave between the time you came in last night and going on your walk this morning."

"There," I said triumphantly.

"But you've been implicated in the disappearance of Mrs. Hargrave over a balcony. That may be your modus operandi for getting rid of people."

"Okay, Grudion. Why don't you cut out the horse crap and

start looking for my wife?"

"My people are on it."

"Good. Now what are you personally going to do?"

He flinched. "Me?"

"Yeah, you. You're always giving me grief and traipsing around spying on me. I want to see some results from you this time. Remember, I'm a paying customer. And I'll give you a hand. Let's start with the cabin staff. They're around the corridor all the time. They might have seen something."

He gave me a weak smile. "Good idea."

We left my stateroom and Grudion marched along the corridor and knocked on an inside door.

I caught up to him as the door opened. Two maids and a steward stood inside, folding bed linens.

"We have a disappearance from Room 10610. Mrs. Jacobson."

One of the maids smiled. "Mrs. Jacobson. She's very nice."

"That's my wife. Have you seen her this morning?"

"No, not since yesterday."

"Have any of you noticed anything unusual? We think Mrs. Jacobson has been abducted."

The other maid put her hand to her face. "That's terrible."

The steward looked thoughtful. "I saw a man accompanying a woman down the hallway this morning. She looked like she was drunk or sick."

"Which direction were they headed?" I asked.

"Toward the front of the ship."

"Can you describe the man?" Grudion asked.

"I didn't really notice him."

"Come on," Grudion said. "Let's check with the staff further up the hallway."

At the next linen room, no one had seen anything. We continued forward and had a little more success.

"Yes," a young woman said, pushing a strand of hair out of her eyes. "I saw a man help a woman into the elevator. He was practically dragging her."

"Did you get a look at him?" Grudion asked.

"His back was to me. All I saw was a brown jacket and a baseball cap."

"How tall?"

"About his size." She pointed to me.

Grudion glared at me. "How long ago?"

"I'd say an hour."

"See," I said. "It wasn't me. You were watching me on the jogging track an hour ago."

"Did you see if they were going up or down?" Grudion asked.

The maid pursed her lips and wrinkles creased her forehead. Then a broad smile appeared on her face. "Yes. After the door closed I saw the lighted numbers change to nine and then eight. Then I turned away."

"That's very helpful," Grudion said. He pulled out his cell phone, punched in some numbers and began squawking in his secret tongue. Then he clicked it shut and strode toward the elevators.

"What now?" I asked.

"I'm having the staff check all forward rooms on decks eight, five and four."

"What about seven and six?"

"Those have bars, the theater, photo gallery and casino. Three of my men will start on deck seven and then move to six."

"I'll check out the casino," I said. "Marion has been very lucky there."

He shrugged. "It's not open. We're too close to Vancouver Island."

"I'll start in the casino anyway and meet you there after you check out deck seven."

I took the elevator down, my old ticker beating like a Lionel Hampton set.

No one was in the casino area—all the tables and slot machines rested like exhausted sentinels in the dim light. So different from the night before with the mob of people coursing through and the sound of Marion and Helen hitting jackpot after jackpot.

I walked around the edge of the room and tried the handle on the door to the hallway I had been escorted down. Locked. At least I remembered that due to my sex-induced super memory. I found one more door and shook the handle. Also locked. Then I sniffed the air like a bloodhound. The old sniffer picked up the faint aroma of chloroform. Success.

I shook the handle again. Then I put my ear to the door. I heard a faint rustling.

"Marion. Are you in there?"

I listened again. A soft moan.

I stood back and kicked at the door.

Bam.

Pain shot through my leg. Damn. I had hurt my foot. I hopped around until the pain subsided. Next I stepped back and raced forward, butting my shoulder into the door. I bounced off like a ping pong ball. My teeth rattled and my shoulder felt like a piece of raw meat.

Rubbing my shoulder and limping, I decided to take the elevator up a floor to find Grudion. I gimped through the photo gallery and spotted him in a bar next door.

"Grudion, this is no time for a drink. I think I've found Marion in the casino."

He strode up to me. "Let's go."

He took off toward the stairwell, and I limped along like *Gunsmoke*'s Chester behind him. I caught up to him in the casino and pointed to the door.

He extracted a key from an elastic tether on his belt and opened the door.

I shook my head. "That was sure easier than my attempts."

Marion lay there in a crumpled pile.

Grudion bent down and checked Marion's breathing and pulse. Then he stood up and punched in some numbers on his cell phone. This time he spoke in English. "Bring a stretcher to the casino immediately."

I leaned over and gently patted Marion's cheek. "You're going to be fine."

Her eyes fluttered and she licked her lips. I heard a faint, "Paul?"

"I'm here." I gave her a hug.

Then two attendants arrived and carefully placed Marion on a stretcher. I followed as they took her in the elevator down to the fourth deck to the infirmary. Then they moved her to a cot. A doctor arrived and checked Marion's pulse and examined her eyes. He extracted a glass vial from a drawer, broke off the top and wafted it under Marion's nose.

She flinched, coughed and her eyes shot open.

"There. I think you're coming to."

He helped her sit up.

"Don't try to stand up yet." He handed her a cup of water and she took a sip.

I sat next to Marion and put my arm around her. "I was so worried about you."

She turned her head toward me and gave a wan smile. "Oh, Paul. I don't know what happened to me."

"That's what Mr. Grudion will try to get to the bottom of. What do you remember?"

"You're asking me about remembering?"

I chuckled. "I'm glad you still have your sense of humor. I had left you in the cabin when I went for my walk."

"Yes. And then I changed and was in the bathroom putting on lipstick when I heard a knock on the door. I thought it was you and you'd forgotten your key card."

"But it wasn't me."

"No. I opened the door and something was thrown over my head. Then a foul smell. That's the last I remember before waking up."

"Did you see your abductor?"

"It all happened too fast."

"So you don't even know if it was a man or a woman?"

"No."

"One of the service crew reporting seeing a man leading a sick or drunk woman, so that must have been your assailant."

"Unless there was another unconscious woman being dragged away this morning."

I hung my head. "This is all my fault. I riled up someone who took it out on you."

After fifteen minutes the doctor suggested we try walking around the room. Marion seemed to have her sea legs again so after one last check of blood pressure and the light in her eyes routine, we were excused.

"I'm getting hungry," Marion said.

"That's a good sign."

She looked at her watch. "Oh, dear. It's too late for breakfast in the main dining room, but we can catch the buffet upstairs."

"That's the cruise life. No murders or abduction will keep us from our eating."

We took the elevator to the twelfth deck, duly washed our hands in the clear antiseptic gel dispensed by a smiling attendant and entered the buffet line.

"Do you want to sit down, and I'll bring some food to you?" I asked.

"No. I'm doing fine."

We loaded up on eggs, sausage, pancakes, juice and coffee and found an open table near the windows.

I had taken two bites when I heard shouting behind me. I turned. "What's going on?"

A man at the next table said, "Someone spotted a whale, that's all."

"Hot damn." I looked out to sea.

Nothing.

I watched for five minutes and then returned to my food.

"I don't understand it. Everyone sees whales and I haven't spotted a cussed one yet."

Marion patted my hand. "Be patient. You'll have your chance."

"But time is running out. We dock tomorrow and at my age this could be my last chance to see a whale. That's provided I survive whoever is after us. I'm sorry that they're taking it out on you now."

"We'll get through this," Marion said. "And you'll see your whale."

"Is that a promise?"

"I can't speak for the ocean, but we can always take a whale-watching trip to Maui."

We finished breakfast without any additional whale alerts.

Back in our cabin I said to Marion, "I need to update Jennifer on my encounter with Karlis Zarins yesterday. Since that granddaughter of mine gave me a heads-up, I need to fill her in on the details."

Marion reached into her purse, fiddled with the cell phone and then handed it to me.

"I know, push the green button," I said.

Marion looked puzzled and then smiled. "That's right. After last night you remember things from yesterday perfectly."

"Thanks to my sexy bride."

Marion actually blushed.

I thrust my right index finger against the green button and the phone did its thing.

Allison answered.

"This is your father-in-law calling from Canada, eh."

"Paul, it's nice to hear from you. What have you and Jennifer been plotting? She's been on her computer, muttering something about Latvia."

"She's my computer bloodhound seeking out information for me."

"Well, here she is."

I heard heavy breathing, and then Jennifer said, "Grandpa, this guy Karlis Zarins I told you about yesterday is a really bad dude."

"I know. I met him after we spoke."

"What? He's there?"

"Yes. He kidnapped me with intent to do bodily harm. I just never expected that a crime boss in Latvia would be Inese's father."

"But you escaped?"

"I was rescued after nothing more than a severe reprimand, but he's not one to mess around with."

"I know. I've found out that he has killed numerous people and is the most feared man in Latvia."

"Not currently. He's now the most feared man in the Pacific Northwest."

"You be careful. Now tell me the whole story."

I recounted my diverted zodiac trip and concluded by saying, "And the worst part was I saw no whales."

"Grandpa, that's the least of your concerns."

"I don't know. It's pretty serious, but several other things happened as well. I was busted for using a counterfeit quarter, and someone chloroformed Marion, abducted her and locked her in a closet in the casino. She's okay now."

I heard gasping and gurgling sounds on the line. Then Jennifer made me go through the details of all the episodes.

"You fall into one mess after another, Grandpa. But back to Inese's murder. We now know that Inese's father is a bad guy, and he's searching for her killer. That means her death could be linked to his crime dealings."

"Possibly. You suspected that when we spoke yesterday. The other scenario is that Gary and Gina bumped off Inese to eliminate a potential competitor for their part of Ellen Hargrave's estate."

"Seems less likely to me. Who would know that Inese came from a crime family?"

"The only one on the ship is the waiter, Erik, who I now know actually works for Karlis Zarins."

"Hmm. So he's either a faithful follower or trying to take over Zarins's operation."

"Either could be the case. With this mess, anyone could have done it."

"And who could have kidnapped Marion?" Jennifer asked.

"Again, no clues other than it being a man, so it couldn't have been Gina."

"Too bad no one recognized the kidnapper."

"That would have simplified things. There's so much I haven't figured out yet. Plus, I don't expect Karlis Zarins to pack his tent and head back to Latvia without some resolution to his daughter's death. And Grudion is like a bulldog. A little misdirected but tenacious."

"You be sure to call and tell me everything, Grandpa."

"You'll be one of the first to hear."

We said our goodbyes, I pushed the red button and handed the cell phone back to Marion.

"Since this is our last day on the ship, we should make one

more trip to the spa," Marion said. "In addition, it will be safer if we're around other people. We also can play bingo again and go to the talent show this afternoon in the theater."

"Sounds like my tour director has my day planned for me. And I'm pretty talented. I can do my forgetting trick and make whales disappear."

"You be good and don't cause any commotion."

"Yes, ma'am."

"And then we land in Victoria in the late afternoon and have our tour of the Butchart Gardens this evening."

We retrieved our swimming gear and made the pilgrimage to the spa. Once ensconced in the hot tub, we let the hot water work its magic on our aging bodies. I looked around the room, verifying that we were surrounded by enough people that no one would try to do us bodily harm.

"I could get used to this life," Marion said, with just her head peeking out of the water.

"You mean being chloroformed and abducted every morning?"

She splashed water at me. "You know what I mean."

Then we dried off our water-logged bodies, donned crisp white robes and plopped down in lounge chairs to relax further.

A half a dozen other cruisers lay in other lounge chairs around us, and I closed my eyes to let the bird-chirping music mingle with thoughts of crazed killers and mob bosses.

Neither Grudion nor I had made much headway in piecing this all together. At least he wasn't breathing down my soggy neck, although who knew, he could have been watching me at this very moment through a video camera hidden near the chirping bird speaker.

I started to doze off and then caught myself. I didn't want to do the Jacobson mental reset today. I had to keep whatever wits I had about me for this evening.

"There it is," a woman's voice shouted.

My eyes popped open.

Two chairs away, a middle-aged white-robed woman with wet hair pointed toward the ocean.

"What's there?" I asked.

"I saw a whale."

Now she had my attention. I squinted and watched the wake behind the ship, expecting Moby Dick to appear at any moment.

I saw an object and my heart started beating faster. Could that be my whale?

Then I looked closer and saw that it was a large log.

"At least it's a good thing our ship didn't hit that."

I kept peering out the window, but no whales appeared.

Finally, Marion tapped me on the shoulder and indicated it was time for us to go tempt the bingo gods.

CHAPTER 20

When we arrived at the theater, the teeming mob was already assembled. We purchased our cards and selected a spot with no Oldsters from Reno in the vicinity. I ordered a virgin tropical drink, but Marion didn't want anything since she felt it would interfere with her focus on bingo.

After the first two games, in which I only had two in a row by the time someone yelled bingo, I said to Marion, "There should be a consolation prize for the poor dumb fart who has the fewest spaces covered. I'd win that for sure."

Marion smiled. "I know. Whales, slot machines and bingo haven't been kind to you."

"Those and murderers, kidnappers and Latvian crime bosses."

We continued playing and on one card I even had three in a row before someone yelled bingo. In the next game my luck remained the same, but Marion began covering spaces like mad.

"Look at this, Paul. I have four in a row already."

"B14," came the next call.

"Bingo!" Marion shouted, standing up.

Bingo echoed through the theater. I noticed that another woman had stood up.

"Both of you come forward." The MC beckoned.

Marion trotted to the stage to be joined by the other woman. The announcer checked their cards, then handed each of them a sheet of paper. Marion and the other woman hugged each other and then stepped to the side of the stage. They appeared to be talking together and laughing. This continued for some time. They hugged again and, shortly, Marion returned.

"Looks like you made a new friend."

"Yes. She looked familiar. Then I noticed her shirt. It said, 'Oldsters from Reno.' "

"Uh-oh. My nemesis group."

"Now, now. Betty is very nice."

"But there's that one guy, Julian Armour, whom I don't get along with."

"Betty will smooth things over. She's Julian's wife."

I shook my head. "Consorting with the enemy."

"We have a lot in common—slot machines, bingo and ornery husbands."

"You gambling women. Do you belong to a cabal or something?"

"Just doing my part to provide financing for the family."

"You're doing a hell of a lot more than I am."

"Don't forget. You earned the free cruise to begin with."

"That's true. Unlucky at gambling and whales but lucky with murders and at love."

She rubbed her hands together. "Now we have more bingo to play."

Marion didn't win again, but she came close once. I, on the other hand, maintained my streak and never covered more than three in a row before some klutz jumped up and did a bingo dance.

"So how much did you win?" I asked after the bingo mania wrapped up.

"Two-hundred-fifty dollars."

"Not bad for a morning's work."

"They deduct it from our bill when we settle up at the end of the cruise."

"Since our cruise is free, maybe we'll actually get money back."

"I don't know. Given all those tropical drinks you've consumed, it may only cover your bar bill."

"I'm the last of the big drinkers. Speaking of which, I better visit the little sailors' room."

When I rejoined Marion, I said, "Between the casino and bingo, you've done pretty well."

"Yes. I figure I'm at least five hundred dollars ahead."

I whistled. "We better move to Reno. You and Betty can collaborate."

"I'm perfectly happy living in Venice Beach with you, thank you."

"That's good. I'm not ready to relocate."

After lunch we headed to the Caribbean Lounge for the talent show. Marion knew her way around this ship like an old pro, so she led me to exactly the right spot. Then she insisted that we sit in the front row to have a good view of the proceedings. I immediately noticed a big group of the Oldsters from Reno on the other side of the front row. Marion waved to Betty, and I slunk down in my seat, not wanting to deal with Julian. The waitress came by and I ordered a non-alcoholic tropical drink and Marion asked for a Coke.

After our drinks were delivered and I had signed for them, I removed the paper parasol and extracted a piece of pineapple on a plastic spear. I was making sure to have lots of fruit on this cruise.

The MC grabbed the microphone and announced that there were eight finalists who would be judged by a distinguished panel including himself, the cruise director, the captain and one celebrity guest who I had never heard of. The winner would receive a two-thousand-dollar coupon for a future Scandinavian

Sea Lines cruise.

"Big bucks are at play here," I said.

"I should have entered you. You could have recounted stories of murder and mayhem."

"Except no one would believe me."

The first routine was a big guy decked out in a grass skirt. The MC announced that he would be performing a Hawaiian war chant.

Marion leaned toward me. "That's Kimo. We met him in the spa earlier in the trip."

"If you say so."

His deep voice boomed out with a cross between singing and yodeling. If I had been his enemy, I'd have been cowed.

Everyone clapped. He bowed and strode back to sit down.

Next on the agenda was a plump young woman in her fifties who sang from the musical *Oklahoma* about being a girl who couldn't say no. I imagined her serenading a plate piled high with steak, lobster, potatoes and cake and then diving in to prove the message of her song.

At the conclusion of her number, she bowed and a rotund guy in the back, wearing a bright Hawaiian shirt that didn't quite cover his stomach, whooped and clapped. I pictured the two of them decimating the ship's larder.

Next a comedian entertained us with stories of his vacation adventures. He hadn't faced dead bodies, but every other imaginable fate befell him including capsizing a sailboat, slipping into a river infested with piranha, being chased by an angry bear (I could identify with that) and being dinner for the world's largest mosquitoes.

Then a young girl twirled and pirouetted, demonstrating that her parents had spent a fortune on ballet lessons.

By now my tropical drink had run through my system, and I was contemplating a quick pit stop. I thought I'd try to gut it out for one more number.

The MC announced the next contenders would be Julian and Betty Armour from Reno. The Oldsters from Reno all stood and shouted as Julian and Betty came to the front of the room. They launched into a George Burns and Gracie Allen routine replete with Julian holding an unlit cigar.

They were pretty good, but all of a sudden I knew I had to visit the restroom. I stood up and darted to the side aisle.

My foot caught a cord. There was a shrieking wail followed by a spluttering noise, and the sound system went out.

I looked back in dismay but raced up the aisle to save myself from further embarrassment.

Later when I slunk back in, a man and woman in western attire were singing a Roy Rogers and Dale Evans song.

The show wrapped up, and the judges put their heads together. The MC then jogged to the front of the room.

"We want to thank this wonderful group of performers. All deserve to be winners and are winners in our opinion. After much deliberation from the judges, we have selected a performer for the prize. Arlene Beaupres from Minneapolis."

Everyone clapped and the girl who couldn't say no came forward to say yes to the award. I was sure that she and her hubby were ready to eat their way through another cruise.

I stood up to leave, and suddenly Julian Armour appeared and thrust his chin inches from mine. "You . . . you . . . ruined our chances. We would have won if you hadn't interrupted our performance."

I put my hands up. "Whoa, just a minute, Julian. It was an accident. I apologize for tripping over the cord."

His face turned red, and I expected to see steam come out of his ears. "It was no accident. You did it on purpose."

Marion stepped in. "I know you're upset, Julian, but Paul didn't mean to hurt you or your performance. And I thought you and Betty did a marvelous job."

Julian's shoulders slumped like someone had let the air out of a balloon. He shook his head as though trying to rid himself of some alien flies buzzing around and stalked away.

"That's one more reason that I need you, Marion. You're much more diplomatic than I am."

She regarded me thoughtfully. "Yes. We make a good team. You attract trouble, and I try to smooth things out."

I opened my mouth to say something, but no words emerged.

Marion patted my arm. "You're a good man, Paul Jacobson, but you do have an uncanny knack for getting yourself in predicaments."

I sighed. "Yes, I do. So thank you for sticking with me."

"I'm here for you to see things through."

"However long I last, which won't be much longer if I don't find a way to avoid crime lords and murderers."

"And irate would-be entertainers."

"I don't suppose Julian will ever look on me in a kindly light after all the encounters we've had."

"You never know. I'll talk to Betty behind the scenes."

"What a woman you are. Protecting me from myself."

"Now I have a task for you."

"Uh-oh. Sounds like payback time."

"Definitely. You're coming with me to the photo gallery so we can find some pictures of us to give to your family and mine."

"Sounds harmless enough."

"I don't know, Paul. With you, any outing can turn into an unexpected endangerment."

"I promise to behave myself."

"Just don't argue with the cashier."

We made our way to the photo shop and perused hundreds of pictures.

"How can anyone find anything here?" I asked.

"Keep looking. We'll find a number of pictures of us."

And Marion was correct as usual. She picked out a photo of us embarking and another taken at a dinner.

Then I found one and held it up—we stood next to a guy in a polar bear costume who was wearing tennis shoes. "Look at this."

"That was taken when we disembarked in Ketchikan."

"Before my wild zodiac ride."

"And before I started feeling sick."

"Seems like a week ago, but it was only yesterday. For a change I can remember it."

Marion leaned against me. "Due of course to the fact that you're a passionate lover."

"Me? It was all your fault. You know I can't keep my hands off you."

"Well, I hope not."

We returned to our room and sat out on the balcony to watch as we entered the port of Victoria. What would be in store for me there? Would I figure out this crazy puzzle of kidnappers, murderers and assorted undesirables? Would I find some resolution amid the rose gardens of Butchart Gardens?

All that could wait. First, I had to pee.

CHAPTER 21

"We need to pack, Paul."

"Now?"

"Yes. The instructions are that we need to leave our luggage outside our room. The staff will remove it tonight and have it dockside in Seattle for us in the morning."

"I guess that's better than schlepping all the stuff off with us."

"I have a carry-on bag for our personal articles. Set aside a change of clothes for the morning as well."

"Yes, ma'am."

While sorting my few remaining clean clothes from the pile of dirty ones, I noticed my hand trembling. It wasn't old age. It was a feeling of foreboding about the upcoming debarkation in Victoria. I had to be on my toes and observant to see if I could fathom exactly what had transpired with this sequence of shipboard crimes. I wouldn't welcome seeing Karlis Zarins if he showed up again. And who had murdered Inese and done away with Ellen Hargrave? Erik and Gary were my two front-running candidates for Inese's murder, but Erik didn't have anything to do with Ellen. Gary and Gina had a motive for killing Ellen and Inese if they thought, incorrectly, that Inese was Ellen's long-lost niece. I was getting close but still no cigar. And that damn Julian Armour. He and I hit it off like oil and water. On top of all the earlier run-ins, I had disrupted his talent show number. I could spend the whole rest of my life, however short, apologizing to him about my misdeeds for all the good it would do.

Well, I would finish packing and then see what was in store for me in Victoria.

After putting our luggage outside the room, we gathered jackets and Marion's camera for our shore excursion and then waited in line to disembark.

"Our last shore excursion," Marion said with a sigh.

We marched down the gangway with the mob of hyper tourists ready to invade Victoria.

"Where to now?" I asked Marion.

She extracted two tickets from her purse and handed them to me. I read the print, which informed me that our meeting point was the parking lot at the end of the pier.

"I assume this means the land end and not the water end of the pier." I looked at my watch. "Right on schedule. We're supposed to gather there in ten minutes."

We strolled along the length of the pier, found the parking lot and then had to figure out which of the twenty or so buses was our magic chariot.

I showed the tickets to a cheerful attendant standing near the curb, and she directed us to the sixth bus in the row.

We clambered aboard and selected seats together near the back of the bus. I looked out the window at the people filing into buses. From my window I could see across the parking lot. A large black limousine waited there.

"Shoot. Too bad that limo isn't for us." I looked at it again. The windows were darkly tinted so no one could see inside.

Other people entered our bus.

"There are Gary and Gina Hargrave," Marion said.

I watched as the man and woman Marion had pointed to selected seats in the middle of the bus. Interesting that with their aunt missing, they were still going on an excursion.

"Uh-oh," I said. "The suspects have arrived."

"They're just on a tour like we are."

Then a noisy bunch entered the bus, and I spotted a T-shirt that said Oldsters from Reno.

"And here come Julian Armour and his sidekicks."

They all sat together in the front.

I let out a deep breath.

"Oh, look," Marion said. "There's Kimo, the man from Hawaii we met in the hot tub."

A large man accompanied by an equally large, attractive dark-haired woman negotiated the aisle.

Marion waved.

"Hey, howzit going?" he said in a loud, booming voice. "You the folks from the spa?"

"That's us," Marion said. "We enjoyed your performance in the talent show."

He gave a whale-sized grin. "This my wife Haddie," he said proudly. "You going to see all the flowers?"

"You bet," I replied.

He laughed. "We want to compare the Canadian flowers to all our plumeria, hibiscus and antheriums."

They took a seat a row ahead of us and on the other side of the bus.

"And there are Andrew and Helen Black," Marion said and pointed.

I saw a couple who had just climbed on the bus sit near the front.

"The gang's all here," I said.

"Well, we have met quite a few people on the cruise."

"Not that I'd remember any of them without your help."

After we were all crammed in, the driver climbed into his seat. He closed the door, started the engine and reached for the microphone.

"Ladies and gentlemen. Welcome to Victoria, the capital of

British Columbia, and known as the Garden City for our year-round mild climate, the best in all of Canada.

"We pride ourselves on our seafood, and the waters of our harbor often teem with pods of orca whales. Did any of you see any as your ship came in today?"

"We did," a chorus of Oldsters from Reno shouted.

"Crap. I missed the whales again."

"We must have been on the wrong side of the ship," Marion said in a whisper.

"I know. The whales are bound and determined to avoid me."

"Now a little background on Victoria for you first-time visitors," the driver said. "Victoria started as a fort for the Hudson's Bay Company back in eighteen-forty-three, founded by James Douglas. Today it represents a blend of British, modern Canadian and native cultures."

We drove along the waterfront as the driver continued his spiel. I watched as a red double-decker bus passed within inches of my nose and then looked out over the harbor at the whales that weren't there.

"We'll stop for thirty minutes here. Two photo opportunities you shouldn't miss. First, the Empress Hotel. Be sure to take a picture of your friends in front of it. Then around the corner is the British Columbia Legislative Building, which will give you the impression of being in London."

The bus pulled to a stop with the hiss of its brakes, reminding me of an angry snake. We all filed out, and I waited until the Oldsters had made their move, and then Marion and I took a different route.

Marion pulled out her camera and captured me in front of the hotel, and I reciprocated in front of the legislative building. With photo evidence of our arrival in Victoria, we sauntered along the harbor and admired the sailboats docked there.

"I once thought it would be wonderful to sail through the Caribbean," Marion said.

"I think the sailboat we're on for the cruise is the smallest one I want to go on."

"You have no desire to have the wind whip through your hair as you tack to Aruba?"

"No thanks. I hate the ocean, and I'm pretty tactless."

I ducked before she could swat me. Then we ambled along the quay before retracing our steps to the bus. As I climbed aboard, I noticed a black limo parked across the street.

As I headed up the aisle, Julian Armour glared at me.

"Hi, Julian. How're they hanging?"

It was a good thing he had the window seat or I think he would have tackled me.

Once relegated to the back of the bus, I sat down.

Our bus driver counted heads and must have decided he had enough victims to continue with the trip, so he started the engine, shut the door, and we shot away like an overstuffed humpback whale, not that I had any clue what one actually looked like.

We traveled through a neighborhood of Victorian homes and the driver resumed his commentary. "Victoria is the western-most city in Canada and home to over three hundred thousand residents."

"Does it ever snow here?" someone up front asked.

"Very rarely. We did have one storm where the city shut down. We weren't prepared. It's so unusual that we don't have snow plows."

"You should live in Minneapolis," someone up front said.

"Or Reno." This was followed by a loud cheer.

After a twenty-minute drive, we pulled into a large parking lot, teeming with other buses.

"We'll be here three hours," the driver informed us. "I'll

hand each of you a Butchart Gardens ticket as you exit the bus."

Marion and I were the last people to leave, but he still had enough tickets for us. I looked at the stub he had handed me, which had a bright red rose on it and the saying, "Over 100 years in Bloom."

"Here's to the next hundred years," I said as we walked toward the turnstile. I looked back over my shoulder. A black limousine had parked across the street. Its doors remained shut.

"That limo has been following us," I said to Marion.

She turned to look at it. "I'm sure there are dozens of black limos around."

"No, I think it's the same one. A limo was dockside, downtown when we stopped and now here."

"Don't get paranoid on me."

"I already am."

"Well, in that case I have a secret for you."

"You have an Uzi in your purse?"

"Almost as good. Perfume."

"Perfume?"

"Yes. I read in a woman's magazine about a perfume called L'Assassin. It smells good but has a secondary purpose. The chemical mixture irritates the eyes so it acts like pepper spray. The article recommended this scent as a protection device. It seems there are places like Canada that aren't too keen on importing pepper spray. And carrying pepper spray on board might be a problem with the cruise line security."

"I'll be darned. You're an armed and dangerous woman."

"Just you remember it."

I didn't know if I felt better or worse with Marion carrying a lethal perfume spray.

With one more glance over my shoulder, I grabbed Marion's hand and we advanced on Butchart Gardens.

After we entered, Marion pointed ahead. "Oh, look. A gift shop."

"Let's see what the place has to offer before we burden ourselves with souvenirs."

Marion pouted. "Spoil sport."

"I wouldn't want you getting loaded down with gifts and not be able to reach your dangerous perfume."

"You're going to stay on that kick and not enjoy the beauty of the gardens?"

"I'm ready for the flowers. But I'm also going to keep my eyes open."

Marion picked up a visitor's guide map at a kiosk, and we both scrutinized it. Then we ambled through Waterwheel Square and followed the path to the left.

"Let's start with the Sunken Garden," Marion said.

"Fine by me. I have a sinking feeling."

We came to an overlook and down below a path meandered through acres of posies.

"This would be quite a paradise if you were a bee," I said.

"It's quite a paradise for human eyes as well."

"Unless you're allergic to pollen."

"Paul, are you going to be positive about anything this evening?"

"I'm positive that I'm nervous."

We descended the stairway into the depth of the Sunken Garden. From down below I looked up at the cliffs that formed the wall of the once-upon-a-time quarry.

"I have to admit this is more attractive than if it had been left as a gravel pit."

Marion patted my arm. "Now you're getting in the right spirit."

Marion checked out the signs that identified the various types of plants and flowers. I let the colors play into my mind since I didn't know a petunia from a hyacinth.

Then all of a sudden Marion grabbed my arm. "Look over there." She pointed.

"What?"

"That man in the gray baseball cap."

I squinted. "I don't recognize him."

"I do. It's Erik, the waiter from the ship."

My old ticker revved up a notch. "The plot thickens."

"I wonder what he's doing here."

"He either has the evening off from the ship or he's here for a different reason."

"The last we heard, he hadn't shown up for his shift in the dining room."

"You're right. I was under the impression that he had skipped out, hiding from Zarins."

"He's not hiding right now."

Marion was right. Erik was purposefully striding through the gardens like he was going to meet someone. Now what exactly was he up to?

"So we have the Oldsters from Reno, Gary and Gina and now Erik here," I said. "All we need are Zarins and his sidekick Valdis."

"Be careful what you wish for," Marion said.

"I wouldn't be surprised if they had arrived in that black limousine."

Marion's smile disappeared. "Now you have me worried."

"We'll see how this plays out. Keep alert and in the meantime, enjoy the flowers."

Marion snapped a picture in the Sunken Garden of me amid the neatly trimmed grass, sculptured hedges, swatches of red, yellow and white flowers and mixture of overhanging trees. I felt like nature boy, senior style. This would be a great place for a geezer to relax on a bench, enjoy the view and dream peaceful thoughts. Provided the geezer wasn't enmeshed in a variety of crime investigations and surrounded by various miscreants wandering around. Part of me felt at peace in these environs and part felt on edge as if a meteor were going to drop out of the sky at any moment.

I looked back over my shoulder.

I wondered if Grudion was following me today. Did he feel he needed to keep an eye on me or had he moved on to better targets? On one hand, I'd just as soon be left alone. On the other, it wouldn't be bad having him around if something happened. And given my propensity to attract trouble, who knew what was in store? And who knew what evil lurks in the hearts of men? The Shadow knew.

We came to a fountain, and Marion took another picture of me in front, probably with water appearing to spurt right out of my head. Kind of like the memories spewing out of my addled brain.

"What does my tour guide have on the list for me next?" I asked.

"The Rose Garden."

"Maybe that will give me a rosier outlook."

And what a place. We meandered through paths surrounded by red, yellow and white roses as far as the eye could see.

"I'd hate to pay the fertilizer bill for this place," I said.

Marion sighed. "All this beauty and that's what you're thinking about?"

"I like the roses. But I can't help but think about the grittier side of things."

Next, we approached an open area with two tall totem poles implanted at the edge of a brickwork plaza. One totem had three levels of animals—a bear face on the bottom, a whale in the middle and a bird with tucked wings on the top. That pretty much summarized my encounter with nature in the Northwest—

chased by a bear, teased by illusive whales and forced to listen to birds chirping in the spa. The other totem had a giant eagle on the top with its wings stretched out, a scowl on its beak and large beady eyes staring to each side.

"Looks just like Grudion," I said.

"No, it's more colorful than he is. Have you noticed that he's usually dressed in white?"

"Not that I remember, but it should make him stand out in this place like a sparrow among peacocks."

"Except for his red hair," Marion said. "That's one characteristic you can always spot."

We continued past a fountain with an entwined fish sculpture, through a Japanese arch and along a path of bright red flowers to a cove. The path ended at a wooden deck that overlooked the water. Half a dozen sailboats were moored across a small bay. As I watched, a seaplane circled and then came in for a landing.

We retraced our steps and found a bench to sit on, holding hands just like newlyweds. After half an hour of making goo-goo eyes at each other, we took another path through ferns and large leafy plants and strolled over a wooden bridge that spanned a bubbling brook. Imbedded in the undergrowth were Japanese sculptures and little pagoda structures.

"Doesn't this make you relax, Paul?"

"I don't know. I keep imagining people jumping out of the bushes."

At that moment I felt a tap on my shoulder.

CHAPTER 22

I jerked my head around and found Gary Hargrave standing there.

"Hi, Gary," I said.

"Don't 'Hi, Gary' me. Why are you every place I go?"

"I guess because we have the same tour. I'm willing to stay out of your way if you're willing to stay out of mine."

"Have you seen Gina?" he asked, obviously still angry.

"We saw her with you on the bus," Marion said. "Did something happen?"

"Yes. She went into the restroom. I was supposed to meet her here, but she hasn't shown up."

"I could check the restroom for you," Marion said.

"I already had a woman do that. Gina wasn't there."

I thought back to the black limousine and the conversation I'd had the day before on the deserted island with Zarins. "I think someone may have abducted your sister."

"Are you involved in this?"

"No. But yesterday I ran into a crime boss who could be responsible for your sister's disappearance."

Gary's shoulders sagged as if he had turned into a rag doll.

"I need to ask you a pointed question," I said. "Did you or your sister have anything to do with the death of Inese or the disappearance of your aunt?"

He looked at me, his face drawn. "Of course not." Then he placed his hands over his face, and I heard sobbing. "I couldn't live with myself if my sister were harmed, particularly after the disappearance of Aunt Ellen."

I raised my eyebrows to Marion, and she nodded. "Do you have any new ideas on what happened to your aunt?" I asked.

He uncovered his face. Tears brimmed in his eyes. "This trip has been a disaster. Both the people I care most about have disappeared. Gina and I have been trying to fathom what could have happened to Aunt Ellen. And now Gina disappears."

At that moment there was a rustling in the bushes, and Karlis Zarins appeared. Then Valdis pushed out of the undergrowth. He held a knife to the throat of a bedraggled Gina.

"Gina!" Gary shouted.

"Stand where you are." Zarins extracted a pistol from his belt.

Gary's eyes grew as large as silver dollars.

"Why did you two kill my daughter?" Zarins asked.

Gary look bewildered. "We didn't kill anyone. Who's your daughter?"

I looked at both Gary and Gina. Gina had an equally puzzled expression on her face.

Then it struck me. "Zarins, I was wrong. Gina and Gary didn't kill Inese. But I think I know now who did."

"I have half a mind to eliminate all of you," Zarins said, waving the gun toward us.

"Not a good idea," I said, trying to keep my voice as casual as possible. "Let everyone go, and I'll tell you who really killed Inese. Then you can do what you need to do and leave in your black limo."

"Black limo?" Zarins eyed me. "Are you crazy, old man? We came in a float plane."

"Then who was in the limousine?" I asked.

I heard a throat-clearing sound behind me and turned to see Ellen Hargrave standing there, tapping her cane on a paving stone. "I was in the limo."

"Aunt Ellen!" Both Gary and Gina shouted simultaneously.

"Who's the old broad?" Valdis asked, tightening his grip on Gina.

"Watch your language, young man," Ellen said.

Zarins waved his gun back and forth. "What the hell is going on here?"

Ellen leveled her gaze at Zarins. "Gentlemen don't point guns at ladies."

"Lady, I don't know who you are or what you're doing here."

Ellen stood as tall as her five-foot-six-inch frame would allow. "I'm Gary and Gina's aunt. Now please have your companion release his grasp on my niece."

"Not until I find out what's going on here," Zarins countered.

"Let me take a crack at an explanation, Mr. Zarins," I said. "This charming lady here is Mrs. Ellen Hargrave, the aunt of Gary and Gina. I believe she staged a disappearance, which we can find out about in a moment, but right now she's obviously concerned about the safety of her nephew and niece. I previously thought that Gary and Gina might have been responsible for the death of Inese and the disappearance of Mrs. Hargrave, but I now admit I was wrong. Ellen, would you care to add to that?"

"You have the facts correct, Paul. I didn't get thrown off my balcony as the evidence indicated. I set that up as a test for Gary and Gina."

"What?" they both exclaimed at the same time.

"Now, now. I shouldn't have gone to this extreme, but I wanted to find out if you were only interested in my money. I pretended to disappear to see how you would respond—if you would be sad or immediately make plans to divide up my money. I'm pleased to say you seemed genuinely concerned that I had disappeared."

"How did you find that out and where have you been?" Gary asked.

"I've had Gladys checking on you." Ellen chuckled. "And I've been hiding in Gladys' room with a 'Do Not Disturb' sign posted, ordering room service and enjoying the view from her balcony. Gladys told the maid not to come in, so no one knew I was there."

I remembered something I'd read in my journal. "Ellen, did you ever discover why you had the wrong medicine that made you sick?"

She chuckled. "Yes. Earlier in the evening I had been in Gladys' cabin. She and I take different medicine, and we had emptied the contents of our purses to find a missing ring. In the process we accidentally switched our medication."

"Okay, lady," Zarins said. "You're a wacko. I see that, but your nephew and niece are still suspects in the death of my daughter."

"I can assure you that they had nothing to do with that sordid matter," Ellen said.

"Yeah, Mr. Zarins," I said. "If you quit waving that gun at everyone, I'll explain who I think killed your daughter."

Before I could say anything else, Julian Armour came charging up the path. Oblivious to everyone else, he grabbed my collar, "I've had enough of you and your meddlesome ways."

"This isn't a good time to renew our argument, Julian."

Out of the corner of my eye I saw Zarins point his gun at Julian.

I knocked Julian over as a shot rang out. I fell on top of him as chips of paving stone sprayed around us.

As I lay on top of Julian, I turned my head to see that all hell had broken loose. Ellen whacked the gun out of Zarins's hand with her cane. Valdis let go of Gina to try to retrieve the gun. Gina kneed Valdis in the crotch, and he dropped the knife and collapsed to the ground.

At that moment Grudion jumped out of the bushes and picked up the gun and knife.

I helped Julian up, and we all stood there like a bunch of cattle that had been zapped by a prod.

"Yah, what's going on here?" Grudion asked.

Everyone began speaking at the same time and pointing at each other.

"Quiet," Grudion roared.

"Let's start with Mr. Jacobson, because he always has such interesting stories."

"It's all very simple. Mr. Zarins is trying to find the murderer of his daughter, Inese. Because of some bad advice I gave him, he thought Gina and Gary Hargrave had killed Inese. Not the case. Then Ellen Hargrave disappeared, and we thought someone had thrown her overboard."

"Like the two times you knocked her down, Mr. Jacobson?"

"Those were both accidents."

Gary cleared his throat. "Actually, at the salmon hatchery it wasn't an accident."

"What?" I said.

"I pushed you," Gary said. "After you knocked Aunt Ellen down during the lifeboat drill, I thought you were out to get her. So when I saw you on the tour at the hatchery, I thought a little payback was in order. Unfortunately, when I shoved you, the result was that you bumped into my aunt."

I shook my head. "See, Mr. Grudion, I'm not the criminal you always suspected."

"Go on with your account, Mr. Jacobson," Grudion said with a disgusted look on his face.

"It turns out that nothing had happened to Mrs. Hargrave other than she went into hiding to see how Gary and Gina would react to her disappearance."

Grudion scratched his head.

"Let me put it in plain Swedish for you, Mr. Grudion. Ellen faked her disappearance to see if Gary and Gina were money-grubbing inheritance-seekers, which they aren't."

"And who is he?" Grudion said, pointing to Valdis.

"He's Mr. Zarins's associate, who's very handy with cutlery." I put my arm around Julian's shoulder. "And this is Julian Armour, another of your paying customers. He and I have had some disagreements in the past, but our relationship is on the mend."

Julian's head nodded up and down.

Zarins stepped forward and pointed at Grudion. "And Mr. Jacobson was going to tell us who killed my daughter before you rudely interrupted our gathering."

"I'd say everyone was a little out of control when I arrived. Go ahead, Mr. Jacobson. Who killed Inese?"

"Well, since you're all so interested," I said. "I suspect that the murder happened in the spa with a hot stone and it wasn't Colonel Mustard or Mrs. Plum, but . . . Erik."

The leaves parted and Erik oozed out of the undergrowth like a giant slug. He pointed a gun at Grudion's head. "Very good, Mr. Jacobson. Now, Mr. Grudion, please drop your weapon and raise your hands."

CHAPTER 23

The gun in Grudion's hand clattered to the cobblestones.

"Grab the gun," Zarins said to Valdis.

"Be happy to," Valdis said as he picked up the weapon from the path.

"Shoot Erik," Zarins ordered.

Instead, Valdis strolled over beside Erik and pointed the gun at Zarins.

"What the hell's going on?" Zarins shouted.

"It's this way," Valdis said. "Erik and I are taking over your operation, Mr. Zarins."

"You can't do that."

"We already have," Erik said.

I pointed to Erik. "You killed Inese in order to lure Mr. Zarins out of Latvia."

"Very insightful, Mr. Jacobson. We knew that Mr. Zarins wouldn't leave his home base unless there was an emergency. I provided that emergency through the death of his daughter."

"You swine," Zarins said. "You were hired to protect and watch over my daughter."

Erik shrugged. "Sometimes plans change. Valdis and I figured that once you were in the Americas we'd find a way to get rid of you and then return to run the business in Latvia."

"Why you conniving crooks," Zarins said, as spittle shot out of the sides of his mouth.

"No," Erik said. "We're entrepreneurs doing a hostile

takeover. Now I'm going to ask all of you to lie on the ground while we take Mr. Zarins for a one-way seaplane ride."

I looked around the group. Marion and I stood closest to Erik and Valdis. I noticed Marion had her hand in her purse.

Suddenly, a whistle blew, and all heads turned toward the sound as a member of the Royal Canadian Mounties, resplendent in Red Serge tunic, brown wide-brimmed Stetson, midnight blue riding breaches with a yellow stripe down the side, brass buttons and white halyard connected to a brown leather holster on a brown Sam Browne belt, came bounding toward us. Valdis pointed his gun toward the advancing Sergeant Preston of the Yukon, but Marion was faster. She had extracted her perfume and dispatched a full blast in the faces of both Valdis and Erik.

They screamed, dropping their weapons. Then all Hades broke lose again. Zarins bolted, knocking over Valdis and Erik as he charged the police officer. Valdis's flailing arms bumped into a pagoda sculpture, collapsing it onto Erik's stomach. The policeman blew his whistle again, but Zarins head-butted him. It was as if the irrepressible force met the immovable object. Zarins's head seemed to disappear into the man's stomach as both crashed into a red wooden bridge, destroying it in a shower of splinters.

Grudion raced over to pick up one of the guns just as Gary did the same. Their heads collided with a resounding "bonk" and Gary ricocheted off, crushing a bed of yellow flowers. Grudion rebounded, knocking Julian over, and came to rest in a bed of ferns. Julian crashed into a young tree, squashing it. Gina tried to run over to help Gary, but tripped over Ellen's cane, fell and knocked Ellen down in a pile of writhing limbs that splashed into the gurgling brook. Valdis seemed to recover from the perfume spray and scooted on hands and knees toward one of the guns.

"Stop him," I shouted, but no one was near or in a condition to do anything.

Valdis's hand reached out to grab the pistol when out of the bushes flew an immense form bellowing out a war cry. The huge body crashed right down on Valdis who let out a loud "Whoomp" and lay motionless. Kimo sat there on top of him with a big grin covering his face.

"Kimo to the rescue, bruddah," my large friend announced.

"Way to go," I said.

The gun still lay on the ground unattended. I noticed Erik regaining control, and then he lunged for the pistol. Kimo was still preoccupied with holding Valdis down and didn't notice.

"Don't let Erik reach the gun," I shouted.

I was too far away to do anything, not that I could have stopped him anyway.

Erik's fingers stretched for the gun when another form leaped out of the bushes, and Haddie bashed into Erik, sending him sprawling. She proceeded to plunk down on his skinny body with success equal to Kimo's move.

I surveyed the scene. Marion and I were the only ones left standing. Then more police appeared, this time in dark blue uniforms, blowing whistles, and I thought I was back in the spa jungle with the world's largest parakeets.

"Just in the nick of time," I said to one beefy young officer who approached me.

Rather than welcoming me with open arms, he grabbed my hands and cuffed me.

"What the . . . I'm one of the good guys."

He wasn't convinced, and I watched as Marion experienced the same indignity. The swarming mob of police plus the one in the Mounties outfit proceeded to cuff all the tangled mass of people.

Before you could say "eh," we were all being led out of the

Japanese garden. I looked back one last time at the carnage. All the flowers and decorations were crushed flatter than the mats after a Grand Sumo tournament.

I asked the officer who was accompanying Marion and me, "How come only one of you is dressed in the red uniform?"

"He was here for a ceremony at Butchart Gardens. Those uniforms are only used for special occasions. He happened to be the first to respond to the report of a disturbance in the Japanese Garden."

"Yeah, we caused a disturbance all right. You've captured a murderer and two international criminals along with all of us innocent bystanders."

"We'll see who's innocent," he said, directing me forward.

We passed a star-shaped pond, but had no opportunity to admire it. Marion and I shuffled along side-by-side with our personal attendant right behind. We entered another garden area where other tourists turned to gawk at our procession. As I stumbled forward, I bumped into Kimo who was being led by another police officer. He had a huge grin on his face. "Hey, bruddah. That was more fun than ti leaf sliding in Iao Valley."

I didn't know what he was talking about, but I was glad someone found the events entertaining. "Thanks for helping us, Kimo. I'm sorry you're being carted away by the police."

"No problem. This the best part of the whole trip so far."

Then I noticed Andrew and Helen with their mouths hanging open. I was too far away to say anything, but I would have waved to them except my hands were constrained.

"It's the Italian Garden," Marion said. "I really wanted to see this one."

"Take a quick look, because I have a hunch we won't see it again."

I admired a cherub statue with water spurting out of a gourd held in its arms. It was embedded in the middle of a pond containing tall papyrus grass, lily pads and pink flowers. In the background a white lattice structure supported emerald green-leafed plants with red flowers.

I turned toward Marion as best as I could. "That perfume of yours sure did the trick."

"Yes. I had never tested it before. Now I know how effective it is."

"I'll remember to bring you and your weapon along any time I have another encounter with the criminal element."

"Paul, I think it's time for you to retire from this sort of activity."

Our taskmaster continued moving us forward as we approached the parking lot.

"Hey, I didn't get my money's worth," I said to my armed guard. "I never visited the Mediterranean Garden."

My comment was answered by a shove, and I stumbled forward.

In the parking area a fleet of police vehicles awaited us. We were not too gently ushered into the back seat, and I plunked my butt down on one side with Marion on the other side, fortunate to have ended up in the same car with my bride.

"You have to give credit to the Canadian police," I said. "They sure are efficient. They wiped us up like snot on a little kid's face."

"I would have liked to see a little more of Butchart Gardens," Marion said.

"Maybe we can take another Alaskan cruise next summer. I still need to spot a whale."

"I don't know. We may want to find a calmer trip next time."

We were driven into Victoria but had no chance to admire the Empress Hotel again. For some reason the driver didn't seem inclined to give us a running commentary like the bus driver had. Instead, we arrived in front of a dull brown building and were led inside. My handcuffs were removed and I had a chance to donate fingerprints. Then I was locked up in the hoosegow. I had a small cell all to my lonesome. On one side of me was Julian Armour and on the other Erik.

I hung onto the bars and wondered how long I'd be incarcerated. This was turning out to be a heck of a way to end a honeymoon cruise.

Then I saw Grudion out in the hallway talking with a police officer. Apparently, he had convinced the constabulary to keep him out of a jail cell. He held out his identification for the policeman to see, and then they engaged in an animated conversation. If Grudion succeeded in securing the release of his passengers, would he help spring me or would he decide to let me rot in jail? Time would tell.

I turned my attention to Julian Armour. He sat on a cot with his head in his hands.

"Hey, Julian," I called.

He looked up, startled. "Oh, Paul. I didn't notice that you were next door."

"Yeah, looks like we'll be neighbors for a while. I want to apologize again for the encounters we've had. I intended no harm."

He let out a deep sigh. "I realize that now. I got a little carried away. When I spotted you in the Japanese Garden, I saw red, and all my anger bubbled to the surface."

"I know how that is. I have a reputation for mouthing off."

He smiled. "And I owe you thanks for knocking me down when that maniac tried to shoot me."

I shrugged. "I'm sure you would have done the same for me."

Julian stood up and came over toward my cell. "In fact, I'm thinking of making you an honorary member of the Oldsters from Reno."

"Oh?"

"Yes. We've never had a member who lived elsewhere, but after I tell the guys what you did for me, I'm sure they'll all support it."

"Well, Julian, I consider that quite an honor."

"How long do you think we'll be in here?"

"I saw Grudion speaking with the authorities. I hope he has enough clout to free some of us. As a passenger, you should be one of the first to go."

"What about you?"

"Grudion has never been a member of my fan club, so I'm not holding my breath."

"I'll put in a good word for you." Then a look of panic came over his face. "My wife doesn't know what happened. She'll be searching all over the gardens for me."

"Maybe Grudion can find a way to get word to her."

His eyes brightened. "She has a cell phone but I forgot to bring one."

I rattled the bars and shouted, "Hey, we have a man here who needs to speak with his wife."

After a few moments a police officer ambled over.

"Mr. Armour here needs to reach his wife. Can you arrange for him to make a call?"

"You his social secretary?" the cop asked.

"Just trying to be helpful."

Julian spoke to the policeman and after some pleading was handed a cell phone. I heard him speak to Betty and then he handed the phone back to the police officer.

"I was right," Julian said. "She was wandering all over the gardens trying to find me. I told her to go back to the ship on the bus and that I would hopefully meet her there."

I looked at my watch. It was 9:50. "I wonder how much time we have before the ship sails."

"We have to be aboard by eleven-thirty and the ship leaves at midnight," Julian said.

"Well, Grudion needs to get his butt in gear then."

I paced the cell. I was raring to leave this joint and clear my name with Grudion. After all the crap he'd given me, I looked forward to resolution. I rubbed my hands together. Inese's murder solved, the reappearance of Ellen Hargrave and even Julian Armour would probably no longer be my sworn enemy. Life was good, but I was still locked in this damn cell.

Then an item I had read in my journal popped into my mis-wired brain: Ellen Hargrave's long-lost niece. It wasn't Inese, but it had to be someone else on the ship. If I could find that out, it would certainly help Ellen. She had gone to all the trouble of testing Gary and Gina. Now she only needed this one other item for closure.

I wandered over to the other side of my cell to where Erik sat, a scowl on his face.

"Cheer up," I said. "I understand Canada doesn't have a death penalty."

"Where I come from I probably would have just been taken out in the woods and shot."

"Where did you grow up?" I asked.

"Estonia."

"How'd you hook up with the Zarins family?"

"After the Soviet breakup, I spent some time in Latvia. Mr. Zarins recruited me."

"Something's been bugging me. Why'd you kidnap my wife?"

Erik gave a sardonic laugh. "You were causing me problems by asking questions and nosing around. I figured a little distraction would give me time to execute my plan to eliminate Zarins."

"Were you always planning to capture him in Buchart Gardens?"

"No. Originally Valdis and I were going to do it in Ketchikan, but then Zarins decided to take you for the zodiac ride. That and I couldn't get off the ship on Friday."

"And you didn't show up for dinner that night."

"No. I had to stay out of the way for a while and prepare my plan to kidnap your wife this morning. I wanted you distracted so you wouldn't cause me any trouble. Unfortunately, it didn't work out that way."

"You can't count on old poops. We have this way of stumbling into things and putting a spanner in the works."

He looked at me with his brow furrowed.

Then I realized he didn't understand the wording I'd used.

"I messed up your plans."

He grimaced. "You can say that again. My only consolation is that they locked you up as well."

"Not for long. Norbert Grudion will work his magic with the Mounties, and I'll soon be riding away. Maybe you have some insight into something else I've been wondering about. Mrs. Hargrave was looking for a long-lost niece from Latvia. The manifest indicated that Inese Zarins was the only staff member from Latvia. Did you ever run across anyone else on the ship from Latvia?"

Erik gave a derisive laugh. "People in the cruise line know so little of what goes on, but the workers find out a great deal. I discovered one other person originally from Latvia." He paused as if waiting for me to respond.

I held my tongue.

"Okay, if you must know, there's a maid named Anita."

I thought back to my journal. "There was a woman of that name who turned down the bed in Ellen Hargrave's cabin."

"That's the one. There's only one Anita onboard."

I chuckled. "Wouldn't that be ironic? Ellen Hargrave has been searching all over for a long-lost niece. Maybe she was right under her nose all along. Still, she didn't mention Anita as the name."

Erik stared at me. "People change their names."

Anyway, this could be something for Ellen to check on if she and I were released from jail before the ship sailed.

I paced back and forth, looking at my watch periodically. I wondered if Grudion was having any success in securing our release. Finally, at ten-forty-five a policeman approached. He held a ring with a set of keys attached. He opened Julian's door and escorted him away.

"Hey, how about me?" I asked.

"Be patient, old man," the police officer replied. Then he and Julian disappeared.

"They'll probably keep you here with me," Erik said. "You've caused so much trouble, they may not want to release you."

I kept examining my watch as the minutes before the ship sailed ticked by. At eleven o'clock the same cop reappeared and inserted a key in the lock to my cell. I had been sprung.

I waved to Erik and headed down a hallway accompanied by my new best police buddy. He directed me to a meeting room and inside sat Julian, Ellen, Marion, Gina, Gary, Kimo and Haddie. Grudion stood speaking quietly to a police officer, outfitted in a dark blue uniform.

Grudion turned as I entered. "Please take a seat, Mr. Jacobson."

I plunked down next to Marion. She grabbed my hand and held it tightly.

Grudion cleared his throat. "A van is waiting outside to take us back to the ship."

Everyone clapped.

"I've arranged for statements to be taken on the ship rather than holding everyone here overnight."

Another round of applause and Julian put his index fingers

between his teeth and gave a sharp whistle.

"I've assured the Victoria Police Department that everyone will cooperate in exchange for return passage to the ship."

All heads nodded.

"Okay, we can leave now."

We stood and marched out to the parking lot. I sidled up to Ellen Hargrave as she waited at the curb, her cane balanced on the sidewalk.

"I have some news for you, Ellen."

"Oh?"

"Yes. It turns out there is one other crew member from Latvia."

Her eyes opened wide. "Who is it?"

"You've met her. The maid Anita."

A broad smile spread across Ellen's face. "I like Anita. It would be wonderful if she were my niece."

"You'll have to talk to her when we return to the ship and find out if she's the one."

"Thank you so much for the information, Paul."

"All part of the service."

We clambered into the van. Once seated, I asked the police driver, "Are you going to give us a tour of the city on the way back?"

Needless to say, all I received for my effort was a scowl.

We reached our gleaming white ship and sauntered aboard as if we had just completed a normal visit to Butchart Gardens rather than the posies-from-hell tour.

As we waited in the security line, Ellen Hargrave tapped her cane. "I want to invite everyone to join me for a late dinner at the Tappan Steak House."

"I don't know if it will still be open," Gary said.

Ellen smiled. "Mr. Grudion was kind enough to call ahead to request a special seating."

As if on cue, my stomach growled. In all the excitement I hadn't eaten since leaving the ship. When used to forced feedings every several hours on a cruise, you needed regular nourishment.

Marion and I stopped by our cabin to freshen up and then joined the others for some feasting. Everyone showed up except for Grudion. I noticed an empty chair next to Ellen.

"Are you saving that seat for Mr. Grudion?" I asked.

"No. He has some duties to attend to. This is reserved for a special guest who will be joining us."

CHAPTER 24

I wondered if Ellen had made arrangements for the Prime Minister of Canada or the Pope to join our celebration dinner.

It all became clear when, shortly, a young woman arrived.

Ellen tapped a water glass with her knife. "Everyone, this is Anita. Mr. Grudion arranged for her to join us so I could have a conversation with her."

As we ordered salads and various cuts of shipboard cow, Ellen and Anita engaged in an animated conversation, complete with laughter and arm waving and ending with a hug.

Then Ellen again tapped her glass. "I have an important announcement to make. Anita Ozols, here, is my niece. We just verified that after she left Latvia, she moved to France, was briefly married and has retained her married name, also replacing her original first name of Ann with Anita. But her birth name was Hargrave."

We all raised our glasses in a toast.

"And in particular I want to thank Paul Jacobson. Through his efforts we were reunited."

Now glasses were raised toward me.

I almost blushed, except I had a mouthful of steak keeping me occupied.

After swallowing, I leaned over to speak to Gina who was sitting on my left. "Aren't you concerned that part of your inheritance is now going to someone else?"

She smiled. "Not really. Aunt Ellen told Gary and me that

after her little test, she would be setting up a trust fund for each of us. I don't think we have to worry."

"That's good," I said. "Sounds like you're happy now."

Everyone seemed in a jolly mood, having escaped jail and seeing Ellen reunited with her long-lost niece. The excitement of the moment prevailed.

Then a thought occurred to me. "I have a question for Anita."

"Yes?" She looked at me seriously, like I was going to make her pass the bar examination.

"If your birth name was Hargrave, why didn't you ever make a comment to Ellen that you had a similar name?"

"Oh, no. I wouldn't have done that. We aren't supposed to discuss personal matters with the passengers."

"In any case it all worked out right in the end," I said.

Over ice cream sundaes, Julian suddenly stood up. "I have an announcement to make. As some of you know, Paul Jacobson and I have had a few disagreements during the cruise. I accused him of stealing my wallet, but tonight when I returned after our adventure in Butchart Gardens, I found it wedged in the back of my closet. Apparently it had fallen there and I hadn't noticed before. Then I got to thinking about passing out in the hot tub and realized that Paul actually saved me then. I got sick when he gave me a bottle of water, but I think it was something I ate earlier and not the water from Paul. He did mess up our performance during the talent show, but I now know that was an accident. After Paul saved my life a second time from that gun-toting criminal earlier tonight, I want to officially thank him." He unfurled a shirt that read "Oldsters from Reno." "I want to present this shirt to Paul so he can always remember our group."

"Won't help, Julian," I said. "My addled brain will forget it overnight."

"Then, Marion, it's your duty to remind Paul."

Marion hugged my right arm. "I'll see that he doesn't forget."

"Now, Paul. You're welcome to come to Reno and visit us at any time."

Everyone cheered, and Julian leaned across the table to hand me the shirt.

"I'll wear this with honor. And if Marion ever kicks me out, I'll come mooch off of you."

Just then Grudion appeared. "I hate to disrupt the festivities, but I need to obtain statements from each of you. This must be completed before we disembark in the morning. I know it's late, but I will move through the proceedings as quickly as possible."

"I don't mind," Ellen said. "Anita and I have a lot to talk over. I'll go last."

Grudion started with Kimo and Haddie.

After they had given their statements to Grudion, they sat down with Marion and me while Grudion grilled Julian.

"Good way fo' end the cruise," Kimo said with his huge grin once again lining his face.

"I haven't seen Kimo this happy all week," Haddie said.

"Thanks again for both of you helping out," I said. "I hope this didn't interfere with your evening plans."

"Hey, we saw most of the gardens," Kimo replied, "and this was more better than sitting on the ship."

Marion and I were then engulfed by huge bear hugs, and then Kimo stepped back. "Next time you come to Hawaii, look us up." He handed me a card. They gave each of us another hug and traipsed off.

After checking to make sure I didn't have any broken ribs, I looked at the card. It read: "Kimo and Haddie Kapala. Private investigators."

"Quite a couple," Marion said.

"I'll say." I shook my head. "If I had known their occupation I would have enlisted their services earlier in the cruise."

Then I had my chance with the grand inquisitor.

Grudion and I sat at the far end of the dining room out of earshot of Ellen and Anita, who were still going strong. Marion had returned to our stateroom, and I had said I'd join her there.

"Now, Mr. Jacobson. Please give me a full account of the evening's activities, starting from the time you left the ship."

"Well, Marion and I took the bus. The first thing I noticed was a black limousine with tinted windows following us."

Grudion raised his eyebrows.

"I saw the same limo when we stopped downtown and when we parked at Butchart Gardens. I thought it might be Zarins, but it turned out to be Ellen Hargrave." I stopped to catch my breath.

"Go on."

"In the gardens nothing unusual happened at first. Then Marion spotted Erik and I began to wonder about him. I did notice a float plane landing in the bay. That I later learned was Zarins and Valdis arriving. Marion and I moseyed into the Japanese garden and that was when all the havoc began. Because of my faulty assumption, Zarins went after Gina and Gary. Then Ellen arrived and explained her vanishing act."

"Elaborate please."

I told how she had staged her own disappearance.

"That's a pretty serious thing to do," Grudion said.

"You can cover that ground with Ellen. Anyway, she appeared in the garden and after her explanation, I knew that Gary and Gina hadn't killed Inese. Then Julian blundered into our little gathering and almost got himself shot."

"I understand you saved his life."

I shrugged. "I just knocked the idiot over at the right time. By then I had concluded that Erik was the murderer."

"How'd you draw that conclusion?"

"As I mentioned to you, we'd seen him earlier in the Sunken

Garden. He'd taken a low profile after my first encounter with Zarins, which seemed suspicious. Someone would have to have gotten pretty close to Inese to stuff a hot stone down her throat. She trusted Erik, so he had means and opportunity. The motive was the remaining part. He explained that when he showed up. He and Valdis were plotting to take over Zarins's operation."

I took a deep breath. "You should have seen the expression on Zarins's face when he realized his two minions were shafting him. But you were there for that part of it. Finally, my bride resolved the situation with a little assist from the perfume spray. That's it. Now I have a couple of questions for you."

"Yes?"

"This thing with the counterfeit quarter. I still don't understand that."

Grudion chuckled. "It was kind of absurd. They were made by a demented, minor low-life."

"A two-bit criminal," I said, putting in my two-bits.

Grudion grunted. "Yah, now do you want to hear this or not?"

I raised my hands. "Okay, okay . . ."

"I suspect that Zarins and Valdis stole a couple of bags and salted them around for the fun of it. The police found half a bag of the quarters in the float plane."

"What crime lords do for entertainment. What will happen now to Zarins, Valdis and Erik?"

"I think the odds are good that they will all spend the rest of their lives in prison. Erik will be tried for Inese's murder. Interpol is after both Zarins and Valdis, who have a list of crimes that would stretch across this room. It's just that Zarins had too good a support structure in Latvia for anyone to reach him. Coming here was Zarins's downfall."

"So Valdis and Erik's plan to lure Zarins away and eliminate him might have worked."

"Yah, without the turn of events that might have been the case."

"Damn. You do good work, Grudion."

"Don't give me that."

"In any case, I should now be off your short list of suspects for all the crimes committed on this cruise."

"That's true." He began numbering off with his fingers. "One. Mrs. Hargrave was pushed down the stairs during the lifeboat drill."

"An accident."

"Two, Mrs. Hargrave falling into the salmon fishery vat."

"Gary pushed me into her."

"Three, Mr. Armour's stolen wallet."

"He later found it."

"Four, Mr. Armour unconscious in the hot tub."

"Drinking and hot tubs don't mix."

"Five, Mrs. Hargrave passing out in her food."

"She accidentally switched pills with her friend."

"Six, the disappearance of Mrs. Hargrave."

"We both heard what she did."

"Seven, the kidnapping of your wife."

"Erik did that."

"Eight, the counterfeit quarter."

"Zarins and Valdis's hobby." I held up my hands. "I got it. So now I'm clean as new-fallen snow."

"Well there is the issue of being in an out-of-bounds area and harassing a bear at Mendenhall Glacier."

"Crapola. I forgot about that one."

"But I have a piece of good news for you," Grudion said.

"I won the lottery?"

"The ranger filed no charges. I spoke on your behalf."

My mouth dropped open. "You actually took my side?"

"Don't look so surprised."

"Well, thanks. So I'm truly free now."

"Not exactly. There is still one crime to resolve."

"Oh?"

"Yes. Detective Bearhurst of the Seattle Police Department will be coming on board first thing in the morning to meet with you and me regarding the murder of the vagrant in Seattle the morning before we sailed."

I felt like a deflated balloon. "I had forgotten all about that. You don't still think I committed that crime, do you?"

Grudion eyed me. "At one time I thought you were responsible for all the incidents I mentioned. We'll see what Detective Bearhurst has to say."

I shook my head. "Thanks for the vote of confidence."

"Cheer up. You're free of all shipboard crimes."

"Lucky me."

So I still wasn't a free man.

Then another thought occurred to me. "What's going to happen to Ellen Hargrave for staging a fake disappearance?"

"That's a serious matter. The cruise line spent a lot of time and money searching for her."

"I'm sure she'll compensate you for that."

"That will certainly help. Then we'll have to decide if we plan to press charges."

"Don't do that," I said. "She's learned her lesson. Just make her pay up and leave it at that."

"Yah, I'm sure that's what will be worked out. After all, she is a paying customer."

"And likely to bring a lot of follow-up business to the cruise line. Grudion, there's one other thing. You have a hole in your security system."

He raised an eyebrow. "What's that?"

I grinned at him. "You obviously didn't enter an indication of Ellen Hargrave being missing in your system that checks passengers' identification when they leave the ship. After hiding, she disembarked in Victoria, and no one stopped her to inquire."

He turned the color of his hair. "I'll have to fix that."

"You do. And let me know if I can help you improve your security in any other ways."

I returned to the table where Ellen and Anita were yakking, and Grudion signaled for Ellen to join him.

I plunked down and asked Anita, "How do you feel finding a long-lost relative?"

"It is very surprising. I didn't know I had an aunt in America. My contract on the cruise ship ends in two months, and then I'm going to visit Aunt Ellen."

"Any plans after that?"

"No. I may stay in the United States for an extended time if I can work out the visa."

"I'm sure Ellen can help with that."

I stayed to kibitz with Anita until Ellen finished her inquisition and then said goodbye to both of them and headed back to my cabin.

Marion was in bed reading when I entered. I should have been tired, but I was still too hyped-up from the adrenaline overdose during the evening's festivities. I looked at my watch. "It's three in the morning. Time sure passes fast when you're having fun."

Marion put her book down and I noticed that it was a mystery and had a picture of a cruise ship on the cover.

"How does that book compare with our recent adventures?"

"Much tamer."

I stuck my head out the sliding door to our balcony, and a gust of fresh air cooled my face. We had to be approaching Seattle. I ducked back in and closed the door. "I'm not sleepy. I think I'll go walk around a little."

257

"Well, you'll have to do it on your own. I can hardly keep my eyes open."

I put on my windbreaker, gave Marion a kiss and left the room. The elevator area was deserted as well as the promenade deck. I went outside and hung over the railing, watching the ocean rush past and listening to the whoosh of water striking the hull. It should have been a soothing sound for me, but my tummy was jittery. I still had one more issue to deal with. It was probably just as well that I wasn't sleepy. I figured I might as well stay up all night—there wasn't much of it left anyway—and I wouldn't do the Jacobson reset. I would keep my limited wits about me.

Somewhere out in those waters, the elusive whales were frolicking. Would I ever see a whale or would Bearhurst haul me off to be locked in the Seattle slammer? No wonder I couldn't sleep when I had that still looming over me as well as whales mocking me.

My reverie was interrupted by a tap on my shoulder. I spun around to find Gary Hargrave standing there.

"Couldn't sleep?" he asked

"No. I decided to count whales instead of sheep."

"Me too. After all the excitement at Butchard Gardens I needed some sea air." He paused. "I owe you an apology."

"Do tell."

"I'm sorry I tried to push you into the salmon vat."

I wagged a finger at him. "You weren't expecting a chain re-action where I'd knock your aunt over."

He hung his head. "I suppose you're right."

"Well, we'll consider it even. I suspected you and Gina of killing Inese and knocking your aunt over her balcony."

He shook his head. "Aunt Ellen is a piece of work. Imagine staging her own disappearance."

"And hiding out for two days just to see how you and Gina

reacted. Quite a devious woman."

"She didn't amass her fortune by being a pushover."

"Except when someone bumps into her on ship stairs or at a salmon hatchery. How about a cup of coffee?"

"Sure."

We adjourned to the all-night café and had a cup of early-morning java. By then a faint glow of dawn was appearing and we could see the lights of Seattle ahead.

Gary told me that he, Ellen and Gina planned to tour the Northwest for a few days once Ellen cleared up her little stunt with the authorities.

Still not sleepy, I shook Gary's hand, wished him well and headed back to my cabin. I turned on the desk lamp and proceeded to update my journal. I could then reread it if I was ever tempted to go on a cruise again.

Fortunately, Marion was a sound sleeper so the light and my pen scratching didn't seem to bother her. Now all I had to await was the arrival of Detective Bearhurst.

Chapter 25

After we docked, I adjourned to our balcony to watch small boats maneuver in Elliott Bay. My reverie was interrupted by a knock on the door. I ambled into the cabin.

Marion stirred but didn't wake up, so I opened the door to peek out.

Mr. Grudion and another man stood there.

"Mr. Jacobson, Detective Bearhurst and I need to speak with you."

I stepped outside. "Let's go somewhere else. My wife is still asleep."

"My office," Grudion said.

He led the way down the corridor.

"You two are early birds," I said, panting to keep up with Grudion.

Detective Bearhurst looked at me. "Seems the same can be said of you. You're already dressed."

"I stayed up all night. At my age I don't need much sleep, and I had an exciting night."

"That's what I understand."

After an elevator ride and short dash down the corridor, we arrived at a secret part of the ship that I didn't remember seeing, although, except for the last two days with my sex-induced-and-lack-of-sleep memory, who could have told?

Grudion unlocked a door and ushered us into a tiny office littered with reports. He cleared off two chairs, and Bearhurst and I sat down facing each other. Since there were no other chairs, Grudion remained standing.

Bearhurst cleared his throat. "Now regarding the matter of the murder of Carl "Curly" Atkins last Sunday."

"You'll have to excuse me, Detective. I have a short-term memory problem. I can't remember last Sunday from squid soup, but I keep a journal as a memory aid. I wrote about finding a body in a garden in Seattle. I only wrote a first name of Curly. I want to make sure we're speaking of the same event."

"That's correct." He looked at me directly, his full, round face thoughtful. "You also contacted me last week suggesting that I check out another street person named Lumpy. Turns out that is Bartholomew Holubar, also known affectionately as Lumpy."

I shrugged. "I remember reading the name Lumpy in my diary."

Suddenly, a smile appeared on Bearhurst's face. "Well, I want to thank you for that lead. There was a red bandanna on the victim. That bandanna had a bloody fingerprint on it that didn't match the victim. When we located Holubar he had a knife in his possession and his right index fingerprint matched the one on the bandanna. When confronted with the evidence, Holubar confessed to murdering Curly Atkins. They had some sort of grudge that got carried away."

My mouth dropped open. Then I regained control. "So I'm no longer a suspect?"

"Well, there is still the matter of you assisting the computer thief at the hotel."

My shoulders sagged.

"Don't worry, Mr. Jacobson," Bearhurst said, giving me a slap on the back. "We captured the thief. He was part of a snatch-and-grab ring and admitted to no inside accomplice. You're one hundred percent clean."

"And to think, I didn't even take a shower this morning."

"And, Mr. Jacobson, I want to express my appreciation again for helping solve the murder." He reached out a big bear of a hand and gave my limp hand a shake.

"I'll be damned. So I'm clear of all charges."

Grudion now smiled. "Yah, completely. Both in Seattle and on the Scandinavian Sea Lines *Sunshine*."

I let out my breath. "That's a big relief."

"And I'd like to give you a little memento." Grudion opened a bag he was holding and handed me a box.

I opened it and found a stone sculpture of a whale mounted on a pedestal.

"Hey, this is great," I said, turning it around in my hands. "I've been looking for a whale the whole cruise and this is the first one I've seen. May I return to my cabin now?"

"Yah. We just needed to close out with you."

"Have a great stay the rest of your time in Seattle," Bearhurst added. "And stay out of trouble."

"Me? I never get in trouble."

Both Grudion and Bearhurst exchanged glances.

I practically floated back to my stateroom.

Marion had awakened, so I showed her the whale sculpture.

"We can add this to the rest of your collection when we get home, Paul."

"Rest of my collection?"

"Yes. You've built up quite a set of gifts from law enforcement officers. A butterfly collection from Hawaii, a picture of the Boulder jail and a receipt for a paid fine for illegal grunion fishing."

"Grunion fishing? I've just escaped from being hooked by Grudion, maybe they're related. I'm sure there are some interesting stories there, but I don't remember any of them."

"But I do. I'll tell you all about it later. Now if you'll give me half an hour, we can discuss it over breakfast."

"Fine. I think I'll take a short stroll on deck while you get ready."

I headed up the stairs while agitated tourists frantically scrambled around, preparing to disembark. I didn't dare go in the cafeteria for fear of having my fingers bitten off by people trying to eat the last remaining food before being forced to leave the ship.

The jogging track was deserted, so I had an opportunity to collect my thoughts in the calmness of early morning. The sun shone, the water glistened, I was clear of all crime charges, I was married to a wonderful woman, I had my health except for a minor matter of some dysfunctional brain cells, and I had survived Alaska. Life was good. If I had just seen one of those damn whales. Oh, well. I had a whale sculpture courtesy of Grudion and the Scandinavian Sea Lines. That would have to suffice.

After circling the deck once, I spotted Andrew Black racing toward me. He screeched to a stop in front of me, gasping for air. "I was worried about you. The last I saw of you, the police were escorting you through Butchart Gardens in handcuffs."

"Yeah, there was a little scuffle in the Japanese Gardens and the Mounties rounded all of us up."

"You going to leave me in suspense or tell me what occurred?"

"Not much happened. A Latvian crime boss and his cohort abducted Ellen Hargrave's niece; Erik the waiter and the cohort turned on the crime lord; Ellen Hargrave, who we all thought had fallen overboard, reappeared having faked her disappearance; Julian Armour blundered onto the scene and almost got himself killed; Grudion appeared; Marion shot eye-irritating perfume at the bad guys; Kimo and his wife Haddie crashed down on some of the criminals; the police arrested all of us;

Grudion convinced the Mounties to release the good guys; Julian Armour became my best buddy; Ellen found her long-lost niece; and all is right in the world except I haven't seen a Goddamn whale."

Andrew screeched to a halt and grabbed my arm. "Just a minute, Paul. I don't want the Reader's Digest version. Tell me the whole story."

"I think they'll kick us off the ship before I can complete that."

"Give it your best shot."

So for the next twenty minutes we walked and I recounted the nefarious adventures in and around Butchart Gardens.

"I must say knowing you, Paul, has made this cruise exciting."

"And I think it's time for this geezer to return home and relax. This vacation has enervated me."

"I'm sure you always find ways to make life around you interesting."

"That's what my bride accuses me of. And I want to thank you for all your support. It was very helpful having someone believing in me and helping convince Grudion that I wasn't Bonnie and Clyde rolled into one person."

"I knew you were innocent of all charges."

"I'm certainly glad that viewpoint prevailed."

"And, Paul, you recognized me this morning."

"Darn right. I stayed up all night so my memory is fine even if the rest of me is dragging a little."

"You're quite the dedicated athlete, being up here this morning."

"I guess the same can be said of you."

Andrew chuckled. "You're right. Everyone else is frantically preparing to depart and we two are strolling around oblivious to all the craziness."

"Two old farts acting like a calm port in a storm of tourist frenzy."

"Helen thinks I'm nuts to charge up here every morning, but it keeps me in shape." He patted his stomach.

"Marion's the same way. But they wouldn't appreciate it if we turned into blimps either."

"Women are never satisfied."

"Can't live with them, can't live without them. What are your plans next?"

"Helen and I will be taking a tour of Seattle and then flying out late this afternoon. And you?"

"I'll have to check with my tour guide. I think we're heading to the airport right after disembarking."

We stopped and leaned on the railing overlooking Elliott Bay.

"This has been an interesting week," I said. "I only wish I had seen a whale."

"Cheer up. You'll just have to come back again." He regarded his watch. "I better go retrieve Helen."

We shook hands and both headed back to our respective cabins.

Marion was out of the bathroom, so I took a quick shower.

Then we took the elevator down for breakfast and survived our last shipboard meal without losing any of our digits before returning to our cabin to retrieve our overnight bags. As we awaited the announcement of our color code to leave the ship, I looked around our stateroom one last time.

"Quite a honeymoon," Marion said.

"And we survived to tell the kids about it."

"Maybe we could hide on this ship and just go on the next cruise," I said, "like Ellen Hargrave hiding from everyone in a different cabin."

"I don't think it would work. Since they scan our ID cards every time we leave the ship, they'd know we were still here."

Mike Befeler

"But they'd have to find us. You now know a good hiding place in a closet in the casino."

"Don't remind me. I'm glad they have that horrible Erik locked away."

"I'm grateful he only chloroformed you and didn't try to kill you like he did Inese."

Marion shuddered. "What a horrible way to go."

"Let's think of more happy things, like how I finally saw a whale, if only a gift sculpture."

Marion patted my arm. "I'm glad that's taken care of."

Then with my sleepless night, I remembered something. "I promised Jennifer that I'd call to tell her everything that happened."

"Well, you can't lie to your granddaughter." Marion fixed up the cell phone for me and I placed the call.

Jennifer answered. "I've been anxious to hear all the gory details."

"How long do you have?"

"An hour before my tennis game."

"I think we can handle it in that time."

"So was it Gary or Erik that murdered Inese?"

"Erik. The slimeball was out to take over Karlis Zarins's operation."

"Like I had suggested."

"Exactly. Your private investigation instincts were right on."

"But, Grandpa, I've decided to be something as well as a private eye."

"What's that?"

"I also want to be a tennis pro."

I chuckled. "Is your tennis game improving that much?"

"Yup. I want to see how far I can go with tennis."

"Give it your best shot and see."

"Now tell me exactly what happened."

I recounted the whole saga: Ellen Hargrave reappearing, Mounties, flying Hawaiian private investigators, crushed posies and Victoria's scenic jail.

"And you're free of all accusations now, Grandpa."

"Yes. Free as a bird."

"So the trip was worthwhile."

"You could say that. I had my beautiful bride with me, and I survived. Only thing is I never saw a live whale. But I think I'm ready for calm Venice Beach after this."

"I don't know, Grandpa. Wherever you go, something weird occurs."

"I'm getting along in years. Maybe things will slow down soon."

"You'll keep going, Grandpa. After all you are a Jacobson."

"That's right. I have to maintain the family reputation and keep up with my granddaughter. You whap the ball hard and straight."

"Okey dokey, Grandpa."

After I finished the call, Marion said, "You should phone our friend Meyer Ohana. He likes to hear from you."

I did the cell phone routine again, and after asking for Meyer, a man's voice came on.

"Is this the old coot who used to keep criminals off the streets in Hawaii?" I asked.

"The same."

"Greetings from the Pacific Northwest, the land of crime and no-show whales."

"If you're not calling from jail, you must have resolved the murder accusation."

"All taken care of. Plus all the problems I ran into on the ship."

"It sounds like a good story there. Since I have nothing to do except listen to television today, why don't you entertain me with your exploits."

"Since it is all fresh in my usually soggy memory, I can do that."

"Does that suggest a little romance has transpired?"

"Yes, but I also stayed up last night so as not to undergo the Jacobson reset. Now if you'll quit interrupting I'll give you the whole scoop." I proceeded to recount my whole cruise saga.

"What a life you live, Paul."

"The operative word being 'live' so far. You never can tell when the grim reaper will collect his due."

"I'm sure you have many years ahead."

"Well, I'll keep kicking until they drag me away."

"Do you want to say hello to Henry Palmer?"

I thought back to what I had read in my journal. "He's the guy who always insults me."

"That's him. It's his way of showing you that he cares."

"I guess I can handle some verbal abuse, particularly since Grudion and Detective Bearhurst are now my best buddies."

There was a pause and then a raspy voice said, "Hello, ass-hole."

I decided to jump into the swing of things, "Hello to you too, butt face."

Henry actually laughed, although it came out like a croak. "It's good to hear your voice."

That floored me more than being insulted. "Yeah . . . well . . . I survived a cruise and will be heading back to Venice Beach soon."

"Marion's too good for you."

"That's better. I was worried for a moment that you had gone soft. And you're absolutely correct—she is too good for me."

We each slung our parting insults, and Meyer came back on the line.

"From what I overheard, you and Henry had a good exchange."

"I suppose he makes life entertaining."

"Like you, Paul. Like you. Give me a call when you're back home. I always enjoy hearing from you."

"As long as I have Marion to remind me of my long-distance friends, I'll be happy to do that. Make sure Henry doesn't end up in jail for libeling someone."

After completing the call, I handed the cell phone to Marion. Her eyes lit up. "I should call my family to remind them that we're flying back this afternoon."

She called, yakked for a while and then shoved the cell phone into my mitt. "Here. My grandson Austin wants to talk to you."

I put the phone to the side of my head. "Are you being polite to my granddaughter?"

"Of course. We spoke yesterday and brainstormed about your experience with the Latvian crime boss."

"I'm glad everyone has been helping."

"So what happened?"

I explained the Butchart Gardens extravaganza.

"Wow. That sounds exciting."

"It was. Your grandmother is hell on wheels when spraying gunk in the eyes of bad guys. I'll tell you more of the details when we return to sunny Southern California."

"Actually, we're having an unusual rain storm today."

"Funny. It's perfectly clear in Seattle."

I signed off and returned the cell phone to be re-stashed in Marion's purse. Then I ambled out onto the balcony to take one last look at Elliott Bay. My head swirled with all the events of the past week. I felt relieved to have all the accusations disappear like the whale I hadn't seen after it breached. I would miss the view from our cozy little stateroom. Not that I'd remember it after I'd next fallen asleep. What a life. I could always choose to not write things in my journal. Then I wouldn't have to be reacquainted with them when I read my missive. Still, it was good to know what I had been through, and Jennifer, Austin and Meyer were all caught up on my exciting week.

Marion joined me on the balcony for an embrace. We disengaged, and I leaned over the railing to peruse the water as a sailboat slipped past.

Suddenly a huge fin appeared. Then a tail flipped out of the water.

"Look!" I shouted. "A whale."

"That's a good-sized one," Marion said. "And how unusual. They aren't usually right here in Elliott Bay."

I watched dumbfounded as the whale breached, dove and then breached again.

"He's putting on quite a show," Marion said.

"I'll be damned. They've been hiding from me all week and then at the eleventh hour, a personal envoy arrives to welcome me back to Seattle."

"You make it sound so personal."

"It is. After avoiding me all week, they're trying to make up for it."

We watched as the whale traversed the sound and swam north. I continued to ogle him until I couldn't see a fin or tail any longer.

"Now my trip is complete," I said.

I looked out where I had seen the whale, glad that my obsession had been relieved. The water sparkled in the morning sunlight like little diamonds dancing on the crest of the gentle swells. Again, the sense of gratitude returned. With Seattle's reputation for rain, I was experiencing a perfectly sunny day with my new bride, both of us fit as old-fart fiddles. And we had survived murderers, a kidnapping, a crime boss, crazy fellow passengers and Grudion. Now all I had to do was disembark without knocking any ladies down the gangplank. I was ready to resume the calm life of Paul Jacobson, retired ex-sailor.

When they announced our color code, we grabbed our overnight bags and joined the other lemmings abandoning ship. On the dock we surveyed a warehouse full of suitcases, perched like gravestones in an indoor cemetery. We wandered among the luggage looking for our color code. Once we found the right area, we retrieved our stuff and had a porter assist us to curbside to catch a taxi.

A cab pulled up and the cabbie jumped out to load our luggage. Just then a street person ambled up. He had a dirty beard, torn clothes and a wild look in his eyes. He reached his hand out.

"Got some change, Mac?"

I looked from side to side. Marion had already settled into the back seat of the taxi, so I jumped in and slammed the door before you could say Grudion and Bearhurst.

READER DISCUSSION QUESTIONS

- How does Paul Jacobson change over the course of the story?

- How does Paul learn to cope with his short-term memory loss?

- How have people you know dealt with short-term memory loss?

- How are the pluses and minuses of aging handled in the story?

- If you only met Paul once, what would you think of him? How about after knowing him over the events of the story?

- What do you think of Paul's sense of humor?

- How does Paul handle adversity?

- How would you handle Marion's situation of waking up and finding your spouse doesn't recognize you?

- How is murder and humor blended in the story?

- What experiences have you had on a cruise?

ABOUT THE AUTHOR

Mike Befeler turned his attention to fiction writing after a career in high-technology marketing. Mike's published novels include *Retirement Homes Are Murder; Living with Your Kids Is Murder*, a finalist for the Lefty Award for the best humorous mystery of 2009; and *Senior Moments Are Murder*. Mike is active in organizations promoting a positive image of aging and is vice president of the Rocky Mountain Chapter of Mystery Writers of America. He grew up in Honolulu, Hawaii, and now lives in Boulder, Colorado, with his wife Wendy.

If you are interested in having the author speak to your book club, contact Mike Befeler at mikebef@aol.com. His website is http://www.mikebefeler.com.